AFTER-IMAGE

A Vicky Bauer Mystery

Other Books by Leona Gom:

POETRY

Kindling
The Singletree
Land of the Peace
NorthBound
Private Properties
The Collected Poems

NOVELS

Housebroken
Zero Avenue
The Y Chromosome

AFTER-IMAGE

A Vicky Bauer Mystery

by

LEONA GOM

SECOND STORY Press

CANADIAN CATALOGUING IN PUBLICATION DATA

Gom, Leona, 1946–
After-image

"A Vicky Bauer mystery".
ISBN 0-929005-91-0

I. Title.

PS8563.083A77 1996   C813'.54   C96-930162-6
PR9199.3.G65A77 1996

Edited by Charis Wahl
Copyedited by Elise Levine

Printed and bound in Canada

*Second Story Press gratefully acknowledges the assistance of the
Ontario Arts Council and The Canada Council*

Published by
SECOND STORY PRESS
720 Bathurst Street Suite 301
Toronto, Ontario
M5S 2R4

Acknowledgements

I would like to thank Kathy Holt and Doug Nepinak for sharing with me their memories of Lahr and Major John Paul MacDonald for taking the time to meet with me and allowing me to tour the Caserne. Errors or distortions in my depiction of Lahr or the DND base are purely my own, and this book is entirely a work of fiction.

Special thanks are due as always to Dale Evoy. Thanks also to Charis Wahl, Denise Bukowski, Ranjini Mendis, and Maureen Shaw for their advice and support.

I am also grateful to the following theorists and film critics, whose ideas have influenced the thinking of my main character: Laura Mulvey, Claire Johnston, Elizabeth Cowie, Raymond Bellour, Christian Metz, Dudley Andrew, Janet Bergstrom, and especially Mary Ann Doane in her book *Femmes Fatales* (Routledge, New York, 1991).

The excerpt from *The Mother/Daughter Plot* by Mariane Hirsch is used by permission of Indiana University Press. The quotations from Freud are from Vols. 22 and 23 of *The Complete Psychological Works, Standard Edition* (London, 1951).

for Dale

THURSDAY

Morning

VICKY BAUER WAS JUST pressing her finger down on the shutter button when she saw the woman being shot. The young couple had walked into her view a few moments ago, and she had been pleased, because they would add something to the picture, a human presence off to the side, with the red roofs of Lahr in the background. The man was wearing a green army uniform, and she'd thought that was particularly appropriate, since the Canadian base was just down the hill about a kilometre from the park, and her grandmother, to whom she was intending to send the pictures, would be as interested in the people as in the scenery.

The young, blond woman took a step back. Her face was dark, shaded, but Vicky could see her mouth open into a small pursed circle and her eyes lift from the gun to the man's face. The woman's right hand rose slowly to her chest. Behind her splayed fingers a red stain began to appear, vivid on the yellow sweater with the white beads in the shape of a bird's wing. Her left hand reached slightly behind her, fumbled at the air as if trying to find something to hold onto. Slowly, she sank to her knees. Her eyes moved from the man's face to where Vicky was standing, frozen, still staring through the viewfinder. Then the woman's left arm lifted, unsteadily, the hand open, reaching toward her.

Vicky let the camera fall, and it thudded onto her chest, jerked to a stop by the strap around her neck. The woman was no longer in the viewfinder, a picture, but deadly real, kneeling in the dark green beauty of the Staatswald with the blood seeping from her left breast, both hands now covering the wound.

Then the man moved. Whether he stepped toward the woman or turned to look behind him, to where Vicky stood beside the path, less than thirty metres from him and only half hidden by the large linden tree, she would never know, because suddenly she was running down the path, the camera banging against her chest, her arms pumping wildly. A large branch from an evergreen tree slashed across her face, but she was barely aware of it. When the path curved slightly to the right, cutting off the view of the city, she risked a glance over her shoulder. Nothing.

The path descended more steeply now, to the edge of the forest, where she had left her bicycle. She stumbled on an exposed root and fell to her knees, whimpering with the pain that shot up her legs, and then she scrambled to her feet and stumbled on. Above her a large bird circled, shrieking.

Suddenly her eye caught a movement in front of her and to the right. She almost cried out but stopped herself in time as she identified the figure as one of the forest workers. Dressed in brown overalls, he was pulling a fallen branch into a half-full wheelbarrow.

She ran over to the man, who straightened and looked at her, frowning. He was large and stocky, with heavy eyebrows and a dark, sun-weathered face. She pointed back up the path, the words gasping from her.

"A woman — she's been shot — please — you've got to help — up there — a man shot her — a man with a gun — "

The forester raised his hands, palms up, and shook his head.

"Oh, please," she cried, grabbing hold of the wheelbarrow, "please." She took a deep breath, tried to calm herself, to remember the right words; she must have learned enough words.

"*Frau*," she exclaimed, pointing. "*Frau*. Dead. Shot."

The man smiled a little. "*Ja. Frau*," he said. He pointed at the branch. "*Arbeit*."

Vicky looked back up the trail. The murderer could be there, just around the bend, behind that tree —

She was almost at the edge of the forest. Once on her bicycle she could be at the base in a couple of minutes, and she could get an MP to come back with her in a car — it would make as much sense as trying to convince this man to help, and what could he do, anyway, against a man with a gun?

"Forget it," she said. The man nodded as though he understood and went back to his work.

The little pause had given her fresh energy, and she sped down the trail in long bounds, her running shoes kicking up a spray of pine needles and dead leaves. A squirrel scuttling up the trunk of an oak tree on her right startled her, but not enough to break her stride. She didn't look behind her, concentrated only on where she was going, counting on the curves of the path to keep her from the sight of a pursuer.

Her bicycle was where she had left it, hidden under a bush, and she jerked it free. She bent low on the seat and pressed her feet, hard, onto the pedals. She risked a look behind her now, but there was nothing on the path except a small whirl of wind shifting the dead leaves. As she turned out of the forest the sudden, familiar rush of traffic noise made her slightly giddy, and she stopped peddling, but the downward slope was still steep enough to shoot her onto Langemarckstraße.

And then there it was, the Canadian Department of

National Defence base, the part they called the Caserne, where the offices of the officers were, and the English-language high school, and the French-language elementary school, and all the CanEx services and the groceteria and the arena and the video store and the Baskin-Robbins — the odd collection of things that were supposed to make Canadian soldiers feel they weren't in a foreign country after all.

She skidded to a stop at the front gate and dropped her bicycle with a clatter against the small booth manned by a security guard who looked too young to be called a man. He glared at her and said in a peremptory voice, "Pass, please."

She grabbed the sill and took several deep breaths. She had to sound convincing. He might remember her from the times she hadn't sounded convincing, from the times she'd been drunk and rude and refused to show her pass with the big "Dependant" stamp across it.

"I don't want to come in," she said. "There's an emergency." She pointed up into the forest. "A woman's been shot. Up there. Get an MP out here."

Before she'd finished speaking, the guard began dialing something on the phone. He turned his back a little to her as he spoke, but she could hear him say, excitedly, the word "emergency." She took a deep, reassured breath, let it out slowly. Maybe she had been expecting him to point at the pile of papers on his desk and say, *"Arbeit."* But of course people being shot was what the army specialized in.

He hung up the phone and looked at her eagerly. "Someone's coming right away," he said. He scratched at his chin with enough force and animation to leave pale red welts.

She nodded. Her legs felt suddenly so weak she had to clutch the sill. She fixed her eyes on the big *Terroristen* poster tacked up in the booth, met the eyes of one of the four young women on it. She remembered, absurdly, hearing an

American tourist in the post office last month say to her husband: "'*Touristen*.' Why would they put up pictures of ten tourists? Maybe they want them to call home. I wonder what '*Vorsicht*' means." Vicky remembered how she had felt: smug, superior, someone who lived here, someone who was studying the language, someone who knew that "*Vorsicht*" meant "danger." But when it had mattered, the only German she could remember was "*Frau*."

A man in a white coat and carrying a black bag, a doctor obviously, was running across the pavement toward her, and he reached the booth at the same time as the jeep coming from the other direction. Two muscular men wearing MP armbands were in the front seat, and the driver shouted at her, "You the one who saw someone being shot?"

"Up there. In the forest." She pointed. "It was a soldier. He ——"

"Get in." The driver stepped out and flipped the front seat forward. She got in the back.

The doctor got in on the other side. "Mrs. Bauer?"

She stared at him. Dr. Lester. Of course. It shouldn't surprise her that he remembered her. Even on his list of all the depressed and neurotic military wives she would be memorable. She doubted he had many patients who had to see him as a condition of not having charges filed against them. The little belt-bag around her waist held at least two bottles of his mood-altering prescriptions.

"Hi," she said.

The jeep was already moving, heading up the hill. "Tell us where," said the MP in the passenger seat. His right hand kept opening and closing on his holstered gun.

She leaned forward. "Straight up into the forest. Take the first right. I think it's called the Randweg. And then maybe a kilometre."

"So what exactly happened?" said Dr. Lester. He sat with his knees together and his bag on his lap. His hands kept opening and closing on the handle in the same way the soldier's did on his gun.

What exactly happened: so she told them, trying to keep her voice steady and objective, although she faltered when she described how the woman fell forward on her knees and seemed to reach her hand out to her.

They passed the spot where she had met the forester. There was no sign of him now, which was just as well because he would probably have tried to stop them from bringing the jeep farther in. The Germans used horses for heavy work, someone had explained to her, because they did much less damage to the forest floor than did mechanized vehicles. Vicky sat rigidly, her eyes darting at the dark forest to her left, imagining a man with a gun taking aim, firing, the glass beside her shattering, the impact of the bullet. What she really wanted to do was drop to the floor of the jeep and huddle there, and it occurred to her that not doing so must mean she was more afraid of the opinion of the men in the jeep than she was of the murderer.

And then they were there. That was the tree against which she had leaned. That was the view of the city she had framed in the viewfinder. There was where the couple had stood. That was where the woman had fallen to her knees.

Vicky pushed her way out of the jeep even before the driver had both legs out. But already she could see there was no crumpled body in a bright yellow sweater and blue jeans lying on the ground.

"It was right here," she said, pointing at the place. "This is where she fell. And the man, he was standing about here — " She paced off a few steps to her right.

The MP who had been in the passenger seat scanned the

forest around them before he slid his gun back into the holster. "Nobody here now," he said.

"But this is where it happened," Vicky said. "I'm sure of it."

The doctor crouched down where she had pointed. "I don't see any blood," he said.

"But it *is* where it happened," Vicky said miserably. "You have to believe me."

The driver had moved only about a metre from the jeep, and now he went back to it, reached inside and spoke into what looked like a walkie-talkie. Vicky tried to hear what he said, but his voice was too low.

Dr. Lester stood up and dusted his hands, even though he hadn't touched anything. He moved over to Vicky, put his arm around her shoulders. She tried not to stiffen or pull away.

"It's okay," he said. "I'm sure you saw *some*thing."

"I saw a woman being murdered."

Another jeep pulled up then, driven by an MP with an officer beside him. The officer, a tall man with curly black hair and a meticulously clipped moustache, made her think for one relieved moment he was Andrew Pilski, the husband of her closest friend here, Annie, and she took an eager step toward him before she realized how superficial the resemblance was. This man was older and thinner, with a tense mouth and a double chin, both seemingly created by his excessively erect posture.

"Ma'am." He extended his hand so she had to take it. Her fingers felt limp and boneless in his hard grip. "I'm Lieutenant Crosby. Would you mind telling me what happened?"

So she told her story again, her eyes drawn repeatedly to the patch of grass and ivy at the edge of the path where the woman had stood. Lieutenant Crosby's eyes kept flicking from her to the forest around them. When she was finished he nodded, his eyes still moving restlessly.

"And the man you saw," he said. "He was a soldier?"

"Yes. He had on a uniform."

"What rank?"

"Rank? I don't know."

"Didn't you see the insignia?"

"No. It was all too sudden. And I don't know what they mean, anyway."

The lieutenant's eyes seemed to narrow slightly. "Isn't your husband in the military?"

"My husband's a teacher."

"I see." A teacher, she imagined him thinking dismissively. But teachers had officer status, so she knew he would have to treat her with respect. At least until he found out her name and record.

As though he knew what she was thinking, Dr. Lester came over to where they stood and drew the lieutenant to the side of the path. Their voices were low, but Vicky couldn't have been more sure of what they were saying. She stared out across the rooftops of Lahr, past the other part of the Canadian DND base, the airfield at the west end of town, and looked at the hazy green hills to the northwest, where the trees were starting to wear patches of autumn colour. Bells began tolling at several churches. She made herself count. Eleven o'clock.

The lieutenant came back. "Mrs. Bauer?" So he'd found out her name, she thought. And everything that went with it. She made herself face him.

"Yes."

"As you can see, there's nothing here now. Dr. Lester thinks you might have seen, well, a couple quarreling, maybe. But I'll have some of the men search the area."

"I know what I saw. I saw a woman being shot."

"We'll have a look around, Mrs. Bauer. You can go back on down to the Caserne."

"Should I file a report or anything?"

"If you want. But I'll be making a report of this as well."

"I'll ask Captain Pilski about it," she said. "He's a friend of mine." Was a captain higher than a lieutenant? She thought so. She hated name-dropping, but rank was what the army understood best, after all. She would have to tell Annie she had used her husband as a reference. She hoped Annie would laugh.

"Oh, yes. Captain Pilski." The lieutenant smiled. It looked forced. "Sure, talk to him then." He tilted his head to the side and scratched at his neck, oddly, by flicking his fingers up, then turned to his driver. "Take Mrs. Bauer back down to the Caserne." The driver nodded, opened the passenger door and stood holding it for her. She had no choice but to get in.

"You'll let me know if you find her?"

"Of course."

On the way back to the base she sat looking out the side window, searching among the trees for a glimpse of yellow. But she felt a kind of strange numbness, a spaciness, as though she might have taken a handful of the pills in her purse, as though she really were the stumbling, delusional alcoholic Dr. Lester probably told the lieutenant she was.

A woman was dead, she thought, as the jeep pulled up beside the gate. And no one believed her. She had been sent away like a child who'd made up a story.

She got out of the vehicle without saying anything to the driver and retrieved her bicycle from where it leaned against the entrance booth. The soldier inside asked her eagerly, "Did they find her?"

Vicky shook her head and got on her bicycle. A car pulled up at the gate and the driver held up his pass for the guard. Vicky looked at the young soldier's face through the windshield. That's him, she thought, horrified. That's the murderer. The guard waved him on through.

Vicky closed her eyes, tightened her fingers on the handlebars. Of course it wasn't him. It was a young man in a green uniform, that's all. The guard was asking her something else, but she reached down pretending to check her bicycle chain and not hear him.

As she bent over, the camera around her neck swung forward, bumping against the crossbar. The camera. She had forgotten all about it, her old, reliable Konica. She straightened, slowly, put her hand over it, pressing it to her chest.

"I think I'll go in," she said to the guard. She dug her pass out of her belt-bag and showed it to him.

"Sure. Go ahead."

She cycled past him onto the base, past the service station and arena on her left, past the offices and snack bars and libraries and laundromats and hairdressers and dentists, until she reached the main LX, the small department store where she could leave her film for processing.

"Tomorrow," the clerk promised her. "About this time."

She left the Caserne uncertainly, thinking maybe she had made a mistake. Maybe she should have given the film directly to the lieutenant. Maybe she should have had it processed somewhere in the city unconnected to the army. The murderer was a soldier, after all. He might be on the base right now, watching her. She tried not to shudder, to look quickly behind her. Well, she'd relinquished the film — it was too late to change her mind. She couldn't remember at what point she had clicked the shutter, or even if she *had* clicked it. The film might be useless. It was only in movies that such convenient evidence turned up.

She should go home, she supposed, but she found herself turning on to Langemarckstraße and heading for downtown, trying to concentrate only on the force of her feet against the pedals, the wind pressing into her face. She dismounted at last at Marktstraße, a pedestrian-only street, and began slowly wheeling her bicycle beside her, peering distractedly into shops. She stood outside a fruit and vegetable store for about ten minutes, looking into the window at her own transparent reflection: a woman in her late thirties, stocky and muscular, in a sweatshirt and slacks, with large eyes and straight black hair in two thick braids that made her look like her maternal grandmother, who still lived on the Blood Reserve in southern Alberta, halfway around the world.

Someone in the store began walking toward the window, and Vicky's reflection merged with that of the woman, who was young and blond. She had to blink hard against seeing a bloodstain spreading onto her sweater.

A pudgy, bald man with a brown mole the size of a grape on his cheek came out of the store and said something to her in German, in a voice that could have been either suspicious or solicitous. She had no idea what he had said, but she answered, "*Nein, danke*," the first German words she had learned. *Nein, danke*: if only she could say that to what had happened in the forest. She turned quickly and walked on.

She found herself, finally, at the ruins of the old brick tower, the Storchenturm, built in the thirteenth century. The Romans had been here long before that, however, between 20 and 200 AD, and had established a camp to guard their ford over the Schutter River, which ran through what was now the city of Lahr. The Roman camp, on the western outskirts of the city, was located approximately where the current

Canadian Forces airfield was. *Plus ça change,* Vicky had thought when she heard that.

She sat down on the low part of the old wall and looked at the ivy climbing right to the small look-out windows at the top of the Storchenturm. It was one of her favourite places in Lahr, this spot, and she came here often, even in winter when the ivy was only spidery threads among the bricks and she had to clear the snow from the wall to sit down. She took a deep breath, feeling it lift her rib cage and shoulders, then let it out slowly, trying not to let it catch.

She wanted a drink. Oh, god, how she wanted a drink. She took the bottle of Valium out of her belt-bag, let her mouth fill with saliva and then took two pills. They weren't as good as a drink but they would have to do.

As she put the pill bottle back in the bag, she dislodged a crumpled piece of paper that fell out onto the stones beside her. It was an old envelope. She smoothed it out on her lap and read what she had written there, just this morning as she was on her way into the forest, when she had stopped her bike at the side of the road and quickly scribbled it down:

> *In chapter 6, challenge the screen-as-mirror theory (check Metz) that's based on the primal "mirror stage" (Freud) in our growth (all that stuff about how the projector is, "significantly," located at the back of the head, where our central sense of self and vision is).* But — *how to account for the fact that in a film one sees everything* except *oneself, the opposite of the mirror?*

She read it again and again, and each time meaning seemed to recede from the words. She knew this observation must have represented some insight, but it all seemed long ago, in a language she could barely remember. "One sees everything *except* oneself, the opposite of the mirror": only moments ago she had seen someone, perhaps a young, blond woman, walking towards her in the shop window, and that image had merged with her own reflection. She shuddered, crumpled the envelope up again and jammed it into her bag. She pulled her bicycle a little closer, leaving one hand on the handlebars and her knees against the front wheel.

A middle-aged couple speaking English stopped close to where she was sitting and then the woman asked her, loudly, "Do you know *wo ist ein* post office?" She mimed mailing a letter.

When Vicky answered in English they exclaimed in delight, and she was compelled to listen to them explain that they were from Winnipeg and here to visit their son who was a soldier. She looked up at them and heard herself say, "I just saw a woman murdered. By a soldier."

They stared. "Oh, my dear," the woman murmured finally. She took her husband's arm.

"You should tell someone," said the husband.

Vicky nodded, dropping her eyes. When she stood up, they both took a step back. She got on her bike and rode quickly away, their appalled whispers receding behind her. The church bells began their interminable tolling. It was noon. Marktstraße began to fill up with people.

You should tell someone. Yes, someone, anyone, everyone.

Conrad would be on his lunch break. She could tell Conrad.

She crouched over the handlebars and sped out of the downtown area, dodging traffic, ignoring a one-way sign, and in ten minutes she was turning into the narrow street in front of the Canadian Cultural Centre; one block farther and she was at the Gutenberg Primary School, one of the two Canadian schools in the city off the base. It looked like any of a thousand such buildings: grey and institutional, more run-down and scuffed-looking than last year, as the army lost interest in maintenance. In a couple of years the whole base, the whole Canadian presence in Lahr, would, after forty years, be gone. They had already begun sending home the CF-18s from the nearby Baden-Söllingen air base.

She left her bicycle outside the main door, not bothering to chain it. The playground was filling rapidly with shouting children; they must just have been released after lunch. Two boys of about nine chasing a ball crashed into her and raced on, barely giving her a glance. She winced, rubbed her elbow, which they had jarred into the doorknob. "Base brats," people called the children, not without reason. She wondered if Conrad would have applied for the exchange program if he had known what discipline problems the children here would be.

And what a discipline problem his wife would be — picked up twice by the German police and handed over to the Canadian military police, once for riding her bicycle drunkenly down Tiergartenstraße and once for writing "Assholes Shop Here" in felt pen on the window of the Sex Shop, to say nothing of her more direct skirmishes with military authority. Such as deliberately wearing uncovered curlers while shopping at the Canadian grocery downtown, in obvious violation of the sign in the window saying, "No Uncovered Curlers," and signed by the base commander. ("So that was *you*," Annie had chortled to Vicky, who was embarrassed to admit she'd acted that time less on principle than on cheap German riesling.) But it was Conrad who'd been reprimanded for not controlling his Dependant, Conrad who would never be able to see any of what happened as funny.

Poor Conrad, she thought, nodding at the grim secretary and heading for the staff room. His two-year trip back to the land of his birth had turned into an emotional maze for him. And now she had *this* to tell him.

The staff room was small and cramped and smelled of scalded coffee. Vicky recognized three of the teachers in the room from last year. Kathryn ("with a 'y'") Oram, the Grade Three teacher; the school librarian, Lynne something; and Paul Garten, the principal, a short and ambitious young man who had come here, like Conrad, to get in touch with his Germanic past and who, although half Conrad's age, had apparently become his closest friend here.

And then there was Conrad himself, her husband, off and on, for twenty years, looking up at her now from the papers he was marking and looking not all that different from when she had first seen him twenty-two years ago, when she went into the staff room at her old high school in the northern village of Worsley, Alberta, to ask for the key to the gym and the vice principal had said to her as she stood waiting uncomfortably, "Have you met our new Grade Seven teacher?" And Conrad had glanced up at her from the papers he was marking with the same expression then as he had now: somewhat alarmed, somewhat mournful, the expression of a man habitually expecting bad news.

Vicky had been just fourteen then, the sort of student the teachers praised because she was bright and industrious and attractive, and apparently able to overcome the stigma of a mother who was native Indian, which, of course, made Vicky a "breed" (the more poetic among the townspeople saying "stovepipe blond"). She didn't care, she told herself fiercely; she was as good as any of them, and she couldn't see all-white ancestry providing that much advantage, even, and perhaps especially, in her own father, an unhappy Irishman with an unspecific grievance against his whole life. After an unsuccessful try at farming two sections mostly of muskeg, he ran the service station until a half-ton truck loaded with barley slipped its brakes at the pump and smashed his right leg.

He could still walk, but his anger and bitterness intensified after that, and he began drinking more than ever. One day he was simply gone, taking their pick-up and their half-Husky dog and leaving behind a note that said, "I'm sorry. Better off without me." He would send them money once in a while, and sometimes, from constantly changing addresses, odd little letters about work he had found, but Vicky never saw him again.

Her mother, losing the conditional respectability marriage to Vicky's father had allowed her, sank into a depression from which she roused herself only for two feeble suicide attempts. These, at least, gained her the sympathy of the town, which she lost again when she tried more indirectly self-destructive behaviour, namely drunkenness and affairs with allegedly happily married men. She began to treat Vicky as a stranger, sometimes calling her by other people's names. Vicky would look at her in a kind of cold horror and think: she's forgotten me. She's forgotten she has a daughter.

Vicky was fifteen by then, struggling to stay in school and surviving on the neighbours' kindness, which was genuine enough but contingent on her dissociating herself from her mother. By Grade Eleven her sense of worth had sufficiently eroded to make her decide to drop out of school, and the generosity of the neighbours feeding and clothing her waned as she turned sulky and unappreciative and promiscuous. ("Just like the mother, after all," they would say sadly, shaking their heads.)

Attempts to locate her father or his relatives were fruitless, and although her mother was finally persuaded to write her own mother on the reserve and ask if they would take her daughter, the letter was never answered. It was likely, Vicky would learn from her grandmother after her mother's death, that her mother never mailed the letter, some pride still restraining her from asking for help from the mother who had so fiercely opposed her marriage to a white man, Vicky's grandmother insisting it meant escape only from the rights conferred by official Indian Status, status lost by women, but not by men, when they married non-Natives.

What would have happened to Vicky then but for Conrad Bauer she didn't want to imagine. He came down to the Grade Eleven classroom where she was cleaning out her desk and said, in a speech that sounded rehearsed, that he had been giving her situation some thought and that, if she promised to stay in school and finish Grade Twelve, she could live in the second bedroom at his teacherage. He would provide her with room and board and a small salary if she would do half the cooking and cleaning, and he would not expect any sexual favours.

Vicky had stood there holding her Social Studies text and stared at him. "All right," she said. Conrad Bauer was not just the only single male teacher at the school but, despite (or perhaps because of) his habitual melancholia, he and his blond, blue-eyed good looks had figured in the daydreams of most of the high school girls. That he was seventeen years older than she only added to his appeal, since she, like most girls her age, had little but disdain for the awkward, giggly boys who were her contemporaries.

It surprised and disappointed her to find that he was sincere about expecting no sexual favours, and it took her several months to rediscover how to please through academic achievement. They might well have continued as they were until she finished high school except that someone filed a morals complaint against him with the school board, and so, shortly after her sixteenth birthday, he suggested they marry. She often wondered what he felt for her then — not the adoring, aching, passionate love she was feeling for him, but it must have been love of a kind. It actually wasn't until they had come to Germany last year that she thought she really understood his reasons for taking her in.

He had not seemed disappointed to find she was not a virgin, although she suspected he was one. Her guilt transformed itself into even more diligent study, and she graduated with the highest marks in the school division, winning three university scholarships. He insisted that she go.

Her first year in Edmonton she missed him so much she could barely endure it, but by the time he got a teaching job in the city two years later she was enjoying life on her own. The sudden arrival of a husband, especially one so much older than she, was hard for her to accommodate, although her new friends were entranced by him, by his seriousness and by his handsomeness, of which he seemed unaware but which made even strangers look at him longer than they should. Her women friends sighed and said he reminded them of Hamlet, of some Gothic romantic with dark, exciting secrets. Vicky had laughed and said glibly, because she had just read it in a novel and it was the kind of thing people said at her age, "Conrad is capable of love but not complexity."

Perhaps because his new school turned out to be the worst in the city, he withdrew more and more from her that year. She found herself deliberately trying to provoke him, calling him broody and moody and paternalistic, wanting him to get angry, to argue, to call her selfish and ungrateful and immature, but he rarely gave her that satisfaction. Their lovemaking was pleasant enough, but it didn't match the frenzied obsessions she saw among her friends or read about in her literature courses.

She asked Conrad what he would say if she had an affair. He looked up from the report cards over which he was labouring, searching for euphemisms, and he sighed and said, his pencil already beginning to write the next word, "If it's what you want, Vicky. I can't stop you." So then she had to have one. It was with her Psychology TA, a thin, hyperthyroid-eyed man living with the department secretary, and it was as passionate and sordid and doomed as Vicky could have wished. She was relieved when it was over, but, relying on the grimly moral novels she was studying, she deduced guilt to be inadequate punishment, so she told Conrad she had to move out. "If it's what you want, Vicky," he said. She felt like screaming at him, although she had learned from her affair that screaming had limited appeal.

They lived apart as much as together for the next ten years. Sometimes the reasons were work-related, Vicky with her honours B.A. chasing out-of-town jobs that never fulfilled their promise; and sometimes the reasons were her own choice, when she found unbearable both Conrad's patient melancholy and her own restless retreats into the unreliable consolations of alcohol and sarcasm. It surprised her, at least at first, that Conrad didn't just find a more agreeable wife with an agreeable job and personality and habits and children. But Conrad did not want to have children, something else she would understand about him only after they came to Germany.

They had been living together for the two years before he decided to take the job in Lahr, so it seemed only logical that she accompany him and use the time to finish, at last, her M.A. thesis on film theory.

As she looked at him now, from the doorway of the Gutenberg School staff room, she felt, as she hadn't for a long time, a welling-up of intense affection for him. He was Conrad, who had saved her, so long ago, when she was just a child in Worsley, Alberta.

"Vicky!" Paul Garten, the principal, said warmly, taking her hand although she hadn't offered it. He was one of those immaculately dressed men whose shirts didn't just look freshly washed and ironed but newly bought an hour ago. "How nice to see you again. Did you have a good summer?"

"Yes, thanks." Being around the teachers always made her feel awkward. Since she had never accomplished a real career, walking into a room full of people who had always made her feel inadequate.

Conrad got up and came over to them. He was still chewing on his sandwich, and several crumbs clung to his grey cardigan. Paul reached over and brushed them off and then he laughed, embarrassed, as though he hadn't realized they were on someone else's clothes. "Well, see you Friday," he said to Vicky.

She nodded. Friday: god, yes. A party at his place. She took Conrad's arm. "Can I talk to you outside?" she asked him.

"I haven't much time," Conrad said, looking at his watch. "I'm on supervision today."

"It's important." She drew him into the hallway. It smelled of old running shoes and ink from felt-tipped pens. But at least they were alone. "I saw a woman murdered today," she said.

"What?"

"Up in the Staatswald. Above the Caserne. I was there taking pictures to send to Gran and suddenly there's this soldier and a young woman and he had a gun and he shot her."

Conrad just stared at her for several moments. "*Shot?* Are you sure?"

"Yes, I'm sure."

"God, Vicky. Are you all right?"

"Yes, yes, I'm fine. I wasn't the one who was shot."

"Did you report it?"

"Of course I did. But when the people from the base got up there the woman's body was gone."

"Did they look for her? Did they do a search?"

"No, not really. I don't think they believed me."

"Well — " Conrad looked away from her, pulling his brows together, pleating the skin between them. She had the sudden feeling he wanted to smell her breath. "What do you want me to do?"

"You can believe me, for one thing," she snapped.

"Of course I believe you. But if the police didn't find anything — "

"But I *saw* it. She was shot."

He lifted his hands a little and let them drop, and she could see him glance surreptitiously at his watch. From outside came the sound of something heavy bouncing off the front door. "Look, I have to go on supervision now. If you reported it I don't know what else you can do."

"Drive back up there with me. Maybe I can find something."

"I can't right now, Vicky. It's the middle of a school day."

"I know that, but this is important, Conrad. A woman was murdered!"

"We'll drive up after school, all right?" He shifted his feet. "Look — I have to go. Why don't you just go home and wait for me and we'll talk about it later?"

"Yeah, sure. All right, then. I'll see you later."

She knew it had been unreasonable to expect Conrad to just walk out of school with her, but still she felt angry. He doubted her, of course he did, and if she couldn't even convince Conrad, how could she expect anyone else to believe her?

Her bicycle had not, she was thankful to see, been stolen or dismembered. She gave it a little shake as though to wake it up and got on and cycled the block to the Canadian Community Centre, which was really just an aging hall whose main cultural activities, aside from movies, seemed to be aerobics classes for the base wives. She used the phone outside the main door to call Lieutenant Crosby, who told her politely that they had spent half an hour searching but had found nothing.

"But I *saw* it," Vicky insisted. "I saw the woman shot."

"Let's hope you're wrong," said Lieutenant Crosby.

"Should I tell the German police? Maybe someone will be reporting the woman missing."

There was a brief silence on the line. "Why don't you leave that to us? Since you say there was a soldier involved the German police would just refer it back to us anyway." He gave a little awkward laugh. "They know we're much harder on our own people than they would be."

That was true, Vicky thought, hanging up the phone. She knew from her own humiliating experience that the German police probably wouldn't want to get involved. If Crosby did report it she could imagine them all laughing, sharing their stories of poor drunken Mrs. Bauer.

She got back on her bicycle and rode the five blocks to her apartment. It was a sunny, warm day, and twice women out sweeping the street in front of their houses smiled at her as she went past. Lahr was the cleanest city she had ever lived in, but she supposed it was no cleaner than any other German city, probably because of women like these, endlessly sweeping their streets, tending their immaculate flower boxes, keeping their windows spotless. She remembered film footage she had seen from after the war, women in Berlin carting away piece by piece the rubble that had been their city.

The upstairs apartment she and Conrad rented from old Frau Daimler was close to a large park, and she usually enjoyed walking her bicycle through it on her way home, but today the thought of going alone into such a place made her detour around.

She turned at last into Haydnstraße, then the drive of the old brick and plaster house she and Conrad had lived in now for more than a year. They had been lucky to get it. Lahr and the nearby Baden-Söllingen base had to house more than 11,000 Canadians, including 8,000 soldiers, relatively few of whom could be accommodated at the base barracks. Rental accommodation depended on the resourcefulness and reliability of one's assigned DND contact person, and since this was often the employee one was replacing a certain disinterest on that person's part was understandable. But the teacher Conrad was replacing was eager to have them take her old apartment so she could sell them her appliances and light fixtures and furniture and wardrobes and dishes, none of which were provided in German apartments. And when Frau Daimler heard her new tenants would not be *Kanadische Soldaten*, of whom she was highly suspicious, but a German-speaking teacher and his wife, she was obviously pleased. Probably it helped, too, that Paul Garten's new wife, Hilda, was a second cousin of Frau Daimler's. In any case, the old woman adored Conrad and would hover around the back door at the time he usually came home from school, eager to engage him in conversation. She was perfunctorily polite to Vicky, who told herself it was simply a communication problem.

Frau Daimler's son, Erich, who lived in one of the northern cities, had been staying with her lately, and, to his mother's delight, had befriended Conrad. Conrad had accepted several invitations to go down "for a glass of Schnapps" in the evening. Sometimes, she thought, the neighbours and Paul and Hilda came over as well. She pretended not to care, but as she sat upstairs trying to work on her thesis the mumble of their German voices was a hopeless distraction. She came particularly to loathe Erich, who, with his heavy brows and large sunken eyes, made her think of the photo of Kafka on the back of *The Trial.*

"I don't know why you dislike the Daimlers," Conrad had said. "They're basically nice people. A bit right-wing, perhaps, but what can you expect?"

She wheeled her bicycle into the small shed at the back, hoping to avoid meeting her landlady, but the old woman was working in the garden, tying a bunch of unhappy looking roses to stakes where they looked like prisoners waiting to be shot.

She looked up, raised her trowel in greeting. She was a tubby, red-cheeked woman in her seventies with her thin, grey hair in a bun. With her perpetual black stockings and dirndl dresses and aprons she looked like the kind of authentic European that tourists would take pictures of.

Vicky smiled and waved, trying not to look as though she was hurrying. She went into the dim back vestibule from which one door led to her upstairs apartment and the other into the main part of the house, unlocked her door, and headed up the staircase.

The apartment was a large, two-bedroom suite, with the north and south walls sloping in to accommodate the slant of the roof. The kitchen had been recently remodeled, which made it ordinary by German standards but high-quality by Canadian ones. Vicky still found herself marveling at its precise efficiency, its ingenious use of space, the way opening one drawer or door could cleverly trigger a complementary one. When they first came here she'd remarked to Conrad that if the term "jerry-built" came from the British expression "Jerry", for Germans, then the meaning of that phrase today should be the opposite.

She slipped the camera, at last, from around her neck and dropped it on the bookcase. Then she pulled the strap of the heavy wooden shutters on the south windows. They clattered open and sunlight sprang into the room. She should have left them closed, she thought wearily, looking around the living room, which was badly in need of a cleaning. She wandered into the second bedroom, which she was using as a study, but the chaos of books and papers was hardly more cheering. She looked at the thirty-two handwritten pages of her thesis, which she had finally titled *Filmic Identification for Women in Early American Cinema*, and she thought: none of this matters. A woman was murdered today.

She turned abruptly back into the living room, slapped a cassette into the portable player and watched the tiny wheels go round and round. If there was music she didn't hear it. Then, not letting herself think, she poured herself a glass of gin and drank it in four large swallows. She felt it running down into her stomach, medicine, making her well, healing the ugly pictures in her head. She poured herself another.

It had been three months since she had had a drink. She was supposed to have stopped. She'd promised Conrad. "I really mean it this time," she'd said.

She phoned Annie, neither expecting nor getting an answer. Annie would still be at work, at the CanEx bar at the airfield.

She thought about calling Andrew at his office at the Caserne, as she'd told the lieutenant she would do, but she pulled her hand back from the phone. She didn't want to talk to Andrew without Annie there for the simple and humiliating reason that she found him too attractive. Last Christmas she had found herself in the hallway with him during a party, and when he'd run his hand up under her sweater she'd actually been faint. Her best friend's husband: she felt like a tramp. He had been embarrassed around her for weeks after that, which she found surprising and rather charming, since she knew such flirtations were hardly unusual here. Sitting around waiting for a war got awfully boring, and amorous dalliances gave the men something to do, as well as, Vicky imagined, allowing them to hone their tactical skills. The women were just as bad, really, according to Annie, who saw things first-hand at the bar. When the troops went out on their six weeks of field exercises during Fallex and the American soldiers came in to run the base in their absence, a high-speed calculator would, she said, have trouble keeping track of the extra-marital orgasms.

So she didn't call Andrew. She had another drink and fell into a drugged sleep on the sofa.

Afternoon

She was awakened by voices — Frau Daimler's rapid, eager German and Conrad's low-voiced replies. Then she heard Conrad's step on the stairs, and she sat up, blinking away the gummy haze of sleep, trying to swallow the curdled-milk taste in her mouth. She grabbed the empty glass on the coffee table and shoved it under the sofa.

Conrad was halfway into the room, setting down his bag of books and papers, when he stopped and looked at her. The slanting sunlight hitting his face exaggerated the wrinkles across his forehead and around his mouth, the pouchiness under his eyes, making him look old and tired. But the eyes fixed on his wife were sharp, a teacher's eyes, trained to spot deceptions.

"You've been drinking," he said.

"I had a horrendous day," Vicky said.

"You promised."

"I saw a woman *murdered*, Conrad. For Christ's sake."

Conrad sighed, sat down in the armchair across from her and leaned his head back. "Do you still want me to go up there with you?" he said.

Vicky looked at him in surprise. She didn't think he'd even remember saying he'd go. "Yeah. Sure."

He looked at his watch. "Well, then let's go now. Before it gets dark."

When they went down the stairs, avoiding the one that creaked so that Frau Daimler wouldn't be alerted, Vicky concentrated on her feet, keeping her hand on the wall to make sure she didn't stumble. Her mind felt fuzzy, slow, but that was because she'd just woken up, wasn't it?

Outside, a cool wind had started to blow, making her shiver. Pedestrians and cyclists glanced up at the darkening western sky swelling with rain, and she was glad she was in a car, the new Passat they'd gotten cheaply through the DND. When they got to the Staatswald they argued about driving it in.

"You're not *allowed* to take cars into the forest," Conrad insisted.

"These are special circumstances, for god's sake. The army brought its jeeps up."

"All right then." He put the car in gear and accelerated up the slope. "Tell me where to stop."

Vicky nodded. Her heart began to beat fast as she stared out the window. Here was the Staatswald, the thick, green, cleansing forest, *die Lungen von Lahr*, the lungs of Lahr, stretching south and east, part of the *Schwarzwald*, the Black Forest, a place that sounded dangerous, full of secrets. It was like visiting a place that had frightened her as a child, that had been returning for years in bad dreams, its landmarks shadowy and faintly distorted. There was where she had left her bicycle; there was where the unresponsive man with the wheelbarrow had stood at the side of the trail; there was the corner where she had thrown a frantic glance over her shoulder. She saw the linden tree against which she had leaned, the quiet view of the rooftops of Lahr, the park bench beside the path and overlooking the city —

"Stop."

She got slowly out of the car, staring at the spot where the woman had stood as though she could make the woman visible to Conrad by the force of memory. She crouched down and peered at the ground, which was covered with dead leaves, a few twigs, some ivy, an underlay of dark green moss. A breeze pulled at the branches above, spreading ragged light and shade, shade and light, across the ground.

Conrad had come up behind her. "Is this where you think she was?"

"Yes. Right here."

"And where was he?"

"About where you are." She placed her hand on the leaves, gently.

Conrad squatted down beside her. "Do you see anything?"

"No. He might have caught her as she fell and carried her away somewhere. And maybe he picked up the bits of underbrush that had blood on them. But you can see how some of the leaves are crushed. As though someone stood on them."

"They just look like dead leaves, Vicky. They've been there for a long time."

Vicky caught her breath. "Look," she whispered.

She moved her fingers slowly, carefully, to one leaf, still half green, which cupped a small white bead. She took it between her thumb and forefinger, held it up to Conrad.

"The woman was wearing a sweater with a beaded design on it, white beads, like this. It proves she was here!"

Conrad stood up, looked around the forest. A gust of wind rattled the trees, pulled loose a yellowing elm leaf that spiraled down to his feet. "It proves you found a white bead, Vicky."

Vicky stood up, too, facing him. "Why don't you believe me? I'd believe you."

Conrad ran his hand over the top of his head, across the hair that had thinned by half in the last several years. "It's not that I don't believe you, Vicky. I'm sure you saw something here, maybe a woman in a sweater with beads, I don't know. But if the army did a search and found nothing, well — what do you expect me to say?"

"I expect you *not* to say, 'Oh, I'm sure you saw *some*thing,' which is what the asshole doctor said."

"But maybe he's right. Our eyes can deceive us — "

"Oh, just tell me to my face I was hallucinating, why don't you?"

She saw Conrad's mouth tighten, his chin raise a little, and she knew it meant he was close to the end of his patience. She wasn't used to it happening so fast. Conrad's patience had always seemed to her virtually inexhaustible. But he had changed since their trip to Dresden last year. Still, he didn't say the cruel things he could have. He didn't say, all right, then, I think you've been hallucinating; I think this is like the time you started screaming because you saw a man crouching in the corner and it was the stereo speaker; I think this is like the time the German policeman brought you home and you told him his hair was blue.

Instead he said, enunciating more clearly than necessary, "I don't think you've been hallucinating. But you've obviously been drinking."

"I wasn't drunk. I had a drink when I came home because I was so upset. That's all."

"*A* drink." His lips turned up slightly at the corners, but it wasn't a smile.

Vicky turned and went back to the car. She had to keep blinking to force away the humiliated tears. After a few moments Conrad got into the driver's side, and then he backed the car up and turned around. They drove down the hill without speaking.

As they passed the Caserne, Vicky said suddenly, "I took some pictures. Maybe they'll show something." She had completely forgotten about them until now.

"Pictures? Where are they?" Conrad threw her a quick glance.

"I left the film at the LX to be developed. They'll have it tomorrow."

"You think the people you saw are on it?"

"I don't know. I'll have to wait and see." She looked out her side window, at the gate into the Caserne where she had babbled out her story. She recognized the same guard in the booth. A few yards farther on stood the ugly, life-size plywood Mountie attached to Miss Toast *Schnell-Imbiss*, a fast-food stand. She realized how hungry she was, that she hadn't eaten all day.

But the thought of going back to the apartment, of trying to sneak up the stairs while Frau Daimler found some excuse to detain Conrad in conversation, of making supper from yesterday's feeble leftovers, filled her with such a forcible aversion she wanted to jump out of the car.

When they turned onto Tiergartenstraße she said, pretending she had just thought of it but sounding so unconvincing she knew Conrad couldn't possibly believe her, "Oh, damn. I just remembered. I told Annie I'd meet her for supper downtown. Do you mind? You can fix yourself something, can't you?"

They were stopped at a red light but Conrad didn't look at her. "Yes, I can fix myself something."

Vicky stopped herself from answering, yes, of course, you cook better than I do. She had agreed, as a condition of having him support her for two years so she could finish her thesis, to do the cooking and housekeeping, and she knew it was more than a fair deal, given her domestic skills. Which made her all the more desperate to get away from him now, from the inadequate and ungrateful self she was with him.

The light went green. "Just a minute," she said. "I'll get out here." She opened the door.

Conrad's eyes were on the rearview mirror, watching the cars behind him. "You want me to pick you up later?"

"No, thanks. I can walk. Or Annie can give me a ride." She got out of the car.

"All right, then." The car behind them honked, and she slammed the door shut. Conrad pulled away.

Vicky turned and began walking toward Marktstraße. When the Passat was out of sight she slowed her pace and finally stopped, leaned against the side of a building. "What a fucking mess," she said to the pigeon that landed hopefully a few feet from her.

She walked on, to the big Rathaus, a word the Canadians, gleefully pronouncing it as Rat House, preferred to "City Hall." She found a phone in the lobby, but when she reached up to put in her money she realized she was still clutching the little white bead in her left hand. She set it carefully on the phone book. A small pearl, with a hole through the middle for the thread. Then she unzipped her bag, put the bead into the envelope on which she'd scribbled her thesis note, and dialed Annie's number.

"You're home! Thank god. Annie, I'm desperate. Can you come and meet me? I'm at the Rathaus. Please, please, please. Tell Andrew you have to see a sick friend or something, it's an emergency. I'll buy you supper."

"All right," Annie said.

The Rathaus was closing, so she waited outside, leaning against a pillar. The sun was behind clouds now and the wind was getting stronger. She hunched her shoulders and shoved her hands into the pockets of her slacks, cursing herself for not bringing a jacket to wear over her sweatshirt.

Three soldiers in Canadian uniforms came down the street, talking loudly and animatedly in French. They must be from the Twenty-Second Regiment, the French Canadians, whom everyone called the Van Doos. It had taken her a whole year to realize that wasn't some inexplicable army slang but an anglicization of *vingt-deux*. Andrew had told her once that the Van Doos probably enjoyed being here more than the English Canadians did because Lahr, in the far south-west of Germany, was only a few kilometres from France, where the French Canadians could escape the isolation that came from being surrounded by a foreign language. They could cross the Rhine into Strasbourg with its clubs and bars and movies every night if they wanted; it wasn't even necessary anymore to stop at the border. Yes, Vicky thought, watching them approach, it would be nice not to feel a foreigner, an alien, accepted by the Germans because of mutual interests but not necessarily liked. She suspected that the students who had protested outside the base every Thursday with signs saying "Canadian Army Out Of Germany" and "Stop NATO" spoke for more Germans than the government admitted. When the base closing was announced, those who expressed regret were doubtless sincere, but only because it would mean a loss of business, of employment.

One of the soldiers said something to his friends that made them look at her and snicker. She thought she heard the word *putain*. She was pretty sure she knew what it meant. She winced but refused to drop her eyes, to let their contemptuous laughter frighten her. She couldn't have been dressed less seductively, but maybe to men trained to think like soldiers any woman standing here would have only one purpose.

One of the men took a step toward her, and for one terrifying moment the soldier, extending his hand slightly now, was holding a gun.

Then she saw Annie's car, a new blue Mercedes bearing the distinctive red and white Canadian plates, turn the corner. Vicky waved and ran down the steps. The men watched her go, then walked on, laughing, elbowing each other like schoolchildren.

It was only when she opened the passenger door that she realized Annie wasn't alone. She was in the passenger seat, and Andrew was driving.

Annie grinned up at her. She had a round, plump face with a wide jaw line and small features that made her look ten years younger than her real thirty-five. She had just curled her hair, unusual for her, and it stood up around her head in asymmetrical brown lumps.

"Hi! Get in!" If Annie's face looked too young for her age, her voice sounded too old. It was hoarse and rough, weathered with cigarettes, often seeming to presage a cough. "Andy has a meeting at the base so he'll drop us at the restaurant and pick us up after."

Vicky got in the back. The Mercedes had that strong, faintly toxic brand-new-car smell. When she looked up she caught Andrew's eyes in the mirror.

"Hiya," he said.

Even the back of the man's head was handsome, for god's

sake. Under his captain's cap with the yellow stripe on the brim she was sure every dark, curly hair was perfectly in place. He exuded confidence, intelligence. It was obvious why he'd done well in the army. Vicky looked away, out the side window, wishing he would hurry up and get them to the restaurant.

And then she thought, but I have to talk to him before he finds out what happened from the lieutenant. So as Andrew pulled away from the curb she leaned forward between the front seats and said, "Could you stop for a minute, Andrew? Something awful happened today and I have to tell you about it."

In the rearview mirror she could see Andrew's eyebrows go up. "Sure," he said. He pulled halfway onto the sidewalk in the pragmatic parking style of the Europeans.

Annie unclipped her seat belt and turned around to stare at Vicky. "If you have to tell *Andy* it really must be awful."

"It is."

And, leaning forward uncomfortably, she told her story again, giving details about the soldiers who went back with her to the Staatswald because she thought Andrew would want to hear about that, remembering this time to mention the pictures, telling them about going up again with Conrad and finding the bead.

"Jesus Christ, Vicky," Annie said, her green eyes so wide Vicky could see her new contact lenses floating in them. "Are you *sure*?"

"Yes, I'm sure." She made her voice calm, assertive. "Although Dr. Lester probably convinced the lieutenant I was crazy."

Andrew had listened to her carefully, nodding occasionally, frowning a little when she described the MPs and the doctor and the lieutenant. She had had the terrible feeling he would laugh, but he was a professional now, doing his job.

"Could you identify the man if you saw him again, do you think?"

"I don't know. It was all so fast. I only got a glimpse, really, and that was just in partial profile."

Andrew nodded. "And you say they did a search after you left?"

"For half an hour. At least that's what Crosby said when I called him."

"I'll talk to Crosby," Andrew said. "I think he's in the middle of a messy divorce so he's a bit distracted these days, but he likes to be thought of as thorough. I'll try to make sure he puts some effort into this investigation."

"Thank you," she said, the words inadequate to her relief. "When I get the pictures back tomorrow, if they show anything I'll come to see you, okay?"

"Yes, absolutely." He glanced at the clock on the dashboard. "Well, we better get going. I'm late for my meeting. I should be back to pick you up by quarter to eight."

Vicky leaned back, did up her seat belt again, and Andrew pulled into the traffic. Annie was still twisted around in her seat, staring at Vicky.

"God," she said. "Are you *okay*? If I'd seen that I'd be a complete wreck by now."

Vicky gave a humourless laugh. "I *am* a complete wreck."

Andrew let them off close to the little restaurant on Marktstraße where they had often met before, partly because they liked its name, *Die Taube*, the dove, which they agreed was nicely ironic in a town with such a hawkish presence. They got a table against the far wall, on which several wood-carved grey doves hung. Two others were suspended from the ceiling. A waitress eager to practise her English took their order.

"And a litre of your house wine, white," Vicky said.

Annie looked at her but didn't say anything. They were both supposed to be on the wagon.

When the waitress was out of earshot, they began to talk in low voices, like conspirators, going over it all again, Annie, fidgeting in her seat even more than usual, asking for more and more details — how tall was he? What kind of shoes was he wearing? About how old was the woman? Was it sunshine or shade? Did the MPs, the meatheads, say anything? Was Vicky sure Lieutenant Crosby didn't believe her?

"I think he must have at the beginning," Vicky said. "But then of course they couldn't find the woman. I can't blame him for being skeptical, especially after Dr. Lester talked to him. I'm sure he convinced him I was just a crazy drunk."

Annie's eyes flicked, just for a second, to Vicky's wine glass.

"I was sober, Annie," Vicky said stiffly. "I had a drink when I got home afterwards. I needed one, all right?"

Annie sat back, startled, raised her hands slightly, palms out. "All right," she said.

"It's just so — " Vicky's voice faltered " — so hard when everyone must think I made it up, or was seeing things — "

"I think you really saw it."

"I wish it were that easy to convince Dr. Lester."

"Oh, him." He was Annie's doctor, too. "You know Lester. He thinks all women are neurotics. That's why the army gave him this posting. He has to keep the ladies shoveled full of diazepam because otherwise, well, they might just pack up and go home. And then who would the men beat up?"

Vicky smiled. "He does think Valium's the answer to everything, doesn't he?"

"What an aaaasshole."

And then they were both laughing, loudly, not caring that

the other couple in the restaurant was looking at them oddly. They were laughing because they were remembering how they had first met, about a year ago, at the Astra Cinema in the Canadian Cultural Centre. There was a subtitled French film on, advertised as being about "a sensitive artist," who, Vicky soon decided, was an immature slug whose treatment of women and a gay neighbour was tediously abusive. During a scene where he wondered aloud if sleeping with yet another beautiful woman would (at least so the subtitles claimed) "dilute my artistic potency," Vicky said loudly, "What an aaaasshole."

There were a few giggles from the mostly female audience, and then, from somewhere near the back, someone applauded.

The someone, of course, was Annie, who at the end of the movie came up to where Vicky was sitting, sound asleep by now, and asked if she'd like to go somewhere for a drink. Vicky, for whom paranoia about the army had already, after four months, become her dominant emotion, would likely have refused if she had been awake enough to realize she wasn't being arrested or ordered to leave. Instead, she blinked and nodded, trying to breathe shallowly so the woman beside her wouldn't smell the gin, and they drove downtown to a *Taverne* not patronized by the Canadians, who preferred their own bars, where the drinks were cheap and they didn't have to mix with the locals.

Annie had been in Lahr three years by then, two of them lived in an awful apartment in the PMQ, the Personnel Married Quarters, before she and Andrew found a private rental north of town. During these three years she had, Annie said, counting them off on her fingers, "three miscarriages, so I finally got the message; one teensy little nervous breakdown the first year; a drinking habit like you wouldn't believe; a nail-biting habit like — " and she held up her hands to show the thick, ugly stubs " — and a weight gain of forty apparently impervious pounds."

Vicky had looked at her in boozy admiration. "So it *is* possible to have a good time," she said.

Annie had warned her that day, with good reason, that she had a mean streak in her, but generally they had been good for each other. They had cut down on the drinking and then promised to stop cold turkey (Vicky saying somberly that night that the German word for "wine," *Wein*, was the same as the word for "cry"); they shared their books and conversations about them; they discussed what an army psychologist in a pamphlet had labeled "An Attitude Problem Among Dependants" and decided he should be court-martialled for stupidity; and they complained about their husbands, but in a generic sort of way, not wholeheartedly, aware of loyalties older and more complicated than their friendship.

The waitress brought their meals. Vicky had forgotten what she'd ordered. There was something schnitzeled and something that wasn't and a green salad. She devoured it all gratefully. Annie picked at her food, saying she wasn't very hungry, but Vicky suspected she was on another diet. She *had* lost weight lately, and Vicky hoped she wasn't trying something awful like diet pills or throwing up or starvation.

Annie pushed her plate away and began rubbing at her eye, dislodging her contact lens. "Oh, shit," she said, picking it off her cheek. She put the lens in her case and then, after several painful-looking tries that made Vicky's own eyes water, she popped out the other lens, put it away, and shoved on her glasses with the taped left temple. "Vanity, thy name is Bausch and Lomb," she sighed. "Honestly, I don't know why we weren't just born blind to begin with."

Vicky had glasses, too, which she was supposed to wear when driving but otherwise didn't bother with. It occurred to her that if the army knew she even owned a pair of glasses it would be another reason to disbelieve her.

Annie looked at her watch. "Andy should have been here by now."

"I hope he's found something out."

But when Andrew did come for them, he looked distracted and upset, saying the meeting, about how to handle the winding-down of the base, had gotten nasty, everyone protecting himself and his turf. He didn't even mention the murder until Annie demanded to know what he'd found out.

"Oh, god, nothing, I'm afraid. I did mention it, but nobody knew anything about it and Crosby wasn't there." He changed lanes sharply and turned up Werderstraße. It had begun to rain lightly, tiny spots appearing on the windshield, but he didn't turn on the wipers. "I left a report form for you in my office. You can come by tomorrow and fill it out."

"Okay," Vicky said, trying not to let him hear her disappointment.

When she got back to the apartment Conrad had already gone to bed. He had left the kitchen in a mess, and it gave her some satisfaction to clean it more thoroughly than usual. As she was letting the water out of the sink, she remembered the glass she had shoved under the sofa. But when she went to look for it, it was gone.

She hung up the dishtowel and went quietly into the bedroom and looked down at Conrad, who lay on his right side facing the far wall. He would always start off sleeping on his back, but as the night progressed he would turn onto his side, pull his knees up and his arms in, like a slowly tightening coil. Vicky could hear him breathing deeply, almost but not quite a snore. She had the urge to go and put her arms around him, but she thought it was sleep he would want more than her erratic affection, so she closed the door and let him sleep.

She wandered through the living room, restlessly, running her hands over the backs of the furniture. When she saw her belt-bag sitting on the coffee table, she remembered the bead she had put in the envelope, so she took the envelope out and went with it into the study. She picked out the bead, slid the envelope into the file folder marked, "Chapter 6: Aesthetic Distance," and set the bead carefully in the paper-clip tray on her desk. Then she sat down and looked at it, in this room surrounded by words she couldn't imagine finding meaningful again. But she would have to, somehow. She would have to try to find her way back into her own life.

On the desk in front of her were the first thirty-two handwritten pages of her thesis. *Filmic Identification for Women in Early American Cinema.* She had promised herself she would write something every day. Just this morning she had begun Chapter 3, "From Spectator to Spectacle." She had the chapter thoroughly and prescriptively outlined, so the writing shouldn't be difficult, although she was uneasy about having so little research.

Practically nothing had been written about filmic identification for women, and few of those who had mentioned it thought filmic identification for women was possible at all. Bellour, one of the major critics, said that woman's place in American film, as in psychoanalysis, was assigned to her purely by the rules of male desire and that women who see such films positively do so only out of their own masochism. It seemed a popular view, proposed by feminist theorists, too. Simply pointing a camera at a woman, said Doane, had become equivalent to a terrorist act; a woman who bought a ticket must deny her sex. Vicky could hardly watch a film now without catching herself when she was enjoying it and thinking: oh, oh — masochism. Yet she agreed with most of Doane's analysis — it was more or less the premise of her own thesis. "Identification for women in early American film is virtually impossible," she'd said on page one. The "virtually" left her a little room, but not much, to consider alternatives.

A headache began to beat lightly at her temples, and she let her eyes go out of focus, the pages in front of her doubling, transparent. Spectator dynamics. Structural-materialist film. Signification. Phatic function. Semiotics. Seeing/being seen = male/female. Lacan. Derrida. Barthes.

It was all unreal, academic, irrelevant. She had just seen a woman murdered. A real-life horror film. One where she wasn't just a spectator but a part of the movie.

The camera would be behind her now. It would have done a close-up on her hand as it dropped the bead into the paper-clip tray, then another close-up on her face as she looked reflectively at the bead. Then it would pull back, show her sighing, bending to her work — and an excited rush of music would play as the camera focused on the page in front of her, and some word, some phrase, would highlight itself and leap magically into the context of the bead, and she would exclaim, "Yes! Now I know who killed her" —

For heaven's sake. She frowned, rubbed hard at her temples, straightened her back. Then she picked up page thirty-two and read the last sentences she had written:

> *To fully understand the conflicted position of the woman spectator — whose identification with female characters is, as we have seen in Chapter One, extremely problematic and whose identification with male characters necessitates a trans-sex or transvestite position — it is useful to examine how within film itself women are similarly*

conflicted. Women may, for example, in film as in life, adopt deliberate disguise. Such disguise could take the form of masquerade, where womanliness is worn to hide the possession of masculinity, where what the viewer sees is essentially a mask.

Vicky stared at the words for a moment and then picked up a pencil and wrote:

Masquerade, yes, that's what I saw, nothing real, play-acting, a woman wearing a yellow sweater and only a mask of blood.

FRIDAY

Morning

"THANKS."

Vicky reached for the pictures. Her hand was trembling slightly. The sad-looking man behind the counter nodded and turned away.

She put the envelope in her jacket pocket and kept her hand pressed against it. Outside the LX store she wheeled her bicycle beside her, not wanting to ride because it would mean having to take her hand out of her pocket. She felt strangely furtive, as though she were smuggling in, or out, a pocketful of plutonium. She should probably sit down right now, here, on the steps of K 11, the CanEx video store, and look at the pictures, but she just kept walking, faster and faster, and then she got onto her bicycle and began pedaling to the front entrance of the Caserne. She barely slowed down as she passed the guard at the gate and turned onto Langemarckstraße.

She had gone several blocks before she stopped. Her heart was pounding, and the tension was winding tighter and tighter in her stomach. She pushed her bicycle along the sidewalk until she came to a bus stop, and then she leaned the bicycle against it and sat down on the bench, putting her hand back into her pocket. She sat there for several moments, watching the traffic go by. There had been a heavy, rain-filled wind the night before, and the air smelled crisp, alpine. She looked up at the sky, cloudless and vividly blue, as though it had been washed clean, and she tried to make herself calm.

Finally she took out the envelope. The sweat on her neck, in her armpits, felt cold and clammy. She opened the envelope, slowly pulled out the pictures. There were only half a dozen because she hadn't finished the roll. She made herself look at them in order, as though they might all be equally interesting. The first was of Conrad standing by the car outside the Gutenberg School; she had actually coaxed a small smile from him. Then there was one of her standing with her arm around the plywood Mountie at Miss Toast in front of the Caserne entrance.

The next one was taken in the park.

Her fingers were damp; she wiped them on her jeans.

The picture was of the trees, a profusion of green, with some autumn reds and yellows sleeving the branches, thick ivy climbing the trunks. The next picture was taken facing northeast, toward the Caserne, although only a small corner of one of the single men's barracks was visible through the trees. The next picture was taken facing northwest, across the city. The shot was overexposed, the red roofs looking pink, but she recognized two of the church spires and the Storchenturm downtown. There was only one more picture.

And there they were. This shot was overexposed, as well, but the two people were reasonably clear. The woman was directly facing the camera, the man facing away but turned a little on his left toward the camera. The woman's right arm was blurry, from lifting it to her chest, to the yellow sweater with the white beads in the shape of a bird's wing. Was there a spot of red on the sweater? Vicky looked closer, holding her breath. No. Nothing.

She looked quickly at the man's hands. His left arm was clearly visible, bent a little at the elbow, his fingers curled against his thigh. And his right hand, the one that had held the gun — it was obscured by his body.

Vicky closed her eyes. What had she expected? It was only in movies that it was so easy. She opened her eyes and looked at the man again, trying to force into sight something gray at his right side, something that could be the barrel of a gun. She kept turning the photo, squinting at it, but there was nothing there, only the dark green of ivy crawling up a tree.

But at least she had a picture of the two people. They were real. If they were real she'd seen someone killed. The picture would not be proof for anyone else, but it was for her.

Her eyes went back to the woman, her small face surrounded by tightly curled blond hair, her mouth open, her eyes fixed on the man. Vicky looked at her face more closely. In her memory she had seen the face as shadowed, shaded, but she thought now the woman must be dark-skinned. And the blond hair? It could be dyed. Or perhaps the woman was of mixed race. Like her.

It was too painful to look at the woman, that hand moving up to her chest, those eyes staring at the man. Vicky moved her own eyes back to him. His head was turned enough to the left that she could see his forehead, cheek, part of his nose and lips. He was of medium height and build, brown-haired, a soldier in uniform. There were thousands here just like him.

She looked at the cuff of his left sleeve. Lieutenant Crosby had asked her something about stripes. She couldn't see any. But up on his shoulder she saw part of a yellow band, perhaps that of a single chevron. What would that make him? A private, probably. She would have to look at the picture under a magnifying glass, maybe have an enlargement done —

Yes, an enlargement. She would be David Hemmings in *Blow-Up*, enlarging and enlarging a detail until it became — what? — a gun? — a spot of blood on a yellow sweater? Of course, she thought, remembering her thesis research, she was only supposed to be Vanessa Redgrave, coming to his studio and baring her breasts, for what reason, if any, Vicky couldn't recall —

She had to stop. This wasn't part of some goddamned movie. The photograph showed nothing except two people looking at each other.

Still, that was something, wasn't it? She would give the picture to Andrew or Lieutenant Crosby or the MPs and they could try to identify the soldier or the woman. If the men didn't have the time or the interest to pursue it she'd give the picture to the German police. It cheered her up a little, the way she could see both a direction and an end to her involvement now. She had something tangible to offer, and then it would be taken out of her hands.

She put the pictures back in the envelope and stood up. And she felt the unmistakable cramp, the dampness in her crotch and underpants, that told her her period had begun. "Shit," she said aloud, thinking, by the time I ride back to the Caserne and put a tampon in I'll probably have not just bloodstained panties but bloodstained slacks, and I can't talk to Andrew or Crosby or whoever like that.

So she decided to go home first and change her clothes. It would take less than half an hour. She put the photographs carefully in her jacket pocket and rode home, fast, cheating at intersections by crossing with the pedestrians, sneaking through amber lights. A man in a muscle car with Canadian plates kept pace with her, briefly, grinning and turning up his rock music that had the beat of a flat tire. She lost him by turning right into an alley, improvising a shortcut.

When she got to the house the back door was open although Frau Daimler was, happily, nowhere in sight. She unlocked the door at the bottom of the stairs and stepped inside.

She heard the sound of paper scrunching, and when she looked down she saw she had stepped onto an envelope. It must have been slipped under the door. Her name was printed on it in large block letters. She stared at it for several moments before she bent over and picked it up. It frightened her — the anonymity of it, the way it had been delivered. The regular mail came through the front door mail slot, and Frau Daimler would leave Vicky's and Conrad's on the little table downstairs in the hall. She had a sudden chilling memory of an article she'd read, about how Colombia's military death squads would send their intended victims invitations to their own funerals. *Sufragios*, the invitations were called.

It took all her determination to start up the stairs with the envelope in her hand, to press her thumbnail under the flap and pull out and unfold the single sheet of white paper inside and read what was on it.

The note was made up of letters cut from a newspaper and glued untidily onto the page. It said: "Your husband ist in on it."

She must have stood there for several full minutes, clutching the bannister, staring at the paper in her hand. Then, slowly, she went into the living room and sat down on the sofa and set the note in front of her on the coffee table. *Your husband ist in on it*. Conrad. It must mean Conrad. He was in on it. On what?

The murder. The note must be referring to the murder.

She pulled her knees up to her chest, hugged them tightly.

The room seemed suddenly to shift, to be dangerously unstable. She remembered the poet Josef Brodsky saying that in the mental hospitals in Russia the walls, windows and doorways were all built just a small degree off square, how that alone became enough to drive one mad.

To drive one mad. Was that the purpose of the note? Who would want to upset her like this? It must have been someone who knew not to drop the note through the front door mail slot, who knew that the back door was usually open or unlocked and which of the inner doors led to their apartment.

Then there was the word "*ist.*" Was it a simple mistake made by a German? Or was it done deliberately, to make her think it was done by a German? The phrase "in on it" seemed to suggest a familiarity with English idiom. The letters themselves looked as though they had been cut from several different newspapers or magazines, and they were in about four different typefaces and sizes, only the "ba," "nd" and "in" cut out together, so it was impossible to tell from which language they might have come.

She went into the kitchen and poured herself a brandy, then another. She held her hand in front of her and watched it tremble, in small spasms.

What she was trying most not to think about was that the note could really mean what it said. It was impossible, wasn't it? Of course it was impossible. Conrad — involved in anything illegal? It was absurd. Involved in a *murder*? The scene from the Staatswald surged again into her mind: the woman in the yellow sweater, the man standing before her with the gun held, unwavering, before him.

Unwavering. Yes, the man had seemed very calm. It hadn't seemed as though they'd had a quarrel, as though there was any passion involved in his action. It seemed so deliberate, like an execution. And where there was an execution there was often a conspiracy. Other people involved. Other people *in on it*.

But not Conrad. Conrad could never hurt anyone.

But could he stand by knowing others were being hurt?

She sat down at the kitchen table and looked out the window at the two huge oak trees in the neighbouring yard. And she remembered what had happened in Dresden.

·

Conrad had been born in Dresden, and after they had been living in Lahr for about three months he told her, suddenly, that since the East German border had basically ceased to exist he wanted to go to Dresden. Did she want to go? Yes, of course she wanted to go. Everyone was talking about German unification, and she was as curious as anyone what it was like on the side that had so abruptly ceased being the enemy, the side that the west claimed as its temporarily misaligned own. The *Wessis* did not exactly seem to embrace the *Ossis* when given the chance, however, and even she had heard unflattering comments from the former about the latter. There was the story, for example, of an Ossi coming to Bonn and greeting an office receptionist with the slogan the government had tried to popularize, "We are all one people," and the receptionist responding coldly, "So are we." There was reason, she knew, for the bitter Ossi jokes about how the only difference between Wessis and Russians was that they could get rid of the Russians.

But for Conrad, she suspected, the reason for going to Dresden was not simply curiosity about a political realignment. He had been six when the British bombed the city. All

he ever told her was that his mother and sister and grandmother and two aunts had died there. His father was killed
on the Russian front — "he fell," Conrad had said, using the
old phrasing that perhaps was a euphemism but that sounded
more horrible, somehow, than "killed in battle" — and
Conrad, after three years in an impoverished orphanage in
Berlin, was sent to Canada and adopted by the Bauers in
Valleyview, Alberta. The Bauers, like many immigrant
Germans, were assimilating as quickly and inconspicuously as
possible, forbidding the use of their mother tongue even in
their own home. On the adoption and school papers they
made sure to anglicize the spelling of "Konrad." Conrad had
a sort of dutiful affection for the Bauers, she knew, but when
they died he had said, shrugging off her sympathy, that he
felt no more an orphan now than he had before. It made her
think about the young and more-or-less orphaned state she
was in when he married her, and she wondered if his own
childhood had influenced that decision.

In any case, she had been happy, one long weekend, to go
with him to Dresden.

As they got farther into eastern Germany she was aware
of him becoming more and more quiet. When they stopped
overnight in Leipzig he was hardly speaking at all, and when
a young couple outside the hotel asked him admiring questions about their Passat and their Canadian plates, he was
uncharacteristically abrupt, barely smiling at their jokes about
how they would trade it for their Trabi, the cheap but notori-
ously inefficient East German car she had seen everywhere.

When she saw Dresden she was surprised and shaken to
still see signs of the war, buildings ending abruptly in rubble.
She supposed the East German government had left them
that way deliberately, for political reasons, to show the brutal-
ity of the Allies. Dresden had been, she knew, one of the

most architecturally and culturally rich cities in the world, which was why it was chosen as a target.

When they neared the centre of the city, she could see more of it had been restored, and new hotels seemed to be under construction everywhere. The Zwinger palace museum complex with its six linked pavilions and baroque gardens appeared on their right. She had read about how the palace had been restored, and she wanted to ask Conrad to stop, to go inside, but when she glanced over at him she saw his eyes fixed rigidly ahead, his face pale and sweating, and she was afraid to say anything at all. They passed the museum and turned right, which led them to the banks of the Elbe River, on a graceful meander of which the city had been built. Florence on the Elbe, it had once been called. Conrad stopped the car, stared at the twisting waters.

"The Marienbrücke," he said tightly. "It was right here."

"Maybe we should buy a city map," she ventured.

Conrad shook his head, kept staring at the water.

"There's a bridge over there." Vicky pointed to the east. "Is that it?"

"No."

But he backed the car up and they headed for it, driving along the river. The rococo yellows and greens of the buildings dazzled the eye, but they couldn't compete with the tension in the car. When they reached the bridge Vicky saw the sign for it, Augustusbrücke, and Conrad, not saying anything, turned onto it.

Across the bridge they kept heading north, through a neighbourhood of new houses, lawns held out in front of them like aprons embroidered with knots of red and yellow flowers. They passed, on a hill to their right, a large cemetery much older than the houses and poorly tended, relinquishing itself to the imperatives of gravity and grass. A row of leaning headstones on the crest of the hill looked like dark thumbprints against the sky.

But it was clear now that Conrad was lost, looking for landmarks that had ceased to exist fifty years ago. Finally he stopped the car and asked a girl playing on the sidewalk for directions. She shook her head at first but then pointed to the east. As they pulled away Conrad said, his voice so low Vicky wasn't sure whether he intended her to hear, "I shouldn't have come."

When they got to the address he was looking for, on the eastern outskirts of the city, it was worse than she'd imagined. There was evidence of a house having been there, once — among the tall grasses and tendrils of ivy she could see a faint outline of a foundation, a stack of crumbling bricks along what could have been the far wall. Two small apple trees were growing beside it, one on either side of the bricks.

Conrad walked over to what might have been the front entrance. He stood there for a long time, not moving, his back to Vicky, who sat, unsure, in the car. At last she got out and went over to him, put her hand on his arm. When she saw the tears streaming down his face, the awful distortion of grief on every feature, she felt helpless and frightened because she had never seen Conrad cry before.

He sank to his knees, terrible sobs twisting his body. She knelt beside him, holding his arm tightly, fearfully.

"I was here," he said at last. "I was here."

And he told her everything, as they knelt there in front of the ruined house like communicants at an altar. How when the bombs began to fall they had huddled together under the kitchen table, his grandmother folding him tightly against and under her, and how, when the bomb hit, his mother had kept screaming and screaming, for what seemed like hours, until she could die, and how it was a full, cold winter day later before someone dug him out from under the rubble, from under the bodies of his grandmother and his aunt, who had come from Berlin to stay with them because it would be safe here, and how he had wandered about the suffocating, burning city for days.

Conrad got up then and stumbled to the car. He put his hands against the door and leaned his forehead against it.

He stood there for several moments, breathing deeply, and then he turned suddenly and said, his voice shaking now not with grief, but with rage, "The bastards. The goddamned bastards. They did it deliberately. The war was essentially over, they knew they'd won. But they did it anyway. They ignored the military targets and went after civilians. If Germany had won the war it would have been the British on trial at Nürnberg for what they did to us at Dresden. And not just Dresden. At Pforzheim in one night they killed half the population. In Hamburg the first firestorm killed 40,000 people, and they were so happy they kept trying to do it again, and they succeeded here, they made another firestorm, three thousand tons of bombs it took, but, oh, they got their firestorm, they killed another 40,000 people. The British have just spent a pile of money for a memorial to the leader of Bomber Command whose policy this was, to hit civilian targets. He killed a hundred thousand children. Don't let them grow up to be Nazis." He jerked open the car door. "Well, maybe he was right. Maybe he should have killed us all."

He got in, slammed the door shut so hard the whole vehicle trembled. Vicky went over to the passenger side and got in. She was afraid to look at Conrad.

"I was talking to Paul," he said, staring straight ahead through the windshield, "about how Germany is the only country that has consistently admitted its guilt in the war and apologized to its victims, and he said Japan, for instance, doesn't have to do it because they had the atomic bombs dropped on them, so they can argue they were victims, too. It's called moral equivalence. My god." His voice caught. "Isn't Dresden a moral equivalent? Isn't my mother's life a moral equivalent?"

He started the motor, shoved the car into gear and pressed down hard on the accelerator. He didn't look back once at the place he had been born, the place he had left his childhood.

They had originally planned to stay overnight in Dresden, but Conrad headed back the way they had come, out of the city. He was driving too fast, tailgating and switching lanes carelessly. They took a wrong turn somewhere and wound up on a small back road with little traffic. The countryside was beautiful, but she was afraid to take her eyes off the road, as though she were the driver. Conrad's anger was filling up the car like an explosive gas. She had never seen him like this, would never have thought him capable of such emotion.

They stopped for the night at Weimar, a small city about half way between Dresden and what had been the old East-West border, at an ancient *Gasthaus* they were lucky to find. Conrad said he was tired and wanted to rest, so Vicky went out on her own and visited the Goethehaus and the Schillerhaus, noting the carefully preserved letters from Keats and Byron, wishing Conrad had come with her, as though this display of old artistic friendships across borders would somehow make him feel better.

When she got back to the *Gasthaus* he was gone, although the car was still there. Worried, she wandered the streets, peering into shops and restaurants, and at last she found him in a dim little tavern a few blocks from the hotel.

He had obviously had a considerable amount to drink, and he looked at her out of red, unfocused eyes that at first didn't seem to recognize her.

"Want a drink?" he asked her finally. He gestured at the waiter, a young black man in a stained white apron.

Want a drink? was a question Vicky hadn't heard Conrad ask her for at least ten years. Too surprised to say anything, she nodded. The waiter came over and Conrad said something to him in German and the man brought over two more large glasses of beer. Conrad took several deep swallows of his immediately, half-emptying the glass. Vicky, hesitating only a moment, did the same. The beer was watery and stale, but Vicky waited only a moment before draining her glass. Conrad didn't seem to notice.

The waiter had gone over to the table beside them where three loud youths with black leather vests and very short haircuts sat. Vicky glanced at them uneasily. Skinheads, *Glatzen.* She didn't understand what they were saying to the waiter, but she could tell by the way he was backing away from them that he was frightened.

Suddenly one of the youths, who had a large blue tattoo on his forearm and wore a thick pewter earring like a clamp, leaned forward and grabbed the waiter's apron, jerking him toward them. Some money fell from the man's tray, and another of the youths pocketed it, laughing derisively. She thought she heard them say, "*Schwarzer*" and "*Schwein.*" There were four older men in the tavern, sitting at two different tables, but although they were watching they made no move to interfere.

"We should do something," Vicky whispered.

"It's none of our business," Conrad said.

"Of course it's our business. Can't you see what they're doing? They're thugs. They're Nazis."

"So am I. They should have killed us all."

"Oh, don't be ridiculous."

One of the skinheads had taken his beer and was pouring it into the waiter's pants pocket while one of the others held him by his belt, pressing him up hard against the table. His tray fell from his hands and rolled slowly across the room, until it hit the leg of Vicky's chair and toppled over. She bent down and picked it up. When she straightened she met the eyes of the waiter. They were large and dark and terrified.

She got up, holding the tray in front of her in both hands.

"Vicky! For god's sake. Sit down. What are you doing?"

She ignored Conrad, began walking over to the other table. One of the youths saw her coming and nudged his companion, who said something and then all three of them laughed coarsely.

"Let him go," Vicky said loudly. They looked startled, probably at the English words as much as at her tone. "Cowards!" she shouted. "Let him go!"

She slammed the tray down on the table so hard the glasses jumped, one of them, half full, overturning. The man holding the waiter's belt jerked away to avoid the running beer and released his grip. The waiter stumbled back.

"You're just thugs, that's what you are. Cowards and thugs!"

They stared at her, their eyes, for one amazing moment, almost as frightened as the waiter's had been. Beer was dripping off the table onto the floor.

She felt a hand on her arm, and she jerked away, not knowing it was Conrad until she heard his low urgent voice. "What the hell are you doing? Let's get out of here."

One of the men had recovered from his surprise by now and he said something to her, pointing angrily at the spilled beer.

"Get fucked!" she cried. "You pathetic asshole!"

Conrad said something in German. She could tell from his tone he was being placating, apologetic. "*Die Frau,*" she heard him say twice. *Die Frau.* The woman. The wife. She was furious, felt like hitting him with the tray.

But she made herself take several deep breaths, let go of the tray, and let Conrad pull her away, to the door. She heard a chair scraping behind her, and for the first time she felt a spurt of fear.

Then she was outside, walking quickly away, half running. Conrad's fingers were clamped on her upper arm like a vice. Only when they reached the end of the block and turned the corner, glancing behind them one more time, did they slow down. They were both panting.

"What did you think you were doing in there? You could have gotten us both killed. They could have had guns, or knives — " He dropped his hand from her arm and moved a little away from her side, as though she were someone he had accosted by mistake.

"Somebody had to do something."

"It was none of our business. Maybe it looked worse than it was. Maybe they were drunk and just having fun."

"*Fun?*"

"What do you know about it?" Conrad demanded. "What do you know about their lives? You can't just cross out the East German border and expect everything to be easy here now. Somebody tells them everything they've been taught all their lives is wrong, so who's to blame them for looking for scapegoats, maybe for thinking they were told lies about Hitler, too? They're supposed to think communism was a mistake, go back to how it was before. Well, Naziism is how it was before."

"How can you make excuses for them? Their behaviour hasn't anything to do with the border coming down. It's simple thuggery, simple racism. Maybe if enough people had stood up to the brown shirts things would never have gotten so out of control."

"How nice it must be to see everything so clearly. Okay, you stood up to that gang in the bar. Very commendable. And next time they'll torment the waiter even worse."

"It was still better to say something. If you don't protest they think you approve, that it's acceptable."

"It's not that simple," Conrad said.

In their *Gasthaus* room they retreated to opposite corners with their books, Conrad with the latest Le Carré, and Vicky, wishing she had brought something more escapist, with the new issue of *Quarterly Review of Film Studies*. She kept reading the same page over and over, but all she could think about was the men in the bar, the unexpected way Conrad had responded. Was he right — had she been foolhardy and naive? Had she just made things worse for the black waiter? She glanced up at Conrad, frowning over his own book, and she realized she had no idea at all what he was thinking.

The next morning they were carefully polite to each other, neither referring to the day before. When they went downstairs for breakfast and had to wait over half an hour for three slices of white cheese and two buns they could have used a chainsaw to cut, they didn't complain. They ate with their eyes cast down, as though they had been chastised.

It was raining heavily as they drove out of Weimar. The water seemed to bounce off the road, turning the pavement into a grey haze. As the wiper momentarily cleared a space before her eyes, she saw a small sign pointing off the road to the right. *Buchenwald.*

"Buchenwald? The concentration camp?" She peered at her road map. "It's not on the map. Why wouldn't they put it on the map?"

"There's probably nothing there now," Conrad said, turning toward the big E40 that would take them back into western Germany.

"I suppose not," Vicky said. But it unnerved her, to think that so close to Weimar with its cultured history there could have been Buchenwald. *Buch* meant book; *Wald* meant forest. Where Goethe and Schiller once walked. And why did her map, bought in Frankfurt, which showed every tiny village both in east and west Germany, not have Buchenwald?

She remembered, suddenly, a movie she had seen with Conrad at the Canadian Community Centre. Called *Europa, Europa,* it was the true story of a Jewish boy embraced by the Nazis as a fine example of Aryan youth. The film had won international prizes, but German critics and award committees trashed it, and few Germans even saw it.

"It's a good movie," she'd said to Conrad. "Why don't they want to face the past?"

"They're tired of it. Think of all those cowboy movies where the Indians are bloodthirsty savages. Didn't they upset you?"

A question of filmic identification, she'd thought. Conrad knew the best arguments. "Well, of course," she said uncomfortably, "but that's different. Those films were lies, distortions."

"Lies and distortions: those are always the prerogatives of the winners."

"But this movie was based on a true story."

Conrad sighed. "All I'm saying is that *you* see the movie and it's absolute evil versus absolute good. And of course you're on the side of absolute good. But the Germans see the film and it's not that easy."

"But surely — now — they can be on the side of absolute good, too."

"And see themselves and the parents they loved cast as monsters?"

"They probably just don't like the fact that the only good Germans in the film are a woman and a gay man," Vicky had said, half making a joke of it.

But as she sat in the car driving back from Dresden she could hear Conrad's voice again, saying, "the parents they loved," and she realized that he must have been thinking of his own parents, and that when he said, "the Germans," he must have been thinking of himself, too. Why hadn't she realized that at the time? It was because his voice had been, as usual, calm, detached, the voice of a man discussing an abstraction. She leaned her head back and closed her eyes, listening to the hammer of rain on the car roof, the hiss of the wipers.

Everything that had happened on that trip had been connected, somehow, but she had stopped herself from thinking about it.

But she had to think about it now. *Your husband ist in on it.*

There had been a change in Conrad since they'd come back from east Germany. Nothing Jekyll and Hyde, she told herself, trying to be amused at the idea; he just seemed more irritable and preoccupied. When he went out with German people, even down to Frau Daimler's in the evening, he would return restless, secretive even. If she hadn't known better she would have suspected he was seeing another woman. But she had her own work to do, her own preoccupations, and mostly she was just relieved that he didn't expect her to socialize with his new acquaintances.

But now, looking at the note in her hand, she made herself coldly consider the worst — that Conrad was involved in something, something awful. What were the gatherings he went to? Did he meet with the kind of Germans who would condone the way the waiter had been treated? Were they what the newspapers at home called the "significant minority of sympathizers"? Were they the kind of people who might still want revenge for what had been done to Dresden? Were they some kind of neo-Nazis?

It was impossible, absurd, a script for *They Saved Hitler's Brain*. Was Frau Daimler saving Hitler's brain in her bureau drawer? Were they cloning Nazis in the basement? She made herself laugh out loud in the empty room, laugh at the bargain-basement plots she was imagining into life.

Yet how could she ignore the note, delivered to her the day after she saw a murder? The note was no joke. She couldn't laugh it into insignificance. Whoever left it had intended to frighten her.

Not knowing what else to do with it, she took the paper into the study, folded it carefully in half and slipped it between pages 104 and 105 of *The Cinematography Reader*. She'd deal with it later, she told herself, after she came back from the Caserne.

Hurriedly she changed her clothes, leaving her blood-stained panties and slacks to soak in the sink, and made herself go back downstairs. If she saw Frau Daimler or Erich, could she ask them if they'd seen anyone leaving the note? They probably wouldn't understand, and if they did they would mention it to Conrad. Unless one of them left the note. They were the most likely to know, after all, when she would be out, when she was likely to return.

She bolted out the back door and onto her bicycle. She was halfway to the Caserne before she let herself slow down.

The sun was hot, and she could feel sweat trickling down between her breasts. She pressed her left arm against her chest, hoping the cotton sweatshirt would blot up most of the moisture.

The guard at the gate, a young woman with a starched-looking face, seemed to scrutinize her "Dependant" card with special care as Vicky waited, fidgeting. She resisted the urge to say something sarcastic (as she had the time she introduced Conrad to someone at a party as her Co-Dependant, remembering only too late that was also the vocabulary of addiction), something about how pointless this checking was, when anyone with a card was allowed to drive in with a load of cardless companions and when the big wire gate at the east end of the compound was often propped open with no one around. Whole armies of terrorists could have sauntered in by now.

But she kept her mouth shut, and at last the guard nodded and handed back her card, and Vicky pushed her bicycle through the gates. Then for one awful moment she froze, completely forgetting why she had come, who she was here to see, what she had to say.

Andrew. Okay. She was going to see Andrew to show him the photo, fill out a report. And the note: would she tell him about the note? If she did it would mean she had chosen not to trust Conrad. No, she couldn't tell anyone about the note. She remembered how she had felt before she left the bus stop to go home, that even if the photo was a disappointment it was also evidence of a sort, something concrete she could give to someone else and she would be out of it. But the note changed all that. She couldn't give the note to someone else and think, it's out of my hands, it's no longer anything to do with me.

Andrew's office was in K-2, which, in spite of its mountainous name, was just a small three-story building not far from the main gate and across from the big Sports Centre and beside the Lahr Senior School and the video store. Like all the buildings on the base, K-2 was built by the French well before the Canadians took it over in the early 1950s, and it was well-maintained but a little creaky, the kind of place she would have liked, actually, if it had been somewhere else.

As she walked up the steps she could see the Commander's Building, which was more or less in the centre of the base and was the most prominent. Square and study and surrounded by its own high wire fence topped with barbed wire — siege architecture, someone called it — it announced itself immediately as being full of generals and other VIPs: not, she had told Andrew once, the strategic way she would arrange things. "How do you know the Commander is really there?" Andrew said, smiling. "Maybe he's actually in a bunker under the Baskin-Robbins." And she had laughed, saying what a good movie title it would make: *The Bunker Under the Baskin-Robbins.*

She hoped he wouldn't joke with her today. The only laughter she would be able to manage would be hysterical.

When she opened the door to his outer office she was glad to see him sitting at the secretary's desk, his fingers laced together behind his head, talking to Phil. Phil Grady was a warrant officer, an enlisted man, and Vicky knew that ordinarily enlisted men would not be hanging around officers' offices, but Andrew and Phil had become friends because of Annie and Claire, their wives, whose families had known each other years ago in Winnipeg.

Vicky had met Phil and Claire a few days after she had met Annie and Andrew, and she had liked them both a great deal — Phil, who was somewhere in his fifties, for his hanging-in-there-until-I-can-retire joviality, Claire for her pragmatic army wifedom and for her motherly charm and social skill that had led someone to dub her "hostess of the Lahr," punning on the German word for "year," *Jahr*. Claire and Phil had seemed a well-matched couple, and Vicky had been dismayed to find out two weeks ago that they were divorcing. "We're just sick of each other," Claire had explained. "It's nothing personal, really."

Phil greeted her warmly, taking her hand. His smile always looked a little warped because of the scar running down his right cheek into his upper lip. It had happened in some accident when he was a teenager, but he enjoyed telling people he was one of the original zipperheads, the name given to the tank operators because of how in war they were often hit and scarred by things flying around the cramped confines of the tank. It sounded like such an ugly word to Vicky, but the men seemed to use it with a certain pride.

"So," he said, "You here to seduce this hunk?" He nudged Andrew, who rolled his eyes and jabbed at Phil with a pencil. In any other circumstance Vicky would have had the time and tendency to be discomfited by the comment.

"Some other time, maybe," she said.

"Vicky thought she saw a woman murdered up in the Staatswald," Andrew said.

Phil gaped at her. "Are you kidding? You think you saw someone *murdered*?"

Vicky nodded. "I did. But they couldn't find her body. Anyway, I got back the pictures I took and one of them shows both people. Here — "

She reached for her pocket. There was no pocket.

"Oh, *shit*!"

"What?" the men exclaimed in unison.

"I went home and changed my clothes and I didn't bother to take my jacket because it was so warm out and the pictures were in my jacket pocket," Vicky said miserably.

"Well, look," Andrew said. "Let's just trot back to your place and get them, then." He glanced at the clock on the wall behind the secretary's desk. Eleven. "I've got a meeting at 12:30 but I'm free until then. I'll drive you."

"I have my bicycle — "

"Driving's faster. We'll toss the bike into the trunk."

As he stood and moved toward the door, a tall, balding man about Phil's age appeared in the doorway. The stripes on his uniform looked the same as Andrew's, so Vicky assumed he was another captain. The three men exchanged salutes, but the newcomer barely glanced at Phil or at her before saying, tersely, "Pilski. I've got to talk to you."

Andrew gave her and Phil a look that Vicky thought seemed rather pleading, and then he said, "Phil, why don't you go get me a car? I left mine with Annie today. I'll join you in a few minutes."

"Yes, *sir*." Phil saluted crisply. Vicky had no idea if he was exaggerating; the army took saluting very seriously. An officer at a party had told her that salutes originated from knights lifting their lances to each other before a joust, and she had laughed, which was not the right response.

She followed Phil out of the room. Behind her the door closed but she could still hear the other captain say, "You've got to help me get ...", and then they were starting down the stairs and the man's voice blurred into an indignantly toned mumble.

"So," Phil said as they turned on the landing, "are you serious? You saw a *murder*?"

"Yes," Vicky said, and she explained, again, what had happened. A day had made the whole thing sound unreal, and she felt she was reciting someone else's story, rather than really remembering.

"Jesus," Phil would interject periodically, shaking his head, as they walked across to the service station.

"What's worst is that probably nobody believed me."

"The picture should help, though, right?"

"Well, it shows I didn't invent the two people." She felt a sudden urgency to tell him about the note, but she forced the words back. Yet if there was anyone in the army she could tell, it would be Phil. There was something about him that had always seemed to her kind and reassuring, not qualities she would imagine the army had encouraged.

Phil spoke to one of the mechanics working on a jeep up on a hoist, and the man trotted off and returned a few minutes later driving a small, white Fiat, produced, probably, in the Fiat plant just outside of town. He held the door for Phil.

"Just like that," Vicky said. "Could I order up a car so easily, too?"

"It only works for officers, I'm afraid," Phil said.

He pulled around to the front of K-2. They managed to wedge her bike into the Fiat's trunk, although they had to tie the lid down half-open, and then they got back into the car to wait for Andrew. The man who'd come in to see Andrew, Phil confided, had had an insubordination grievance filed against him and was desperately trying to enlist support, so it might be a while before Andrew could get free.

Vicky nodded, thinking she could be halfway home by now on her bicycle. People addicted to cars could never appreciate the efficiency of bicycles. She watched three soldiers lazily painting K-11, the Canex video store. Last week she had seen some graffiti on it that had made her smile: "Join the army and see the next world." Elsewhere someone had written, "Old soldiers never let you forget it." Of course both slogans were painted over within a few hours, but the army was probably using them as a reason to repaint the whole building.

"Why are they bothering?" Vicky asked, nodding at the painters. There was a smell of turpentine in the air.

"Well," Phil said, "you know what they say: if it doesn't salute you back, paint it."

Vicky laughed. "No, really, why bother, if the base is supposed to be closed in a couple of years?"

Phil sighed. "I know. We just have to keep the men busy."

"I saw this movie once," Vicky said, "where some officer is reviewing the troops and he says, 'Soldiers in peacetime are like chimneys in the summer. What do you do with them?'"

Phil watched the three soldiers. "There's a lot of peace-keeping work, of course. But you'd be surprised how many people think we shouldn't be involved. It's good for PR, they think, for keeping defence budgets up, but our real business is warmaking, not peacemaking."

Peacemaking: Vicky thought about the primate study she'd told Annie about a few weeks ago. It looked, not at aggression, which had been studied a lot, but at how things were resolved afterwards so that the troop could live together. The researcher found that in chimps and other monkeys the protagonists would later approach and groom each other and fondle each other's genitals, to loud squeals of approval from the rest of the colony. "Fondle each other's genitals!" Annie had exclaimed. "How marvelous! Andy took a conflict-resolution workshop last month and they didn't teach him *that* technique!"

At another time Vicky might have told Phil about the study, and they would have laughed and agreed how sensible the behaviour was, but today all she did was nod and say vaguely, "Of course." She gestured around her and asked, "What are the Germans going to do with this place once you all leave?"

"Who knows? It would make a good concentration camp. The Germans have the know-how, after all."

Vicky stared at him, surprised at the cynical comment. But in spite of herself she looked around the compound and thought, *Buchenwald,* suddenly imagining it, unspeakable tortures behind the familiar windows. She thought about the three thugs and the black waiter in Weimar. And then she thought about Dresden.

"The Germans weren't the only ones who committed atrocities in the war," she said. "The Allies firebombed cities full of civilians, calmly planned the murder of a hundred thousand people at a time. Conrad was born in Dresden. He had to see his whole family die."

"Oh," Phil said meekly. "I'm sorry. It must have been awful for him."

"It was."

They were silent, not looking at each other. Maybe she shouldn't have lectured Phil like that, she thought, knowing he couldn't try to rebut her because she had used Conrad in her argument. She wasn't sorry for what she'd said, though; it was the truth, after all. But now they had to sit here uncomfortably, as though they had quarreled. She cleared her throat, just to puncture the silence.

A light gust of wind blew a tinfoil food wrapper across the pavement in front of the car, and a crow swooped down for it. A second, smaller crow flew in from the roof of K-16, the Senior School gym, and the two fought over the paper, cawing in angry, gargly voices at each other. The first crow managed to get airborne with the wrapper in its beak and flapped off toward the Staatswald. The other, deciding not to pursue, flew back to the roof.

"It wouldn't have been worth it," Vicky said. "It was just a piece of paper."

"What?"

"I was talking to the crow. I said the tinfoil wasn't worth fighting over."

"Oh," Phil said. "The crow. I thought maybe you were, you know, speaking metaphorically or something."

Vicky laughed, and then Phil did, too, and it eased the awkwardness between them. Still, Vicky was relieved when she saw Andrew come down the steps. The other captain was still with him, talking urgently, gesturing, and Andrew made several unsuccessful movements to get away before he was finally able to step free of the voice the man seemed to keep throwing over him like a lasso.

"Sorry I took so long," Andrew sighed. "Ferguson is hysterical."

"I suppose I'd be, too, in his position," Phil said.

He got out of the car and Vicky realized that he wasn't intending to come with them. She wished he were.

She and Andrew said little to each other on the way to her apartment. The nearer they got the more uncomfortable Vicky felt. She told herself it had nothing to do with being alone with Andrew, but when she looked over at him she couldn't bring herself to move her eyes farther than to his hands on the steering wheel, to his long fingers which he was drumming lightly on the wheel, those long fingers with the dusting of dark hair between the knuckles. *Peacemaking*, she thought suddenly, *fondling each other's genitals*, and she had to swallow hard to stop a mad laugh from escaping. When Andrew pulled up in front of the house she opened the door before the car had fully stopped.

"Do you want me to come up with you?" Andrew asked.

"Oh, well — " She had just assumed he would; she wasn't sure why. "If you want," she finished lamely.

"Okay." He followed her around to the back. His footsteps

crunching the gravel behind her made her feel like bursting into a run. Why hadn't she just told him to wait in the car? Maybe he was thinking she had invited him up for reasons that had nothing to do with getting the pictures.

Frau Daimler's son, Erich, was in the back yard, running sandpaper along two boards suspended between sawhorses. His Kafkaesque eyes looked up at Andrew with undisguised curiosity.

"'n Tag," he said.

"'n Tag," Vicky said, stepping quickly through the back entrance. The hallway smelled of cleaning products, of ammonia. As she unlocked her door she could hear Andrew say something in German, and Erich's reply, and then Andrew again, and some laughter. When Andrew came inside and began to follow her up the stairs she said, "I didn't know you spoke German so well."

"I don't really. I took some courses."

"So did I. All I can say is 'hello' and 'good-bye' and 'shit-head.'"

"Well, that should about cover it."

Vicky was ignoring atavistic urgings to apologize for how messy the apartment was. With her bloodstained panties and slacks soaking in the bathroom sink, she just had to hope Andrew wouldn't need to use the toilet.

"My jacket's in the wardrobe," she said. "Wait, I'll get it." She walked quickly across the room, trying to think of what she would say to be most convincing when she handed Andrew the picture.

Her jacket was there. The pictures weren't.

Incredulous, she shoved her hands again and again into the two pockets. The envelope wasn't there.

"It's gone," she cried.

Andrew came over to her. "What? The pictures are gone?"

"Yes! I *know* I left them in here."

"Maybe they fell out."

"Yes — they must have — they've got to be here somewhere — "

Frantically she began to search the apartment, retracing her earlier steps: from the stairs to the sofa, then to the kitchen, the bathroom, the bedroom, the wardrobes, and the study, of course the study, where she'd hidden the note.

But she found nothing. Andrew had been making a half-hearted attempt to help, picking up the sofa cushions and dropping them quickly; she supposed if she'd been in the army he could have had her court-martialed for the dirt he found under them.

"They're just gone." She felt like crying.

"And the negatives — "

"Were all in the same envelope."

"Maybe they fell out of your pocket somewhere between here and the Caserne."

"I'm sure they didn't. I remember I had my hand in my pocket when I came in the back door and they were still there then."

"Well, I dunno, Vicky — what do you think happened to them?" Andrew sat down on the arm of the sofa and hooked the ankle of his right leg over the knee of his left. He picked up his hat from the coffee table and turned it slowly in his hands as he looked at her.

"I don't *know*. It doesn't make any sense."

"Your door was locked when we came in, wasn't it? I mean, I suppose it's possible they might have been stolen."

A chill crawled up her back, came to rest in her neck like a knot of ice. "Stolen. Oh, god."

"So was your door locked?"

"Yes. But it would be easy to force. And there are a lot of

keys for it around. Frau Daimler has several, and Conrad — ”
She stopped, but that was worse than finishing the sentence,
however feebly, because it left Conrad's name dangling there,
like a noose she had tied at the end of a rope of insinuation.

She crouched down in front of Andrew, not caring how
foolish she might appear. "You've got to believe me, Andrew!
There *was* a picture. I know how it must look — first the
woman's body disappears, then I say I have a picture but it
disappears — ”

Andrew got off the sofa and crouched down beside her.
He put his hand under her elbow and stood up, pulling her
to her feet.

"I believe you, Vicky."

"*Do* you?"

He hesitated, just for a moment, but long enough for her
to notice. "Well, I can't imagine why you'd lie."

"There's another possibility. I could be completely crazy."

"Oh, I doubt that. Not *completely*, anyway." And then he
put his arms around her and laughed a little. Vicky could feel
the vibration in his chest passing through into hers.

He began stroking her back. She felt his warm breath,
quickening a little, on her neck. His hair smelled clean, freshly washed. Oh, god, she thought: get a grip. She pulled back,
away from him, from the pulse of desire in her groin.

"I'll go down with you and get my bike out of your
trunk," she said. "And maybe I'll cycle back the way I came.
Just in case I did drop the envelope on the way."

"Sure," Andrew said, his voice not giving away anything
of what he might be feeling. "Good idea." He picked up his
hat and anchored it carefully on his head.

They went down the stairs, careful not to touch, to walk
too close to each other. At the bottom of the stairs she saw
Andrew look at the lock on the door and frown.

"That's pretty poor," he said. "Even I could break in here without you knowing. Can't you get your landlady to install some kind of deadbolt?"

"I could try," Vicky said. Of course it would have to be Conrad who asked Frau Daimler.

Erich was still outside sanding his boards, and he looked up at them and smiled. Vicky could imagine what he was thinking. How long were they upstairs — half an hour, three-quarters of an hour? Long enough. She wondered if he would tell Conrad.

"Wait," she said to Andrew. "Could you ask Erich if he saw anyone come to the back door in the last two hours? Is your German good enough?"

"It might be." Andrew turned to Erich and spoke to him in German. Erich said something, rapidly, but the shaking of his head made his meaning clear enough.

"*Danke*," Andrew said. He turned to Vicky. "'Fraid not. But I think he said he came home only a few minutes before we did. Either that or he said, 'The last two students ate all the wood in the grocery store.'"

"That makes as much sense to me as anything else lately," Vicky said.

When Andrew had gone she rode her bicycle slowly back to the bus stop where she'd first looked at the pictures, scanning the streets and gutters for the white envelope, but it didn't surprise her not to find it. She realized she never did fill in the report form Andrew was going to give her, but she supposed it didn't matter, anyway. Even if Andrew did believe her, without proof, without the picture, they would just stick her report away in the "Delusional Woman" file. Maybe such a report had already been filed for, about, her.

When she got back home she searched the apartment carefully again. Nothing. She had to face it. Someone had come into the house and stolen the pictures. By leaving them here when she went out she couldn't have been more accommodating. Someone could have been watching the house. Maybe the same person who'd left the note. Or someone could have followed her to and from the Caserne, been watching her at the bus stop. Someone. The murderer? She shuddered, glanced involuntarily down the stairs. Had she locked the door? Not, apparently, that it mattered.

Why had she left the film for processing at the base in the first place, where the murderer could plainly have watched her? And then why hadn't she looked at the pictures as soon as she got them, taken them right over to Andrew or Lieutenant Crosby? Instead, she'd bolted off the base like some giddy rabbit and then gotten sidetracked by her goddamned period. If the murderer had been following her, he could logically have assumed she was heading home with the pictures to leave them there; why else would she take them home instead of returning to the base a few blocks away? And when he saw her go out, wearing different clothes, he would have thought it was worth coming in, having a look around. What other explanation was there? The only people who knew she'd left the pictures here were Phil and Andrew. Phil was with her the whole time, and Andrew was in his office talking to the other captain.

She poured herself a gin and tonic, a large one, one she used to call, in the days when it was funny, "a noticeable drink," and then she jammed a tape in the cassette player and turned the volume up loud, not caring what it was, something classical, maybe even one of the Haydns they'd bought because they were moving to Haydnstraße and doing things like that had seemed part of a happy new adventure.

In the study she looked around, slowly, despondently, at the muddle of papers. She opened *The Cinematography*

Reader to page 105, half-expecting the note to have disappeared, too; but, no, there it was. She closed the book, not touching the note, and went to the window and looked out, but her eyes only fell to the dry, gray soil in the window box. When they'd moved in it was lively with flowers which they'd told Frau Daimler they'd look after, but Vicky had managed to kill everything off within a month by first forgetting to water and then over-watering. The impatiens she'd planted the next summer had survived only three weeks. If Frau Daimler had spoken to Conrad about it he hadn't passed the complaint on to her.

She sighed, turned, and left the room, closing the door behind her.

Afternoon

She made herself a ham and cheese sandwich and ate it carelessly, standing in the kitchen and letting crumbs fall to the floor. Then she wandered around the apartment again, half-heartedly straightening cushions and books and dishes, running her thumb over dusty surfaces until she had a little accumulation of gray felt which she wiped on her jeans. As she passed the phone she dialed Annie's number, idly, knowing she wouldn't be at home. When Annie answered she was so surprised she almost hung up.

"This damned sciatic thing," Annie said. "My boss was furious, but, shit, I could hardly walk this morning. I think there's going to be a change in the weather. My leg always acts up before it rains. Is that pathetic fallacy?"

Vicky laughed. "I think it works the other way around."

"Well, who cares? It means I have an excuse to take drugs."

She did, Vicky thought, sound rather, well, hearty. Vicky told her about the pictures. She wanted to tell her about the note, too, but she pressed her fingernails into the palm of her hand, concentrated on the pain and thought, no, don't.

"Jesus," Annie said. "You really think someone could have taken them?"

"It's the only explanation that makes any sense. Even Andrew thought it was a likely possibility." She had been uncomfortable telling Annie about Andrew coming up to her apartment, but Annie had only said, "Good. I'm glad he could get a car."

"So what are you going to do now?" Annie asked.

Vicky sighed, twisted the phone cord between her fingers. "Maybe I should just have another goddamned drink."

"Why don't you come over? We can sit in the garden and fondle the squirrels."

"That sounds nice." Annie's new house, rented "on the economy" as opposed to being owned by the army, was one of the nicest Vicky had been to in Lahr ("I wonder who Andy had to fuck to get this," Annie had said, appreciatively), and the thought now of sitting in her garden fondling the squirrels had a lot of appeal. Instead Vicky heard herself saying, "But Conrad will be home soon, and I did promise to cook him a meal this year."

"Okay. Be a good little *Hausfrau* then. Call me if you change your mind."

"I will."

She hadn't realized until she'd said it that she *was* waiting for Conrad. Her mind seemed to brace itself against what she would say to him, but she knew that even if she said nothing at all she had to look at him coldly and objectively and ask herself if he could really have become such a stranger to her. Could she look at him and think: he might be involved in a murder?

When she heard his key in the lock and his step on the stairs she fought down a shiver of panic. Act normal, she told herself, running into the kitchen and starting to open drawers and run water and take things out of the refrigerator, although it occurred to her that such a gush of domesticity was hardly normal.

When Conrad came into the kitchen she was peeling potatoes, carefully, at the sink. She turned and made herself smile. The smile felt as though it had too many teeth in it. But this was just Conrad, she told herself, her old, familiar Conrad, looking exhausted, dropping with a sigh onto one of the kitchen chairs.

"Hi," she said, her voice sounding too high-pitched.

"Hello." He bent down and undid his shoelaces. "So. What's the story with the pictures? Did they come?"

She concentrated on the potato, but her hands were trembling so she put the paring knife down, pressed her right palm onto the counter and pivoted to look at Conrad and said, "Yeah. One of them showed the man and the woman. It didn't actually show him, you know, firing the gun, but it did show the two people."

"Really?" He straightened, one of his shoes in his hand. "Where is it?"

"Well, that's just it." And she began to tell him everything that had happened. Except, of course, about the note. Although she could feel herself yearning to tell him, to say, wait, I'll get it, to run to the study and show him, and that would solve it, she would have decided to trust him and that would be that, the truth would be almost irrelevant —

She made herself go on, trying to judge his reactions, looking for skepticism or guilt, hoping now to see the former because it would preclude the latter. He listened, intently, turning his shoe once or twice in his hands.

When she was finished she felt weak, as though she would sink to the floor without her hand anchoring her to the counter. Conrad sighed and set his shoe on the floor against the wall. "So what do you want to do now?"

Had he believed her? Maybe that mattered less to her now than whether *she* believed *him*. She wanted to go and put her arms around him, to be fifteen again and trust him as though no other possibility existed. But she only stood there and said, "I don't know."

"Well, you've told Andrew, you've told some of the others. It's up to them to pursue it."

Vicky nodded. She pried her palm off the counter and sat down, picking up the dishtowel she'd left on the table and pleating it between her fingers. "And how was *your* day?" she asked.

Conrad grunted. "Hell. That Marshall kid. At noon hour I caught him ripping down the artwork in the hall, and when I yelled at him he took up a karate position and kicked me in the leg so hard I nearly collapsed. Look." He rolled up his pants and she could see a deep, purpling bruise.

"God," she exclaimed, momentarily forgetting everything else. "Can't you get him expelled or something?"

"We send him home for the day, and his parents get furious at us because it's all our fault — can't we handle an eight-year-old kid?" He rolled down his pant leg. "I think his father is rather proud of him — he's turning into such a good little soldier."

"You should be able to get a kid like that out of the school. He's dangerous."

"We've got a dozen more just like him. Paul thinks we should just chain them all up in the basement every day. I told him it was a great plan."

In on it: "it" was the plot to chain up a dozen uncontrollable children in the basement of the Gutenberg Elementary

School. She began to giggle. She couldn't stop.

Even Conrad at last had to give her a little smile. "I don't think he was joking."

"I hope not." If only it were really something like that, something silly.

.

They were just finishing supper when Conrad said, "We have to go to the party tonight, don't forget."

Vicky's fork stopped halfway to her mouth. "Party?"

"You know. At Paul's. He mentioned it to you again yesterday."

"Shit. I forgot."

"Well, you said you'd go. It's a bit late now to tell him you won't."

"All right, all right. I'll go."

She wore, to be mollifying, the dress Conrad had bought her for Christmas. It was a little young for her, with puffy sleeves and a hemline ten centimetres above the knee, and when Annie had seen her in it she had laughed and exclaimed, "Barbie!" But when they went downstairs Conrad said she looked nice, and she supposed she did, in a Barbie kind of way. Conrad looked nice, too, in a Ken kind of way; he was still as slim as when Vicky had first met him, although he stooped a little now, perhaps from all those years of bending over children's desks. His face, though, was relatively unlined, and Vicky couldn't help comparing him to Phil, who was about the same age as Conrad but whose face was a mass of wrinkles, as though it were slowly collapsing inward.

They managed to tiptoe out the back door without alerting Frau Daimler. When they were getting into the car

Conrad said, "When I came home today, Erich was in the back yard, and he told me you had a soldier visit you."

"A soldier visit me." Vicky jerked the door open. "That bastard."

"Oh, I don't think he meant to imply — "

"Of course he meant to imply. He wanted you to think Andrew and I were having a quick little fuck. That nosy creep."

"I'm sorry I told you. I thought you'd be amused."

"Well, I'm not. I don't know how you can stand the man. What do you talk about with him, anyway, when you go down for your evenings with them?" She caught her breath. Why had she asked him that, now? Did she think she might trick him into saying, *Oh, we sit around planning the Fourth Reich* —

Conrad shrugged, backed the car out onto the street. "His mother does most of the talking."

"So what do you talk about with her?"

"Not much. It's just ... nice for me to hear the language again, to speak it myself. When the Lehrmans or the Gartens come over we play cards sometimes. Games I used to play as a kid."

"You play *cards*?" She watched Conrad's face, trying to see behind the words. He looked uncomfortable, but that didn't mean he was lying, did it? Maybe he was just embarrassed to admit he was doing something purely for fun.

Traffic was light, and they got to the Gartens', on the southern fringe of the city, in less than twenty minutes. Paul and his German wife of three years, Hilda, owned a large, gabled house with a latticework front and lovely stained-glass windows that had been installed when the house was built more than a hundred years ago by Hilda's great-grandfather.

Vicky and Conrad were among the last to arrive. Vicky

recognized most of the teachers from the school, Kathryn with-a-y Oram, Lynne something, another man and a middle-aged woman who looked familiar but whose name she couldn't recall, and two teachers from the elementary school at the Baden-Söllingen base whom she'd met last year. There were probably also a few people from the other Canadian elementary school in Lahr, the Westend Junior, and maybe, judging from the accents, some Germans as well. With the various spouses there were probably about thirty people, standing in little, hunched clusters that reminded her of the way cows would huddle together, heads facing in, during rainstorms.

Paul and Conrad wandered off, talking about some change in the report cards. Hilda, an earnest, smiling woman of about thirty with an enormous bosom and thick auburn hair pinned up with nervous hairpins that were threatening to spring free, managed to append Vicky to two men from one of the Canadian schools and two women who were probably their wives. The women wore almost identical dresses, one red and one blue, with low necklines and lacy sleeves. Vicky looked longingly at the bottles of wine and glasses arranged on a sideboard. One of the men, who wore the top two buttons of his shirt open to expose a thin, gold chain and so much furry growth it looked like chest hair on steroids, began an anecdote about a parent-teacher interview that involved the mother making a pass at him. Vicky sidled away, poured herself a big glass of white wine, and was back for the punchline: "So I said to her, 'I do think we should put your son's needs ahead of our own right now, Mrs. Kastner.'"

"You didn't!" shrieked the woman in the red dress. "What did she say?"

"Well, she implied I was imagining it all and walked off in a huff."

"I wish she'd come into *my* classroom and run her hand up *my* arm," said the other man.

"Oh, *you*," said the other woman, obviously his wife, and they all laughed, Vicky as well, as though it had been hilarious.

"Are you a teacher, too?" the first woman asked her.

"No. I'm just Conrad's wife." Immediately she was annoyed with herself for saying that, because it was a fake and snobbish humility; she had never thought of herself as "just Conrad's wife."

"Oh, yes," said the woman. "Conrad's at the Gutenberg School, isn't he?"

Vicky smiled brightly and nodded. She suddenly realized she had forgotten to ask Conrad if he'd told anyone what had happened to her yesterday, but it seemed likely he hadn't, for which she was deeply grateful. Just the thought of having to repeat the story yet again, to answer more incredulous questions, made her want another drink very badly, and when the man with the chest hair began another anecdote, she sauntered back past the wine and refilled her glass. It was good wine, she thought, feeling it run happily down her throat. It was very good wine.

She topped up her glass and took a handful of peanuts and wandered across the room collecting little pieces of conversations (" — pulled their kid out already so — ", " — no CD player to — ", " — ship *that* home — ") and letting them, not unpleasantly, clatter about in her head. "I don't mean to cast aspersions on her character," a woman was saying loudly across the room, "but really." Vicky smiled. As a child she had misunderstood the phrase as "to cast nasturtiums," and for a long time she thought it must be a rather nice thing to do.

She began looking at the women's shoes, trying to

remember the categories she and Annie had used one day as they sat cattily watching passersby at the outdoor restaurant beside the Storchenturm. Tonight she didn't see any I-don't-give-a-shit runners or even, except for her own, any low-heeled okay-I-give-a-little-shit loafers; but there were a lot of I-may-be-a-feminist-but-don't-count-on-it pumps, and even two pairs of flimsy fuck-me-anytime spike sandals.

In one corner, three people were gathered around a half-filled bookcase, heads lowered towards one of the shelves, and when Vicky looked more closely she was astonished to see they were snorting cocaine. The man who had just finished handed the little tube to the woman beside him and, while he moved a bit in front of her to shield her from view, he seemed amazingly casual about it. Vicky knew that hard drugs were available here, but still she was surprised to see teachers using them. She wondered what would happen if they got caught. She looked down into her glass of wine and murmured to it, "You're positively out-classed here, my dear."

"Pardon?" said someone beside her, and she laughed foolishly and said, "Nothing."

The woman who had just finished snorting the coke was looking up, a radiant smile on her face, and she caught Vicky's eye. Vicky returned the smile, one of acknowledgement, complicity. She wanted suddenly to go over to the woman, to ask, "May I try it?" and the urge, the anticipation of what it would be like, was so strong she actually felt herself tremble. Would she have gone over, if Hilda hadn't come by just then and made some cheery comment about how Paul appreciated Conrad's help with the volleyball schedules? When Hilda moved on and Vicky looked back at the trio by the bookcase they had gone. She was both relieved and disappointed, that paradox of the human condition, of being saved from oneself.

Hilda Garten's young son from her first marriage was passing through the crowd with a tray of drinks, and Vicky adroitly exchanged her empty glass for a full one. Eventually she made her way across the room to where Conrad and Paul were talking to Kathryn and one of the Baden-Söllingen teachers and a bored, trapped-looking man whose function was also obviously spousal.

"Vicky," Paul said warmly, drawing her into the group. "How're you doing?" He was wearing a navy blue suit and tie, the only man in the room dressed so formally.

"Fine," she said.

"We were just discussing Conrad's war wound."

She looked blank.

"Where the Marshall kid kicked him. Didn't he show you?"

"Oh, yes."

"Army teachers should get full combat pay," Paul said. "We bloody well deserve it."

"I had a kid last year who *bit* me," said Kathryn. "I had to get a tetanus shot."

"Well, at *least* we don't have a lot of black students like the American teachers do," said the Baden-Söllingen teacher, gesturing dramatically. His cufflinks were the size of bookends. "Talk about hassles."

"I have one black kid," said Kathryn. "He's acting out all the time. The other kids hate him. He's a real problem."

"Maybe the other kids are the problem," Vicky said.

There was a moment of awkward silence, and then Paul, putting his fingers around the knot in his tie as though to stop it from leaving, said, "Well, sure, there's a racial aspect here, no question. But this kid really *is* a behaviour problem."

"So would you be if you were in a class full of kids who hate you," said Vicky.

"Well — 'hate' is too strong a word, perhaps. Kathryn?"

"Oh, yes, I mean, they don't *hate* him. They just don't really like him — "

"Do you talk to the kids about it?" Vicky persisted. "About what racism really means?"

"Well," said Kathryn, pushing her fingers nervously into her stylishly tousled hair, "I have to be careful. I'm not allowed to be too assertive about it. Their parents — "

" — are probably racists, too. So do you try to do something with the kids to counteract it?"

"There *are* things in the curriculum .... " Kathryn threw a pleading glance at Paul, letting it linger en route for a few seconds on Conrad. It was that glance that made Vicky decide, what the hell, why should I let it drop, why should I let her get away with it?

"Do you think that's enough?" she demanded.

"Well, Vicky," said Paul, smiling in a way she took to be avuncular, "Kathryn's doing quite a good job with that boy. Besides, I think we may be talking less about race than about problematic households that happen to be non-white. You don't know what it's like in some of these classrooms."

"Don't I?" Vicky drained her glass and set it down sharply on an end table. She could see Conrad wince and serve a hard look at her, but she lobbed it back and continued talking. "Did Conrad ever tell you I'm half Indian? Do you really want to know what it's like from a kid's point of view in 'some of these classrooms'? Well, I can tell you that putting a few things in the curriculum isn't enough. I can tell you that blaming a 'problematic household' is a cop-out — " Her voice was getting louder and more angry, and she made herself stop.

There was an embarrassed silence around her. Conrad's drunken wife, she could imagine them thinking: poor

Conrad. Paul was fingering the knot in his tie again, turning it back and forth now like a doorknob that wouldn't open.

Finally it was Kathryn who ventured, meekly, "I didn't know you were half Indian. I mean, you don't look Indian."

Vicky could actually hear Conrad draw in his breath, and Paul looked quickly across the room as though searching for help. But, Vicky realized, surprising herself a little with the insight, she would only make things worse for herself by giving a sarcastic answer when one was so obviously but innocently invited, so she made herself smile and say, "I suppose not."

Kathryn smiled back. "I'm half Italian, but you'd never know it, either."

"Really?" Vicky said, smiling. She picked up the glass of wine on the end table beside her and took what she hoped was a demure sip, although she realized before she set it back down that her glass had been empty and that she had taken her demure sip from what was probably Kathryn's glass. She continued smiling, demurely, and then Paul began talking about his trip to Italy, a humourous anecdote about the fast drivers, and she almost complimented him on his graceful segue from her own social misdemeanors.

Conrad waited about twenty minutes, until another couple was leaving, before he took hold of Vicky's arm and said, "Let's go."

Vicky nodded, aware he was probably not asking for her agreement.

In the car Vicky folded her hands tidily in her lap and fixed her eyes on the little medallion they had bought in Munich and glued onto the dashboard. *Komm Gut Heim*, it said. Come Safely Home.

"Well, say something, for god's sake," she said at last, when they were halfway home.

"What shall I say?"

"Say I was drunk and disgraceful, that I behaved badly in front of your friends."

"Do you think you did?"

"Stop acting like a psychiatrist. Tell me what you think."

He was concentrating on his driving, his face somber, enameled by the moon. When he finally did answer, what he said surprised her.

"I don't know what I think," he said.

When they got to their apartment the lights were still on downstairs, and as they opened the back door Frau Daimler opened her door into the hallway at the same time and looked at them in mock surprise as though she really expected them to think it was coincidence.

"*So spät, Kinder!*"

Vicky thought she understood the words, and she said, smiling broadly, "It's neither very late nor are we children."

Frau Daimler nodded uncertainly, then looked at Conrad, expecting, probably, a translation. Conrad said something in German Vicky didn't understand, but from Frau Daimler's laugh and cheerful answer Vicky was pretty sure it wasn't an accurate translation.

"*Gute Nacht,*" she said, and started up the stairs. She didn't think the woman answered her, but she couldn't be sure.

She was in the bedroom getting undressed before she heard Conrad start up the stairs. He came to the door of the bedroom and said, "That was rude."

"What?" Vicky's hand stilled on the button she was undoing. She had no idea what he was referring to.

"She was just trying to be friendly."

"Oh, that." It seemed silly to get into an argument with him about Frau Daimler when he hadn't chastised her for her behaviour at the party, so she only said meekly, "I'm sorry."

"She's just a lonely old woman," Conrad said.

"She has Erich. She can't be all that lonely."

"Erich is her stepson. Her own children were killed in the war."

"Oh," Vicky said. Oh: when you have to reply but have nothing to say.

Conrad turned and went into the living room, and she heard the TV go on. She hated it when he watched TV because, since it was all in German, it shut her out so completely. Maybe he was doing it now for just that reason. She had been surprised and disconcerted, as perhaps Conrad had been, to find that, after all those years away, he was still fluent in the language. She put on her pajamas and sat beside him on the sofa. He was still dressed, hadn't even taken off his shoes. His hands lying palms up on his lap seemed strangely lifeless, like empty gloves.

"What's on?" she asked. When they had first moved here he had sometimes translated for her, or, when she was taking German classes, encouraged her to follow the language herself, but they had both lost interest in this eventually.

"Some movie," he said. It was American, dubbed, and she was astonished to see it was an old Second World War movie. There was Robert Mitchum leaping into a jeep, his mouth speaking angrily, and only a little out of sync, in German.

"Why on earth would they want to show *this*?" Vicky asked. "Surely no Germans want to see old third-rate U.S. movies about how Germany lost the war."

Conrad didn't move his eyes from the screen. "Paul's cousin works for Pro 7, one of the private stations, and he says these films are very successful."

"I don't understand. *Europa, Europa* was ignored here, yet there's an appetite for *this* stuff?"

Conrad shrugged. "It's because the films are old, maybe.

And the Germans who watch don't particularly identify with the German characters. They identify with the action, the excitement, the famous Hollywood stars."

"Well, that's very interesting," Vicky said. On the screen a land mine blew up, overturning a tank.

"Another satellite station has even been broadcasting *Hogan's Heroes*. The theory is that people are distanced enough now to see the characters as caricatures."

"Maybe it has something to do with the dubbing," Vicky said thoughtfully, biting at a hangnail. "When someone speaks your language, identification is easier. Women find it hard to identify with women in film not just because of the visuals but because those women are speaking a foreign language, men's versions of what women would say. Maybe if we dubbed those voices into what women *really* could or should say, we could identify with them."

"I suppose."

Vicky sighed. Conrad's interest in the conversation had clearly waned. He kept watching the screen. Planes were flying across it, dropping bombs. "Come to bed," she said finally.

"Later."

Vicky sat for a while longer, trying without much interest to lip-read what Mitchum might originally have been shouting at two muddy soldiers huddled in a trench, and then she got up abruptly and went into the study. Where the small bead lay in the paper-clip tray. Where the note about Conrad was pressed between the pages of a book about artifice and illusion, about moving pictures. Her neck began to ache, the muscles slowly tightening, making her feel as though a tree were growing in her spine, spreading branches up the back of her head. She sat down and put her head onto her arms on the desk.

She thought about the evening, the party, letting the film of it run in her head, trying not to be a character but to be the director, the editor, the camera, the camera that never lies, no, the camera that always lies; trying to cut herself out of the picture, the way she would like to cut the woman in the yellow sweater out of the picture, to cut the picture out of the picture, and someone had done that for her, had removed the picture, had made the whole thing unhappen.

She was just encouraging her headache. She sat up, rubbed at the back of her neck, at her forehead. She would feel wretched tomorrow, she could tell. She picked up the file labelled "Aesthetic Distance" and jotted down what Conrad had told her about the old war films and what she had said about dubbing women's voices. Maybe she could do something about historical perspective affecting identification, too — "Aesthetic Distance" would be a thin chapter; she couldn't afford to discard any ideas. But that would be Chapter 6; she'd worry about it when she got there. She closed the file and put it back between the folders for Chapters 4 and 5 ("The Close-up" and "Hitchcock: Women Who Knew Too Much") and the folders for Chapters 7 and 8 ("Mother/Daughter" and "The Movie Male: Masculinity Gone Mad").

She was supposed to write something on her thesis every day. Did the notes she'd jotted count? Couldn't she let it go, just for tonight? God knew she had enough excuses —

She made herself pull over the pad of blue-lined paper on which she'd been working. Page 32. Chapter 3. From Spectator to Spectacle. All right.

But when her eyes dropped to the last words she had written, her handwriting large, scribbled, barely legible, she caught her breath, felt her hand lift itself away from the page.

Masquerade, yes, that's what I saw, nothing real, play-acting, a woman wearing a yellow sweater and only a mask of blood.

She turned the pencil over and began to erase, carefully, concentrating, trying not to wrinkle the paper, and then she opened the file with her notes for Chapter 3 and replaced the erased words with the ones her outline prescribed.

> *Freud, of course, has postulated just such a necessity for women's masquerade. "In the course of some women's lives," he says, "there is a repeated alteration between periods in which femininity and masculinity gain the upper hand."[1] Elsewhere he says, "In females, the striving to be masculine is ego. But it then succumbs to the momentous process of repression."[2]*

SATURDAY

"D'YOU THINK THERE'S much racism in the army?" Vicky wiggled her toes in the child's wading pool Annie had found and filled with water in her backyard.

"Sure." Annie hiked her chair a little closer to the plastic pool, immersing her feet. She was wearing dark green sweat-pants and a not-quite-matching green pullover with fraying cuffs. The clothes looked loose on her, Vicky thought; Annie *had* been losing weight. Annie cleared her throat and let drop to her lap the knitting she was half-heartedly squinting at. She had apparently abandoned both her contact lenses and her glasses. "I would think racism was required," she went on. "The whole concept of war and armies is contingent on xeno-phobia, *n'est-ce pas*? How could you have a motivated soldier if you couldn't make him think of the enemy as the Other — the Gook, the Chink, etc.?"

"I can see that, but I was wondering if you thought it existed much, well, on a more individual basis among the sol-diers. Something the army didn't switch on and off according to who the current enemy is."

Annie shrugged and picked up her knitting again. It was supposed to be turning into an afghan. She'd started it three months ago when she quit smoking, but it was still barely the width of a scarf. "Yeah, sure. Christ, there are always fights between the English-Canadians and the Van Doos. And they're supposed to be in the same army."

"I was thinking of racism based just on skin colour."

"Of course it's there. Why are you asking?"

Vicky fixed her eyes on the pink turtles cavorting on the plastic pool. "Well, I think the woman who was shot was black."

"The woman who — " Annie sat up straighter. Her lawn chair creaked. "She's *black*? You didn't mention that before."

"I didn't realize it until I saw the picture. And then I began to think that maybe she was shot because of that."

Annie's chair creaked again as she leaned back. "It's possible, I guess."

"I've been thinking of that time Conrad and I were in Weimar and the way that waiter was treated by those skinheads, and, well, Jesus, you hear more about it all the time, don't you?"

Annie sighed and tilted her head back and closed her eyes. "I know. God, it's hard to understand how those people must think. Remember in *Hannah and Her Sisters*, Woody Allen says, 'How should I know why there are Nazis? I don't even know — "

" — how a can opener works.'" They completed the line together, but it didn't make them laugh.

"Still," Vicky said, "we hear so much about incidents in Germany only because Germany has 'a history.' But it also has the most generous refugee and immigration policy of any western country, and at least here hundreds of thousands of people march in protest against a racist murder. At home who gives a shit? Even the police are beating up blacks and Asians and Indians." Indians. She wished she hadn't said that, although that was whom she was thinking about more than anyone. Maybe Annie would think she meant East Indians ("tame Indians," as someone had explained nastily to her as a child, as opposed to "wild Indians"). It seemed important, somehow, that she not appear to be talking about herself, about a personal paranoia.

"I know," Annie said. If she had made the connection with "Indian" she didn't let on. Vicky was watching Annie's fingers on the knitting needles. She saw, suddenly, a stitch slip off the left needle. Annie didn't notice, kept knitting. Should she say something, Vicky wondered; was dropping a stitch serious?

"I suppose it's just that need to degrade someone, so they can feel superior," Annie went on. "Women of any colour, of course, are useful for that. Did I tell you what the enlisted men call the women they work with, the women who are soldiers like them, who are supposed to be their equals, their friends?"

"I'm afraid you did. They call them 'split-asses.'"

"Nice, eh? I was reading about the Tailhook investigations. Made me sick. Boys learning to be men by learning to hate women."

"Maybe what should surprise us is that not more women get murdered."

"Well, let's not think about it, kid," Annie said. "We'll only get depressed."

A movement at the corner of the house, a small brown creature, caught their eyes.

"A bunny," Annie said.

"A rabbit," Vicky said at the same time. They laughed. The rabbit crouched low and froze halfway across the lawn, staring at them.

"It's weird how they can watch you from the side," Annie said. "We see them in profile but they're looking right at us. One eye is, anyway."

"It's that predator/prey thing. Animals like humans have

eyes facing forward so they can hunt, and animals that get hunted have evolved eyes to the sides to watch for danger."

"I didn't know that."

"Biology 101."

"Shoo," Annie said, waving her hand in the direction of the rabbit. "We're danger. Go hide." The rabbit didn't move.

"We're not dangerous enough, I guess," Vicky said.

"This evolution thing." Annie paused, squinting at the rabbit. "Given human behaviour, men's eyes should face forward but women's eyes should begin to move to the sides."

"Pretty profound."

"Women's Studies 2001." Annie flexed her ankle, rubbed at her thigh. "God, this sciatic thing is bad when I have my period."

"I've got mine now, too. Maybe that means we're spending too much time together."

Annie lifted her right leg out of the wading pool and winced as she set it on the grass. "Huh?"

"Oh, you know. That stuff about how when women spend a lot of time together their periods get synchronized. Some other trick of evolution."

"Oh, yeah. Jesus, what's the survival value in that? So that when one stud comes to town he can service them all on one trip?"

Vicky laughed, forced her eyes not to flick to the upstairs window of the house where she had heard Andrew working at the computer, the chatter of the printer. The window was half open, and she knew he might be listening to them.

Annie lifted her other leg out of the pool. When she bent over to roll down the cuffs of her sweat pants, the rabbit bolted across the yard, disappeared into the lilac hedge. "Shit, my leg hurts. I'm going in to get some aspirin or something. Want another coffee?"

"No, thanks." She watched Annie hobbling into the house, carrying the knitting. She should have said something about the dropped stitch. It was too late now.

She thought about going home; maybe she and Annie *were* spending too much time together. If she went home she could work on her thesis, since Conrad was away for the day in Offenburg at a volleyball tournament with some of the other teachers from his school. The German teachers seemed to be great lovers of volleyball, and she had begun to pronounce the word the way they did.

"Folleyboll," she murmured idly, thinking, I'll stay just a little longer.

She curled her toes in the plastic pool and looked around the beautiful garden that the Pilskis' landlord came over and tended for them. There were several large oak and linden trees, ivies crawling lushly up trellises, a whole corner of the garden full of heavy-headed roses in a variety of colours. All the downstairs windows had flower boxes full of impatiens and primulas and geraniums and small white daisies. She dabbled her fingers in a small bed of nasturtiums beside her chair. Impulsively, she picked a flower, pinched off the top of the little spout under the blossom and sucked out the nectar, its bittersweet taste of childhood. She dropped the blossom back into the flowerbed. Casting nasturtiums. She smiled.

A bird in one of the oak trees was singing an amazingly complicated song. Above her head she could hear the computer making odd chirping noises of its own, and she smiled again, recognizing all too well the sound of a shift from real work to a computer game.

She leaned her head back, closed her eyes, let the sun fill her face. "Folleyboll," she murmured. "Folleyboll."

"What?" Annie had come back out. She sat down beside her.

"Nothing. Just thinking how nice it is here."

"Yeah. It's great having a whole house to ourselves."

"How's your leg?" Vicky sat up and looked at Annie, who had propped her leg up on the side of the plastic pool.

"Better. I took some Tylenol 3s the dentist gave me. And half a Valium. And a sinus pill." She pushed back along her nose the glasses she'd put on. "God, how did people live before prescription drugs?"

"You better watch out how you mix those things."

Annie sighed. "Yeah, right. I might fall and drown in the pool."

Vicky laughed. She had expected a more caustic rejoinder, along the lines of look-who's-talking. But, she would have protested, she hadn't had a drink all day, and here it was afternoon already. But the thought of it, a drink, any god-damned drink, made her throat tighten; just the thought of it made her hand quiver as it reached for the empty coffee cup.

Andrew came out of the house then, squatted down beside them at the pool. He was wearing a red tank top and shorts, and the sight of him made Vicky want a drink even more. His body didn't have a muscle out of synch. He made her feel fat; he made her feel excited; he made her feel ashamed. All of which, she thought, pretending to take a sip from the coffee cup, were probably typical female reactions. She tried to keep her eyes from his shorts, the way they stretched tautly across his buttocks, between his legs. She remembered, bizarrely, reading that only in animals in which the female has the capacity for orgasm are the testes of the male carried outside the body, possibly so they can stimulate the female. Vicky felt her face redden: probably some other primitive sexual signal, she thought.

"So what're you girls talking about?" he asked, letting one hand drop into the water. "Men?"

"There *are* other topics of conversation," Annie said.

"Yeah? Not as interesting, I bet." He took his hand out of the pool and wiped it on Annie's sweatpants.

"Hey!" She slapped at his hand.

Their voices were casual, joking, but Vicky felt an ambiguous hostility behind their actions. She had never let herself think too much about what their lives were like together. Annie had complained — but then so had all the army wives — that her husband didn't talk enough to her ("With me if he has any thoughts at all they're agoraphobic," she'd grumbled), and once she'd made a vague reference to an affair Andrew had had, but Vicky did not encourage her to tell her more. Maybe she didn't want to know such things about Andrew. Maybe it was because she would have to exchange confidences about Conrad, and her feelings for him seemed so eccentric and variable that she didn't want to commit herself.

Your husband ist in on it. What feelings for Conrad did she have today?

Andrew stood up. His knee cracked and he rubbed it. "Well, back to work," he said. He stretched his arms over his head. The tank top rode up a little on his flat stomach.

"Okay," Vicky said. "I won't stay long."

"Stay as long as you want. You're not disturbing me. Well, unless you want to." He winked at her, in the disconcerting way he had of simply dropping one eyelid while keeping the rest of his face perfectly still. Then he turned and walked back to the house.

"He flirts with you," Annie said when he was inside. Her voice was cold.

Vicky laughed nervously, tried to make her answer light. "He flirts with all the women. It's nothing personal."

"Nothing personal. Thanks for the reassurance."

"I didn't mean it like that — "

"You encourage him."

"Annie! I don't!" It was, she told herself, trying not to get upset, just Annie's mean streak that had made her say that.

Annie had warned her when they first met about her mean streak. Vicky had laughed, because it was a phrase her father had used about her, not without cause, when she was a child: "You've got a mean streak in you, little girl." Vicky had tried to imagine what it looked like. It would be red, that seemed likely, and it must shoot through her sometimes like a bolt of lightning. She never actually caught it happening, but she didn't doubt that it did.

Certainly Annie's mean streak was like that, a bolt of lightning. They would be having an ordinary conversation when suddenly Annie would say something like, "You have a bad habit of pretending you know more than you do." But then she would laugh, and usually (but not always) apologize, and they would go on to something else, and Vicky would forgive her because, well, Annie had warned her, hadn't she, and it was exciting, in a way, to be with someone who was not always nice and safe and socialized, and maybe her criticisms were tactless but not untrue.

Like now. How much truth was there to Annie's accusation? Vicky could imagine her betraying pheromones filling the air, floating up to the open window where Andrew had been sitting.

She should have told Annie about the dropped stitch: not telling her suddenly seemed significant, a bad error in judgement.

"I *don't* encourage him," Vicky said, carefully, when Annie didn't say anything. "You're my *friend*, for god's sake."

She had almost said, "best friend," but she'd stopped herself. It seemed too pushy. And maybe what she would have meant, anyway, was, "best friend here," as opposed to when they went home. She had a sudden vision of how it might be with Annie, their letters getting farther and farther apart, reduced finally to a one-line greeting on a Christmas card, and the thought of it actually brought tears to her eyes.

"You're so *important* to me," she said. "You're — And now, with the murder and everything, I don't know what I'd have done without you."

"You'd have done fine," Annie said. Her voice may still have been a little grudging, but the coldness was gone from it. "You didn't need me."

"Of course I did. I still do."

Annie kicked her foot lightly against the wading pool, making the water shiver. "I know it must be hell, having that business on your mind all the time."

"I keep thinking there's something more I should do," Vicky said. She felt relieved and a little guilty to have routed the conversation away from Andrew, away from Annie's irritation, but talking about the murder was hardly more pleasant. She stood up and walked around the plastic pool, rubbing her hands together as though they were wet or cold. "Now that the picture, inadequate as it was, is gone," she said, "I feel even more that it's up to me, that my story is all there is, you know? Maybe I should still report it to the local police."

"I thought the army did that already."

"I suppose so. But the local police haven't talked to me. Not that I've exactly built up credibility so far with them, but maybe I should at least talk to someone there."

"If I were you I think I'd just try to let it go," Annie said.

"What do you mean, let it go?"

"I mean it's going to make you crazy if you don't."

"I have to know I've done all I can."

"Okay, but I'd let the army look after it. Andy will keep checking on it. He won't let it just be buried."

Vicky slid a glance at Annie. She wondered if Annie had brought up Andrew's name deliberately, as a kind of apology. "I'd appreciate that," she said.

But now that she had thought about going to the local police, she couldn't get the idea out of her mind. When she left Annie's, arranging to meet her at the Astra Cinema in the evening for a new movie the Cultural Centre had brought in, she began cycling toward the German police station. It was more or less on her way home, she told herself; she wasn't committing herself to stopping there.

She turned onto Turmstraße. Two blocks farther and there was the station. She'd often cycled past it. She wondered if Turmstraße might have taken its name from this building, which was indeed a *Turm*, a tower, a small castle of three stories, with a conical roof and flower boxes in the recessed windows. It looked more like a quaint museum than the Kriminalpolizei station.

She stopped in front of the door and leaned her bicycle against the side of the building. If she did go in, what would she say? Her German wasn't good enough to explain. *Guten Tag. Kann jemand hier Englisch sprechen?* She mouthed the words. Even if she found someone who spoke English, what then? They would recognize her name — *ja, Sie sind die* drunk wife of the Canadian teacher. *Ja, wir kennen Sie!*

She had just reached for her bicycle again when the door opened and a young man in uniform came out.

"*Entschuldigen*," he said. He smiled and held the door open for her.

"Uh, well, no," she said. "I was just leaving."

The man looked a little surprised, but he held onto both his polite smile and the open door. "*Wollen Sie nicht herein?*"

"Oh, what the hell," she said. She took hold of the door. "*Danke.*"

"*Sicher.*" He released his hold, nodded, and headed off down Turmstraße, whistling something she recognized from a Disney movie.

Vicky held onto the door for several moments. "What the hell," she said again, and went inside.

The dark-haired woman behind the main desk let her say only a few clumsy words in German before she interrupted. "English, yes? I can speak English if you wish."

"Oh, yes, please." Vicky laughed nervously. It sounded like a horse whinnying. "I, uh, I'd like to talk to a police-man."

"I am a police*wo*man," the woman said. She smiled, whether in genuine encouragement or the opposite Vicky wasn't sure. She had a large, full-lipped mouth and even teeth, although one of her incisors was noticeably chipped. "Am I acceptable for your talking to?"

"Oh, yes, of course! That would be fine."

The woman stood up and Vicky realized how unusually tall she was, almost two metres. Her erect posture made it clear she appreciated the advantage of her height. "Come to my desk, yes?" She gestured behind her at one of several unoccupied desks. "We can talk there. I am Frau Klug. I am a — *wie sagt Mann das?* — a constable?" She put the accent on the second syllable.

"*Con*stable."

"*Con*stable. *Genau.*"

Vicky followed her to the desk and sat down. *Klug*, she remembered, meant "smart." She hoped it was a good omen.

A man carrying a stack of files walked by and glanced at her, and she turned her head aside, in case he might be one of the policemen who had arrested her and then turned her over to the DND. She had no memory at all of what the men looked like.

"So. How can I help you?"

"Well, I .... " Her mouth was dry as drought. How should she begin? And then suddenly she thought of a way. "I'm wondering if you have a missing person report on a young woman, perhaps a black woman, who would have gone missing on Thursday?"

"Gone missing?" Constable Klug looked puzzled.

"Disappeared. Was reported missing." She could hear her voice rising, in the annoying manner of people who thought someone who did not speak their language had a hearing deficiency.

"Ah, yes. I understand. Is this missing woman a relative? A friend?"

"Well, neither, actually." Trying to find something out without actually telling her story was obviously not going to work. "You see, I was up in the Staatswald on Thursday and I thought I saw, I mean I *did* see, this woman being shot, by a soldier."

"Shot?" The constable's eyes widened. She leaned forward a little.

"Yes. I reported it to the base, to the Caserne, immediately, but when they sent people up to look they couldn't find anything. But I *did* see it. I'm absolutely certain. I was taking pictures up there, actually, and one of them showed both the woman and the man, right after he shot her." She had made the picture sound better than it was, but then it didn't really matter, did it?

"Did you bring with you now this picture?"

"I'm afraid it was lost, or stolen."

Constable Klug sat back slightly in her chair. "This is all most interesting. I will write down your name — " She picked up a pencil and looked inquiringly at Vicky.

"Vicky Bauer."

"And I will check with my *Boss* — yes, that is the same word in English? — to see what information we have. Perhaps he can ask the Kommissar."

"The ... Kommissar?"

The constable smiled, displaying her top teeth. "It is what we call our supercomputer in Wiesbaden. At the Bundeskriminalamt. It is perhaps like the FBI? The BKA has now perhaps twenty million files, and costs hundreds of millions of deutschmarks to run. It is very good especially with information about terrorism."

"Well, I don't imagine this case has anything to do with terrorism."

"But, still, I will talk to my Boss. Perhaps he knows about this missing woman. Please wait here, yes?" She stood up, the piece of paper with Vicky's name on it in her hand.

Vicky nodded. She would wait here, yes.

Constable Klug disappeared into one of the offices down the hall, and Vicky got up and went over to the window, sidled her thigh onto the desk beside it and looked out, reassured to see her bicycle still standing by the door. The man who had been carrying the files was sitting at one of the corner desks, engaged in a phone conversation to which his only contribution was the occasional grunt. At one point he sat forward abruptly and began frisking his desk for a pencil, but upon finding one he only toyed with it, tapping it irritatingly on his desk in little arrhythmic bursts. He was the only person besides Constable Klug Vicky had seen in the building — the Kriminalpolizei in Lahr were obviously not overworked. But there must be others, secluded in offices, like Constable Klug's *Boss*, who was probably even at this moment reading god-only-knew what files on her. An eye muscle began to beat beneath her left eyelid. She blinked hard several times, trying to squeeze it away, but it wouldn't be dissuaded.

The constable came back then, and Vicky hurried to her seat like a misbehaving student caught by the unexpected return of the teacher.

"I have found no report on a missing woman, I am afraid," said the policewoman, sitting down behind her desk and propping her elbows on it. Her gaze was uncomfortably direct, more of a stare, really, and Vicky could read nothing behind it, no clue as to what either the local records or the *Boss* or the Kommissar in Wiesbaden might have told her.

"I see. Well, did you ... was there anything else, about this case, I mean? A report from someone in the army, from the Caserne?"

Constable Klug shook her head. "No. I did not find such a report from the *Kaserne*. Was such a report made?"

"I thought so. Lieutenant Crosby said, well, I thought he said they would, I thought they would file something with you."

"Yes. It is usual so to do, especially when the crime could involve a German citizen. A German national, as you say. I will look again for this report."

"It's possible they didn't bother to file it because they didn't find anything, they didn't find a body." Why had she said that? She had basically told the woman they hadn't believed her.

"They should still have made a report." She opened a drawer in her desk, pulled out a file folder and extracted a page. "You will make a report for us, yes? You will tell me in English and I will write for you in German and then we will — *wie heißt das?* — we will investigate."

"Yes," Vicky said. "I'll be happy to make out a report."

"It is only unfortunate," the constable said, reaching for a pen, "that you do not also have the photo. But — let us begin."

So Vicky went over it all again, carefully, telling everything except about the note about Conrad, while Constable Klug wrote it down. It took over half an hour. When Vicky hesitated at signing it, the policewoman said Vicky could add a disclaimer saying she had made an oral statement in English and didn't read German.

"So," said Constable Klug when Vicky had finished. The woman stood up, her height making Vicky feel she had shrunk. "Thank you for coming. We are not all at the Polizei so frightening, *nicht wahr?*" She smiled her large-mouthed smile, corrugating her cheeks.

"No," said Vicky, smiling back uncertainly, not sure what the comment meant or if she had answered correctly. Was the woman referring to Vicky's previous encounters with the German police, when, apparently, they *had* been frightening? Vicky had always been too drunk to notice. "Well. Please let me know if you find out anything."

"Yes. *Natürlich.* We will let you know if we find out anything." She extended her hand, and Vicky shook it, expecting a bone-shuddering clasp, but it was surprisingly mild.

When she was back outside, getting on her bike, she took a deep breath of fresh air and thought: I did the right thing, coming here. At least now there was something on record. Even if the German police believed her no more than the army did, she had done her best to get justice for the murdered woman. As she headed out on Turmstraße, she went over her meeting with the constable: *had* the woman believed her? It was impossible to say. Besides, even if she did, there was still no proof. *It is only unfortunate that you do not also have the photo.* Yeah, right.

She turned onto Goethestraße. The traffic wasn't heavy, but fast, and she kept to the right, accelerating her pace, enjoying the feel of the muscles in her thighs, the pull and release, the way it made her feel healthy and strong. When she had first come here and bought the bicycle she could barely pedal around the block without gasping.

And then, suddenly, the bike was out of control, hurtling onto the sidewalk, ripping her feet from the pedals.

She knew instantly she had been hit from behind. She struggled to keep her hands on the handlebars, to stop from falling, but the curb was too high, and when she was thrust over it the bicycle skewed to the right, leaning too far to be corrected. She felt the momentum tear her free, and she flew across the sidewalk, her left foot missing by only a few centimetres the steel pole supporting a street sign. She landed heavily on her right side on the grassy border between the concrete sidewalk and a hardware store. The bicycle skidded toward her, the rear wheel grating into her stomach.

The way she was lying she had a perfect view of the car that had hit her. It stayed in the same lane and kept going. But all she could tell the police later was that the car was small and red, that there was only one occupant, and that the license plates began with WA and were red letters on white, identifying them as belonging to someone in the Canadian army.

·

It could, she thought, pouring herself another drink, have been a lot worse. The car, apparently, had not hit her hard, must, in fact, have barely bumped her, because there was little damage to the rear fender. If the bicycle hadn't jumped the curb she might even have been able to control it, to stop herself from falling. And of course landing on the grass meant her injuries were only bruises instead of broken bones.

The policeman whom the clerk in the store called to the

scene had insisted, however, on taking her to the hospital for x-rays. When they had offered to find Conrad in Offenburg at the volleyball tournament she had assured them it wasn't necessary, and when they persisted in trying to contact someone for her she had given them Annie's name.

"Jesus," Annie had said, her face white, staring at her on the gurney as they wheeled her out of Radiology. "Oh, Jesus."

"I'm okay," Vicky said. "Really. Nothing broken."

"You could have been killed," Annie said, biting at her thumbnail.

"Well, I wasn't," Vicky said, making her voice sound more cheerful than she felt. "Now take me home before someone figures out there's no exchange rate on Canadian medicare in this hospital."

She wished later she had asked Annie to come up to her apartment with her. Left alone with her bruised right leg and stomach, she could only hobble around the living room and think about what had happened.

An accident. Surely it was just an accident. If someone had really been trying to hit her he could have chosen a less busy street, with less likelihood of witnesses. It was just an accident, a driver not paying attention, maybe drunk, then panicking and being afraid to stop. She couldn't let herself think it was deliberate, someone following her from the police station, thinking cold-bloodedly that he would hurt her, how badly didn't matter, warning her to leave things alone, because she could be killed, too, as easily as this —

No. It was an accident, a careless driver who was in a hurry and had a few too many and didn't stop. She remembered a med student telling her about the "zebra diagnosis" axiom: when you hear hoofbeats, think horses, not zebras. Think the obvious, the uncomplicated.

She took her drink to the sofa and sat down. The hospital

had given her a tranquilizer and she knew she wasn't supposed to drink on top of that, but she didn't care. It was warm in the room, but she was shivering. She pulled her knees up to her chest and circled her arms around them. Relax, she said to herself, relax. After a while she set the empty glass on the coffee table and lay down and closed her eyes.

The phone jarred her awake. When she stumbled to it, forgetting her bruised leg, she cried out from the sudden pain shooting up her thigh.

"Hello?"

"Hello. *Ist* this Frau Bauer?" It was a woman's voice, with a strong German accent.

Ist. There had been that slight extra "t" sound between "is" and "this." *Your husband ist in on it.* Vicky's mind snapped alert.

"Here is Constable Klug." This time the "is" was clearer.

"Oh, yes, of course."

"I have heard from the foot-policeman of your, your *Unfall,* your ... accident. He told me you said my name when he talked with you."

"I did? Oh, I guess I must have. I remember telling him I'd just come from the police station. I suppose I was sort of in shock."

"Yes, yes, *sicher,* I understand. I am very sorry about this accident. Are you well now? Are you all right?"

"No bones were broken. I've just got some bad bruises."

"*Ach.* I am very sorry." She paused. "What I want to ask you is, the driver of the car — you did not see him?"

"Just the back of his head. It was all so fast. I think it was a man, and that he had short, dark hair, but that's all I can say."

"I have wondered — " she paused again " — if you think this man could be the man in the Staatswald, the one you saw shoot the woman."

"Well, yes, it did occur to me." She was simultaneously chilled and relieved to hear the policewoman voice her own fear.

"I will pay attention to this," Constable Klug said firmly. "I will make it with the investigation."

Vicky wasn't sure quite what that meant, but it sounded positive, so she said, "Thank you. Thank you. I really appreciate your taking this all seriously."

"And you will be careful, yes?"

"Yes," Vicky said. "I'll try."

When she hung up the phone her hands felt like ice. She pressed them between her legs. If Constable Klug thought she might have been deliberately hit, didn't that make it more likely to be true? Wasn't it better to be paranoid than really in danger? *You will be careful, yes?* That was a warning, too. What if Constable Klug was just making sure she got the message? What if Constable Klug, too, was "in on it?" Wasn't it logical that whoever hit her was told where she was by someone in the police station?

But perhaps someone had begun following her earlier, right from when she left home in the morning. She'd taken the bicycle path most of the way to Annie's — a person in a car would have found it difficult, but not impossible, to tail her. Maybe he'd started following her from Annie's; somehow he knew where she was. But who knew that except Annie and Andrew? Was she going to start suspecting them, too? Well, why not — she was suspecting everyone else she knew. Weren't the least likely suspects the guilty ones? Conrad was the least likely suspect she could imagine, and look at what she was thinking about him. She wished she could laugh, but she only sat there looking at her hands pressed, hard, between her thighs.

She felt so damned cold.

Annie had assumed she wouldn't want to go to the movie, but Vicky said she'd rather do that than stay home alone waiting for Conrad and licking her wounds — and being afraid, she thought, but didn't say, just as she didn't say, oh, you and Andrew didn't tell the murderer I was over at your place, by any chance, did you? So Annie came over in her new, blue Mercedes and picked her up, and they limped into the theatre.

"What happened to *you* two?" exclaimed a woman who had lived in the same PMQ as Annie had.

"We fell off our horses," Annie said, and they all laughed.

The movie, which Andrew had seen on a plane and assured them they would enjoy, was called *The Butcher's Wife*. It started off interestingly enough, but degenerated into a banal and predictable romance.

"I wish you hadn't told me all that stuff about how the camera is male," Annie said on the way home. "I can't see a movie now without being aware of that, of how women viewers are pushed out of movies. I mean really, did you notice how in that allegedly erotic scene between Demi Moore and Jeff Daniels she's the one who's come to *his* place in the middle of the night, but she's still wearing a sexy negligee while he's completely clothed?"

"Hey," Vicky said. "That's a given."

"And then they cut away from Moore for a few seconds so that when the camera returns to her the negligee is mysteriously gaping open up to her crotch."

Vicky wished she could match Annie's energy tonight but she was thinking: only four more blocks and then I'll have to see Conrad, tell him what happened.

"It's like that famous sexist painting by Manet," Annie went on. "'Lunch on Herb,' I used to call it, you know the one."

"'Lunch on — ' Oh, '*Déjeuner sûr l'herbe.*'"

"Right. It's this picnic, where the woman is naked, the men fully clothed and having this conversation, but the woman only sits there, excluded, looking seductively at the artist. It's like today the artist is the camera, but the woman is still the same."

"Yeah," Vicky said. "The woman is still the same."

"I guess it won't change until women get to make their own movies."

"Even then, some critics argue, the whole pointing-a-camera-at-a-woman thing is so loaded with patriarchal meaning women can't escape being objectified."

"Well, at least we can change the *stories*. We can make things turn out right. And I don't mean driving women off a cliff at the end." *Thelma and Louise* had been the movie two weeks ago.

"Yeah," Vicky said. "We can definitely work on the endings."

Annie pulled up in front of the Daimler house and Vicky got out. There was a full moon, so bright it seemed to put a phosphorescent sheen on everything. The Passat, she saw, was in the garage, parked beside her bicycle, which the policeman who had taken her to the hospital had brought back for her. When she unlocked her door she had the feeling the door to Frau Daimler's suite might have cracked open, but she resisted the urge to whirl around and look. She stepped quickly inside, grimacing at the sting of pain the abrupt movement gave her leg.

"Vicky?" It was Conrad's voice, from the kitchen.

"Yeah." She limped up the stairs. Conrad was sitting at

the kitchen table in his pajamas, marking papers. He finished the one he was on before he looked up at her.

"How was the movie?"

"Disappointing. How was the folleyboll?"

"Not bad. We made the quarter-finals so we have to go back tomorrow."

"Well. Congratulations." She went to the fridge and poured herself a glass of milk.

"Are you okay? You're limping."

She sat down opposite him, trying not to wince as she bent her knee.

"I was in an accident with my bike. A car ran into me."

Conrad's red pencil dropped from his fingers. "Are you all *right*?" He looked concerned, alarmed. Could he be faking? Could he really be involved, in however small a way, in something that would injure her? She couldn't meet his eyes, ashamed of what she was thinking but afraid, too, that if she looked closely enough she might find a flicker of guilt or collusion or fear, fear because whatever he might be "in on" was out of control.

"I'm okay. They took me to the hospital for x-rays but I was only bruised."

"What *happened*?"

"I decided to go to the German police, to tell them in person about the woman being murdered, and on the way home this car came up behind me and hit the bicycle. I was lucky I fell onto the grass and not the sidewalk."

"But — I saw your bicycle downstairs. It looked all right."

"Well, it isn't," she said, trying not to sound irritated. "The pedal on the right side is cracked and the whole frame may be bent. If you don't believe this happened, ask the police. There was a witness."

"Of course I believe it happened."

"Well ... good."

"Was it ... all the car driver's fault?" And she saw his eyes flick to the bottle of gin she had foolishly left standing on the kitchen counter.

"Yes," she said, clenching her teeth on the "s." "It was a hit-and-run. I had *not* had a drink. I had one after, when I got home." *One*, she thought, was a euphemism, but she was telling the truth where it mattered.

"Well," Conrad said, "the important thing is that you're okay." He picked up the red pencil and began to toy with it. "Did you or the witness get the license number of the car?"

"No. But it was a Canadian plate. I could see that much. The policewoman I talked to earlier called to say she thought there might be a connection between this and the murder I saw."

Conrad's pencil stopped moving. "Really? My god."

"Yeah. My god," Vicky said, gratified to have shocked him, and he *was* shocked, she was sure of that, as she looked at his pale face across the kitchen table.

.

Conrad's faint snores drifted through the open study door. Vicky got up and closed it. She stretched her arms over her head, trying to pull the pain away from her lower back, but it didn't help. She had just spent an hour reading a chapter of Irigaray, and she couldn't remember a word. She sat back down at her desk, opened her file on Chapter 3, and pulled the notepad toward her. Okay. Spectacle. Spectator. Masquerade. Freud.

Twice she began writing, and twice she turned the pencil over and erased the stiff, unsatisfying words. Finally, just so she could tell herself she'd done *some*thing today, she turned to her outline of the chapter, and after the sub-heading "woman as inert/artifact" she inserted:

What Annie said about art — use more painting references to pad out this section, e.g., Manet's "Lunch on Herb."

SUNDAY

CONRAD HAD INSISTED she keep the car today, even though they had managed to push the pedal on her bicycle back into place and discovered the frame wasn't bent enough to affect its use. Conrad had asked Paul Garten for a ride to Offenburg, and Paul was happy to oblige. When he came to pick Conrad up, wearing a white T-shirt and shorts that bore the creases of a recent ironing, he brought along an apple strudel from his wife.

"Hilda assures me her strudel will make you feel better," Paul said.

"I'll rub it on the bruises," Vicky said, and then felt ashamed because it sounded ungrateful, and she wasn't ungrateful. "Do thank her for me," she added hurriedly. "Really."

"Now, just because you have the car doesn't mean you have to go anywhere, you know," Conrad said, starting down the stairs behind Paul.

"Well, I have to now," Vicky said. "You've made the combination sound inevitable."

"Ice," Paul said, opening the door. "On that ankle. And keep it elevated. You can prop it up on the dashboard in the car as you drive."

"Yes, Mom," Vicky said.

After they had gone she ate a piece of strudel, and then, because she did have the car, after all, she winced her way downstairs. Her right leg hurt when she bent it, and the ankle was swollen, but she was in better shape than she'd expected to be. It was a relief to walk through the hallway without worrying about running into Frau Daimler or Erich — Sundays at this time they were always at church, perhaps the same Catholic church that even now was beginning its protracted, amplified tolling a few blocks away. The Germans, she had discovered, had a high tolerance for this particular hourly noise, with several churches often vying to outdo one another.

She got in the car, dug out of the glove compartment the glasses she was supposed to wear for driving, and began to drive aimlessly through the downtown, which was virtually free of traffic.

She turned onto Friedrichstraße, headed east, then turned right, mostly by reflex, onto Langemarckstraße. She stopped outside the base, and then, because the guard began eyeing her suspiciously, she drove inside, holding up her identity card, which he barely glanced at.

She stopped at the snack bar, bought a hot dog and ate it in the car with the door open and her legs sticking out. She watched the young soldiers wandering by and stared at their faces, looking for the profile she might recognize.

A young woman wearing a short skirt, high heels and white socks was wheeling a pram toward the CanEx video store. Adrienne. Vicky slouched down in her seat. She'd met Adrienne at one of Claire's lunches. Adrienne and Vicky and Annie had gotten into a cranky discussion of *Top Gun*, about whether it was just a propaganda film for the military, Adrienne saying so what if it was and then adding something that made Vicky smile now just remembering it.

"Tom Cruise was, like, so fantastic in that movie. You know, they were so grateful to him they named the cruise missile after him."

"What?" Annie stared at her.

"It's true."

"Maybe the cruise control on cars is named after him, too," Annie snorted.

"Well, maybe it is."

Vicky was feeling a certain sympathy for Adrienne by this time, having herself often enough dangled from the end of an untenable position, refusing to let go.

"For Christ's sake, Adrienne," Annie said. "Tom Cruise is just an *actor*. The cruise missile is called that because of how it *operates*."

"I'm sure their names are related."

"I'm sure your *parents* are related," Annie said.

Later, when Annie was driving Vicky home, Vicky said, "You were pretty hard on her."

"Are you kidding? She was asking for it. As the song says, 'If you don't like my peaches, don't shake my tree.'"

"I think it was talking about sex," Vicky said.

"Sex, propaganda, cruise missiles, what's the difference?"

Adrienne was going inside the video store now and Vicky straightened up and swallowed the last of her dried-out hot dog. She wished Annie were here. Even when her peaches had a mean streak in them Vicky still liked to shake her tree.

But as she sat there, rolling the napkin from the hot dog into tight little spirals, she realized she had something she wanted to do. Maybe she had been intending it, unconsciously, all morning.

She drove off the base and turned left onto Langemarckstraße. Onto the road into the Staatswald.

Since it was Sunday she wouldn't have to worry about

meeting forestry workers who might tell her she couldn't bring her car in, so she drove quickly up onto the Randweg, telling herself her reasons for being here were more important than the rules. Her heart began a quickened drumbeat as she approached the spot where she'd seen the shooting. There was the tree against which she'd leaned. There was the view of the city she'd framed in the viewfinder. There was where the couple had stood.

She stopped the car but didn't get out. The car felt safe; the forest around her, its dim, green silence, seemed dangerous, full of secrets. She sat there for a long time, the car idling. What had she expected to find? Something in the air, perhaps, the way spiritualists said happened with violent events, the lives of the victims torn away so suddenly their spirits still lingered, mute and uncomprehending? She had had an Irish friend at university who said that she sometimes felt presences from the past in certain places and that her mother and other people she knew had the same experiences. They called the phenomenon "singing."

Vicky lowered the front windows. A cool, piney breeze pulled through the car. But there was no presence, no haunting perfume, no pale shape coalescing in the air, reaching out ghostly arms to her.

She put the windows up. But as she shifted the car into gear she felt a sudden sadness, acute as physical pain. A woman *had* died here, violently, and no one seemed to care.

She continued up the Randweg looking for a place to turn around, but, although the road had two tracks, it was not meant for a car and she was afraid of getting stuck in the soft ground if she left the tracks. The road kept getting narrower and more shaded and damp. There was an exit somewhere up ahead, she knew, but she began to doubt that she could make it that far. Already on the last curve she had felt the tires spin on the slippery leaves and pine needles, and the road was still going uphill.

At last she stopped, put the car in neutral and sat there for a moment with her foot on the brake. What would Conrad say if she had to tell him she'd left his car stuck somewhere up in the Staatswald? It would mean another police charge for bringing the car up here in the first place.

"Shit, shit, shit," she said to the steering wheel.

She would back down, she decided, and just hope there wasn't anyone else coming up behind her. She could turn around at the place the jeeps had, or, if that seemed too difficult, she could back all the way down; it wasn't that much farther.

She shifted into reverse and released the brake. The car began to roll backwards.

It took her about half an hour of inching back, her neck getting so stiff she thought it could snap right off, before she neared the look-out and the place where the jeeps had been. She was relieved to see that it seemed large and dry enough for her to manoeuvre the Passat around. Carefully, she backed against the trees as far as she dared, braked, spun the wheel hard to the right.

She shifted into first gear and turned her head. What she saw through the front windshield made her slam her foot on the brake and scream.

A young, blond woman was sitting in the exact spot the other woman had stood. Her legs were pulled up into a half-lotus position and on her lap was a sketch pad. She was holding a thick charcoal pencil and she had, obviously, been sketching the view of Lahr. But she had turned now, and was looking at the car that had backed against the trees behind her.

It wasn't just the shock of seeing the woman there that had made Vicky scream. It was what the woman was wearing.

Tight blue jeans. And a yellow sweater with a design of white beads in the shape of a bird's wing.

They sat there for several moments, staring at each other. Then the woman turned back to her sketching, her head moving slowly up and down as she looked from the view to her paper.

Vicky couldn't move. Her right foot was jammed so hard on the brake pedal she might have been teetering at the edge of a cliff. Her mind was empty, thoughts evaporating before they had time to form.

The young woman looked at her again. Vicky forced herself to smile, and then she concentrated on pulling her foot off the brake pedal. She had the clutch in, and the car began to roll forward, toward the woman, who stiffened, looked alarmed. Vicky braked again, quickly, but she could see the woman's legs unfold and then curl under her as though she might be getting ready to stand, to run. She pulled the sketch pad up a little toward her chest.

Vicky made herself turn off the motor, get out of the car. Her smile was still glued on and she was sure it looked hideous, but she couldn't make her face relax. Her mouth was so dry her tongue felt velcroed to the roof of it. She walked toward the woman, who watched her with obvious unease, perhaps even fear, on her face.

"Hello," Vicky said. Her voice sounded croaky.

"Hello," the woman said. She had a round, chubby-cheeked face with a large mouth and blue eyes that seemed to squint when they blinked. Her skin was tanned but might have been fair enough to belong to a natural blond.

"You ... do you speak English?"

"Oh, yes."

"I ... I'm surprised to see you here. I thought — you see, I thought, a few days ago, a woman was standing right here where you are, and I thought, well, a man shot her."

"Shot her!" The woman's hands tightened on her sketch pad.

"Yes — I'm sure that's what I saw. And she was wearing that sweater, the exact same sweater, you are."

The woman lowered the sketch pad and looked down at her sweater. "It is perhaps common. I bought it in a big store in Frankfurt." Her English was careful, with only a trace of a German accent.

"Well, it's — I mean, it's just such a coincidence. Were you here a few days ago, on Thursday?"

"Yes, I think so," said the woman, after a slight pause. "I came up here several times last week."

"Was anyone with you on Thursday? A man?"

"No. Perhaps a man came by and we greeted each other, that is all."

What should she say now? She had to ask the right questions, but what were they? "Do you live in Lahr?" she asked finally.

"No. I am from Frankfurt. I am only visiting friends here."

"Could I ask your name?"

The woman lowered her eyes to her sketch pad and ran her forefinger up and down its edge. "Is it necessary for you to know this?"

"Yes, yes, it is. You see, I might need to tell the police — "

"The police!" Her eyes flew up to meet Vicky's, and she blinked several times in her hard, squinty way, as though she were looking into sudden bright light.

"Yes. Of course they would want to know about you." Vicky was bluffing, but she had to pursue the advantage she had apparently gained by mentioning the police.

"All right." The woman hesitated. "My name is Hannelore. Hannelore Schneider."

"Could you give me your friend's address here, and phone number? And your phone number in Frankfurt?"

The woman ran her forefinger again up and down the edge of her sketch pad. Her nails were cut short but well manicured, with freshly applied red polish. Church bells sounded somewhere below them, and she looked toward the sound. She waited until the bells stopped before she answered, still looking out across the city.

"I will telephone the police myself, if you wish. Later."

"I can drive you down now." But taking the woman to the police with what she had just said would hardly help Vicky's case. She'd outsmarted herself. So now she had to hope the woman would refuse, that she wouldn't want to get further involved —

"I would like to stay here and finish my drawing. While the light is good. I have not so much time left in Lahr. Also I have my bicycle here." She gestured at the bushes beside her. "I do not need a ride."

"Well — can I give you my name and number, then? So you can call me if, if you remember anything?"

"Yes, all right. But I know nothing more than what I have told you."

"Well, in case you do. My name is Vicky Bauer. The phone is in my husband's name. Conrad. With a 'C,' not a 'K.' Do you want to write it down?"

"I will remember."

"Well, then." Vicky shifted her feet. She was sure that if she left now she would never see the woman again. But what choice did she have? She couldn't force the woman to tell her anything more. She couldn't run down to the Caserne and demand the MPs arrest the woman for, apparently, not being dead after all.

"Please call me before you leave for Frankfurt," she said

finally. "It's important. A woman was killed."

"Vicky Bauer. I will remember."

"Conrad Bauer. The phone is in my husband's name."

The woman nodded, lowered her sketch pad, and began to resume her drawing. Vicky had taken enough art courses to know the work was amateur, perhaps, but not faked. Vicky could recognize the skyline, the church steeples, the Storchenturm, the distant hills of the Schwarzwald.

"Well, then," Vicky said. She put her hands in her pockets, took them out again. The woman glanced up, her lips curled in a slight, dismissive smile, her hand not lifting from the drawing. With her other hand she tilted her sketch pad slightly away from Vicky. She couldn't be making it clearer the conversation was over.

Vicky stood for a moment longer and then turned and walked back to the car. She was sure the woman was watching her go but she didn't look back. She started the engine, shifted into gear. As the car pulled alongside the woman, Vicky rolled down the window: she had to find some final words, something compelling enough to make the woman pay attention.

"You're not safe, you know. No matter what you think, you're not safe."

Vicky was gratified to see the sudden fear on the woman's face, the way her eyes seemed to grow larger. Her lips parted slightly, but she didn't speak. The two of them stared at each other for several moments, and then the woman lowered her face again to her drawing.

Vicky let the car roll ahead, down the road. She kept her eyes on the woman in the rearview mirror until she was obscured by the trees, and even then, all the way down to the park entrance, and onto Langemarckstraße, Vicky kept flicking her eyes up to the mirror, hoping to see — what? — a figure on a bicycle following her, reaching a hand out and calling, "Wait!" But of course she saw nothing, only the thick, receding forest.

Opposite the Caserne she stopped, turned the car off. Her left hand still gripped the wheel so tightly she had to concentrate to make it relax, release.

What the hell had *happened*? She had just seen a woman resembling the murdered woman, in exactly the same spot and wearing exactly the same clothes. But it *wasn't* the same woman. Was Vicky meant to think it was? It seemed likely. The woman couldn't possibly have been there by coincidence. She must have been sent. By whom? The murderer? Who else would go to such lengths to — to what? To make Vicky think she was crazy? Or was it another warning? Like the note under the door, like the bicycle accident that was no accident?

And how did the woman know to be there at exactly the time Vicky decided to go into the Staatswald? She had told nobody of her intentions. But she *had* sat in the Caserne for over half an hour, eating her hot dog, watching the soldiers go by. If someone had followed her from there, perhaps with the woman and her bicycle, there would have been ample time for the woman to establish herself with her drawing while Vicky was conveniently getting her car bogged down higher up the road. But how did they know she'd come back and not persevere to the other exit? Maybe they knew how bad the road was. Maybe the woman had been going up there every afternoon, just in case. Maybe she was there to be noticed by other people, passersby who could claim they had seen a blond woman in a yellow sweater in the Staatswald days after Vicky had apparently seen her murdered —

Vicky put her hands to her head and pushed back her hair, hard, from both sides of her face. She was finding it difficult to breathe, as though someone had his hands around her neck.

It was all so bizarre. Nobody would believe any of this. But that's what the murderer counted on, wasn't it? That nobody could possibly believe her now. That even she herself wasn't supposed to believe her now.

She had to stay calm. They wanted her to panic, to babble her improbable story. Or they wanted her to disbelieve her own eyes, to be like the people who thought the first moon landing was faked, filmed in a TV studio. And could she say for sure they weren't right? If the movies had taught her any-thing it was that she couldn't believe her own eyes.

She put her hands back on the wheel, fixed her gaze in the rearview mirror, made herself think about the woman, what they had said to each other. I wasn't strong enough, Vicky told herself, aggressive enough. I did exactly what they expected me to, which was to drive helplessly away. I should have shouted, demanded answers, accused her of being an accessory to murder. The woman was capable of being frightened — I should have followed up on that. I should have refused to leave, or only pretended to leave and then followed her.

Maybe it wasn't too late. Maybe she was still there, wait-ing until she was sure Vicky had really gone. If she had left the park via Langemarckstraße Vicky would have seen her.

Her fingers were shaking as she turned the key in the ignition. She made a U-turn on Langemarckstraße and pressed the accelerator to the floor. The Passat leapt up the hill. She slowed as she entered the park, envisioning the woman coming down the road toward her on her bicycle. Vicky leaned forward tensely, her eyes trying to bend them-selves around the next curve, to find a flash of yellow.

But when she eased the car around the last curve before the spot where the woman had been sitting, there was no sign of her, of her sketch pad, of her bicycle. She could have gone anywhere into the forest, Vicky thought, up any of the narrow walking trails, or she could have continued along the Randweg to the next exit; a bicycle could easily have made it through the soft spots where the car had had trouble. She had vanished, just as the murdered woman had.

She sat looking dully out across the city for several moments, and then she turned around and headed down the hill.

She had just passed the Caserne when she saw Phil coming up the stairs from the path that ran along the Schutter river, which formed part of the northern border of the Caserne. He was dressed in a jogging outfit, and there were scoops of sweat under his arms. His bald spot gleamed as though the sun had been polishing it. Ordinarily Vicky would have been pleased to see him, but today was hardly an ordinary day. Phil had already seen her, however, so there was no way of avoiding him. He trotted up to her side of the car and she rolled down the window.

"How're you doing?" he asked, leaning his arms on the sill. The ammoniacal smell of his perspiration almost made her eyes water. "Any more news on that woman you saw killed?"

The words were in her throat: *there was a woman in a yellow sweater, in the Staatswald, pretending to be her* — She swallowed. It would sound crazy, delusional, exactly the way the murderer wanted.

"Afraid not," she said.

"That's too bad." Phil shifted his arms a little, releasing another wave of perspiration. "So what are you doing up here today?"

"Oh, Conrad's out of town for a volleyball tournament, so I'm just out for a drive."

"Looking for a soldier to pick up, eh?" He winked, making the scar on his cheek jump.

Vicky laughed. Looking for a soldier. Yes, she was. "Well, you know what us army wives are like."

Phil dropped his eyes, and Vicky remembered his divorce. Her comment must have sounded tactless, although, as far as she knew, the divorce had nothing to do with Claire having looked for another soldier.

"Yeah, well," he said. He rubbed his thumb along the metal car window frame. "I'm glad you're still talking to me."

"Why shouldn't I be?"

He looked up. "Then you haven't heard?"

"Heard what?"

"Well .... " He paused, turned his eyes away. "Claire is being, to use her word, 'deported.'"

"Deported? What do you mean?"

"It's army policy. Once someone stops being a dependant, the army refuses to be responsible for them."

"But wasn't she going to stay until the kids finished the school year? And what about her job? She's still a regimental secretary, isn't she?"

"They fired her. Only military dependants are eligible for such positions."

"But that's outrageous! She followed you from posting to posting for twenty years, she raised the kids, she worked for the army, and this is her payoff? To get fired and deported?"

"I know," Phil said. "They'll put her up in a hotel in Canada for seven days, and that's it. She has to have found a new home by then. She's blaming me, but it's not my fault," he added plaintively. "It's army policy."

Vicky bit back a sarcastic reply. She couldn't afford to alienate Phil. Besides, he was probably right; it wasn't his fault. She knew it had happened to other army wives. It was army policy. Everything was army policy.

She said good-bye more tersely than she intended and pulled away, then made herself smile in the rearview mirror and wave. Phil waved back and then began jogging gracelessly towards the Caserne entrance.

She would have to phone Claire, Vicky thought, and tell her — what? — I'm sorry, this fucking army? Nothing useful. Yet she was relieved, in a way, to have something else to think about as she drove home. The word *Schadenfreude* came to her mind and she wondered if it might mean not so much a taking-pleasure-in-the-pain-of-others as just a distraction from one's own miseries.

When she got back to the apartment she decided to phone Annie, promising herself she would hang up if Andrew answered, and that if Annie answered she wouldn't tell her what had happened in the Staatswald today.

"Yeah?" It was Annie.

"Hi. It's me."

"Oh, hi," Annie said. "Hey, I just heard from Claire. You won't believe what's happened to her."

"I ran into Phil today. He told me."

"That bastard."

"It's army policy," Vicky said. "How much can he do about it?"

"He could try insisting the army let him claim her as a dependant until the school year's over, for Christ's sake. He could do something besides ingenuously shrugging. But he's a good old army man. I think he's secretly glad about this."

Schadenfreude. "I thought this was an amicable divorce."

"Amicable divorce. An oxymoron if there ever was one. Anyway, she moved out yesterday. She's at the Europa Hotel, that grotty hole."

"Does she have any recourse at all? Grounds for an appeal, a grievance?"

"She tried that. They told her it wasn't gender discrimination because the same would happen if it was a male spouse of a female soldier."

"But the fact that 99 percent of the spouses are women — "

"Of course," Annie said.

Vicky sighed. "I better start being nicer to Conrad."

"It's no joke."

I wasn't joking, Vicky wanted to say but didn't.

"There are hundreds of women here," Annie went on, "staying with abusive husbands because they're afraid. Not just of the husbands but of the army. The army can take away everything."

"It sucks."

"It sucks real good. Well, what else have you been doing today besides talking to Phil? Where did you see him, anyway?"

"At the Caserne. I was — " And then she was telling Annie everything, about the woman in the yellow sweater and what they had said to each other and how she went back to find her and she was gone.

"Oh, god," Annie said. The words sounded as though she'd said them on an indrawn breath. "What does it *mean*?"

"They want me to think I imagined everything, the murder, everything."

"Did you try to call Frankfurt, to see if there really was a Hannelore Schneider listed?"

"Why bother? Of course there wouldn't be. It's a phony name."

"Are you sure, are you absolutely *sure*, this wasn't the woman you saw before?"

"Yes," Vicky said, trying not to be upset at the question. "I am absolutely sure."

"It might be better if you *weren't* sure. I mean, if you

could tell yourself, yeah, it was the same woman, I must have made a mistake — "

"I *didn't* make a mistake! Not that time, not this time!"

"Okay, I know. I just mean, I wish it *were* a mistake. This is all just getting so bizarre. Curiouser and curiouser, as Alice would say."

Vicky made herself laugh. It wouldn't have convinced anyone. "I feel more like the Red Queen. She says: We have to run twice as fast, but I'm already out of breath."

"Look, I'll tell Andrew and he could — "

"No! I .... Oh, shit, I don't know. Tell him, don't tell him, what does it matter?"

"Oh, Vicky," Annie said. "I wish I knew what to say."

After she had hung up, Vicky felt slightly nauseous. She thought she could taste the hot dog she'd eaten at the Caserne. When she swallowed, her tongue felt too large for her mouth. And it was, wasn't it, she'd heard that somewhere, that the human tongue, unlike the small tongues of other primates, was so huge and unwieldy, bending at a right angle down into the throat, that it would likely have resulted in human extinction because of the way it interfered with swallowing, allowing food to go astray into the trachea, except that it also allowed the production of language. Language, oh yes, the miracle of speech. A rodent, a bird, an ant could communicate danger to its species and be believed.

She lay down on the floor and put her legs up on the couch. It was supposed to relax her. She laid her arms across her face, her eyes.

It might be better if you weren't sure.

The woman being shot: Vicky imagined on her the face of the woman she had just seen. It was possible, wasn't it? They were the same height and build. The first woman had looked dark-skinned, but it might have been only shadows after all. And when she'd reached out to the man, perhaps she *was* only greeting him, a passerby making a comment on the view, on the sketch pad in the grass at her feet. The gun in his hand was a book, a camera, a hat; the bloodstain was another trick of the light, a red leaf falling from a tree. The photograph had shown nothing. And everything the young woman had said and done today — couldn't it all have been said and done by an innocent person sketching in the forest and interrupted suddenly by a frightening stranger raving about murder, about yellow sweaters? Wouldn't Vicky, too, have looked alarmed at mention of the police; wouldn't she, too, have decided the best way to discourage this babbling intruder was to turn back to her work and try to ignore her?

Are you absolutely sure? She couldn't be, could she, not absolutely, not if she could ask herself these questions.

And the note about Conrad, the theft of the pictures, the bicycle accident — could she argue them all away in her mind, too? The accident was only that, an accident. The pictures had simply fallen from her pocket as she rode home; the note was just a cruel joke by a student or by an MP who'd done it on a dare, urged on by drunken friends as the latest story about the crazy Mrs. Bauer spread around the base. Or how about that she had written the note herself, one of those movies where the hero searches for the killer and finds out at the end it's himself? Herself. Herself cannot be the hero but can definitely be the split personality.

She sat up, abruptly, banging her elbow on the coffee table. Tears began running down her cheeks, and loud, awful sobs broke from her throat. She sat there, her hands limply at her sides, and cried.

What she wanted, needed, was to get drunk. Not to have a drink, but to get drunk. Blindingly, passing-out drunk. To make it all go away. To make herself go away.

She blew her nose and washed her face in the bathroom sink, avoiding looking at herself in the vanity mirror. Then she poured herself a gin and tonic and drank it in three big gulps that made her throat hurt. She poured another, took it into the living room and turned on the TV, daytime housewife programming, just like at home only in another language, kitsch 'n' sink, someone called it. She pushed the Off button with her foot and went back into the kitchen, sat down at the table by the stack of unanswered mail, bills, fliers, memos, Conrad's unfinished marking — a messy pile they never managed to eliminate. She pulled from it the letter to her grandmother she had begun last Thursday.

> *Dear Gran,*
>   *Hi! Thought it's about time I wrote to tell you we are still alive and well here. Conrad's year is a little easier than the last, and I am still grinding away at my thesis. It's lovely in Lahr now, the trees all turning colour —*

Vicky picked up a pen and continued the sentence.

> *— and I went out to take some pictures to send you but instead I saw a murder, at least I thought it was a murder, but now I —*

She threw the pen down and wadded up the paper and tossed it into the sink. What did her grandmother care, anyway? Vicky had been in her mid-twenties before she visited the old woman on the Blood reserve not far from Lethbridge, and, while the woman had been welcoming enough, she had also sighed and said she had fourteen grandchildren, or was it fifteen, and she had a hard time keeping track of them all. Vicky had met one of her cousins on that first trip, too, a darkly handsome youth with a confident smile, and they were having an interesting discussion about environmental issues when he told her she "talked white." Every time she had gone back to see her grandmother she remembered those words and wondered if he was right, if she would always be an outsider there, because her mother had married a white man and because Vicky had, too.

"Your mother thought she was marrying up," one of her aunts told her, "and look what happened. She lost her status, everything."

Vicky had nodded, wanting to defend both her mother and herself but not knowing how. She had continued the visits, more infrequently as time went on, but needing that connection, that sense of family. It was the same reason, she supposed, that she continued to write to her grandmother who rarely, any more, answered.

Well, she would write her some other time. She had something more important to do now. She had to get drunk. She finished the drink she had and poured another, making it half gin this time.

On top of the stack of papers on the table was a pile of arithmetic exercises from Conrad's students. He had finished correcting all but four of them. Vicky retrieved the red pencil from the floor where she had knocked it and continued the marking.

"Good for you, Kristi," she said. Kristi had gotten them all right. Vicky drew a little happy face in the corner. "Poor Kevin," she said. "I hated math, too." Kevin hadn't finished even half the questions, and three of them were wrong. Shelly and Robert each had only one wrong, so she gave them happy faces, too.

At the bottom of the arithmetic sheet was the outline of a woman in a long dress carrying a bouquet of flowers. Some of the children had begun colouring the drawing, and Vicky thought this was a good idea, so she opened the kitchen drawer where Conrad kept some of his school supplies and took out the box of crayons and began colouring, bending low over the papers, staying within the lines. The flowers were tricky, some of the petals so small. She made the woman's dress a different colour on each page.

She refilled her glass. She could feel the familiar, comfortable blurring. The pink crayon skidded outside the line defining one of the flowers.

"Oh, damn," she said. She had to be more careful. She did the whole next page more neatly and it made her feel better. She made another drink, started another paper. When her crayon slipped outside the lines again she had the impulse to wad the page up and throw it away, as she had her grandmother's letter, but she stopped herself just in time. She sat looking at her mistake and felt like crying again.

The phone rang. Vicky wrinkled her nose at it, as though the phone had just farted.

It rang several times before she decided to answer. She took her glass with her into the living room. It would have to be a short call; her glass was almost empty.

"Yeah?"

There was a pause. "Hello? Is this Vicky Bauer? This is Constable Klug."

"Oh. Yeah. Right."

"I am telephoning to let you know that I have investigated your story — " Inveshtigated, she pronounced it: like a drunk, Vicky thought, suppressing the urge to giggle. She slapped her hand over the mouthpiece. " — saw no one."

"What?" She must have missed something.

"He saw no one."

"Who saw no one?"

"The forest worker."

"The — who did you say?"

"The forest worker."

"Oh. What forest worker was that?"

Constable Klug cleared her throat. When she spoke her voice was very slow and precise. "The forest worker you saw in the Staatswald."

"Oh, *right*. That forest worker."

"I thought you would want to know."

"Okay. Right. The forest worker. He saw no one."

"He remembers seeing you but no one else."

"The forest worker saw me but no one else."

"Yes. I spoke to him myself. This morning."

"Okay. I see. I get it. Great. The forest worker saw me and no one else. Just the news I need to make my day complete."

"I'm sorry — "

"Well, I'm sorry, too. I'm sorry I didn't close my eyes and see nothing. I'm sorry I said a word to anyone. I'm sorry the forest worker saw no one." She couldn't stop. The words kept coming out. "I'm sorry I came to this country. I'm sorry I was bloody-well ever born."

There was a long silence on the line. Finally Constable Klug's voice said, carefully, "Are you all right, Mrs. Bauer?"

"Yes, yes, I'm fine. I'm great. The forest worker saw no one."

"Perhaps this is not a good time to speak. Perhaps we will speak again some other day."

"Yeah, sure, some other day."

"I will hang up now, Mrs. Bauer. Good-bye."

Vicky stared at the phone, humming, in her hand. What had she done? She had sounded irrational, moronic, hysterical. She had sounded drunk.

Why had she even answered the phone? She was supposed

to be past drunk by now. She was supposed to be oblivious. She was supposed to be one toke over the line, sweet Jesus, one toke over the line.

She tossed the receiver in the direction of the telephone base and refilled her glass in the kitchen. Then she lay down on the sofa and stared up at the ceiling.

Everything was going so wrong. She had wanted to be like the David Hemmings character in *Blow-Up*, confident and tough and solving the mystery, but she was just screwing everything up.

And then suddenly she remembered the ending of *Blow-Up*. The character returns to the park; the dead man he photographed has vanished. He wanders around, disoriented, and then watches a group of mimes begin an imaginary game of tennis. When one of them hits the imaginary ball out of the court, apparently onto the grass beside him, and gestures to him to return it, he slowly bends down, picks it up, and throws it back. The point being, Vicky thought, that the character now no longer can, or cares to, distinguish between the real and the illusory. A disappointing ending, the critics had said, a cop-out.

"Yeah," Vicky said out loud to the ceiling, which was starting to blur. "A cop-out." Maybe that was how her story would end, too, with an imaginary tennis ball. She'd be bouncing it off the walls of her rubber room.

Or maybe the ball was there, the dead body there, only if she saw it. Sure, why not? Didn't recent evidence in physics show that matter acquired characteristics only by observation, that a particle didn't even have a location until the experimenter decided to look for it in a particular spot? Until observed, it was just a spread-out wave, an idea. The basis of everything was subjectivity. The tennis ball, the dead woman, the second woman, this room, this house — she was imagining everything into, out of, existence.

The ceiling was starting to look like something underwater, shimmering. A spread-out wave. She closed her eyes, took a deep breath. When she exhaled she burped, bringing the taste of the hot dog, tinged with apple strudel and gin, into her mouth. Oblivious. Please. Sleep. Sleep was supposed to be the best of both worlds: you got to be alive and unconscious at the same time. Or was that the worst of both worlds? Amnesia would be better. The amnesia of a fugue state. She'd read about that. A temporary memory loss brought about by anxiety. An escape.

·

Conrad was shaking her. "Wake up," he said.

Vicky struggled up from sleep, pushed at it as though it were a heavy, black door. Conrad was kneeling on the floor beside her where, she saw through squinting eyes, he was mopping up something spilled on the carpet.

"Oh, shit," she said, sitting up. Her head felt swollen, bruised.

Conrad didn't look at her. He finished sponging up her spilled drink with the dishcloth and went into the kitchen. She stood, unsteadily, and followed him, her heart limping along in her chest. She was incredibly thirsty. When she licked her lips her tongue felt like a rasp.

Conrad had stopped at the kitchen table. He turned and pointed at the arithmetic assignments. "What did you think you were doing here, Vicky?" His voice made her wince. He was really angry this time, no doubt about it.

"I finished your marking and then I started to colour the pictures."

"Look at this." He picked up the last paper she'd done

and held it in front of her face. "A kindergartner can keep in the lines better than you did."

"It's not that bad." Although it was, she had to admit, making herself look at the way the yellow crayon had coloured the woman's skirt in big zig-zags that overlapped on both sides. She couldn't remember doing that, but she must have.

"What on earth were you thinking? What will I tell the kids?"

"Your crazy wife broke out of the attic?" This wasn't the kind of argument she knew how to have with Conrad. He was supposed to sigh long-sufferingly and change the subject and that would be that.

He slapped the paper down on the table. "I just don't know," he said. "I just don't know." He turned abruptly to the sink and began wringing out the dishcloth. The sight of the dripping liquid made Vicky remember how thirsty she was.

"What's this?" Conrad reached into the other sink and picked up the wadded-up letter Vicky had tossed there. "Another one of my arithmetic papers?" He began to uncrumple it.

"It's just a letter to Gran I didn't finish."

"I don't know why you bother. She never answers."

It was a hurtful and unexpected thing for him to say. Conrad had always encouraged her to visit her grandmother, to stay in touch.

"She's an old woman," Vicky said. "It's hard for her to write."

Conrad glanced at the letter, handed it to her. "You want it?"

She shook her head. He crumpled it up again and threw it in the garbage can.

"I was thinking about some advice she gave me," Vicky said.

"What was that?"

"She said, 'You shouldn't have married a white man.'" Vicky said it lightly, but she realized immediately it was a mistake.

"If I told you my grandmother said, 'You shouldn't have married an Indian,' that wouldn't be funny, would it? Why should this?"

"Well .... " She cleared her throat, tried to concentrate, to make what she said sound passably intelligent. "When an underclass says insulting things about the people who've got power, the remarks are just defensive, not dangerous. Like women making jokes about men. Those jokes don't have the power and threat behind them that men's jokes about women do. So when we Indians say things about whites, well, they're just — "

"'We Indians.' You're as white as you are Indian, for god's sake. You use your Indian blood only when it's convenient, when you want to impress or shock somebody, like you did at the party Friday."

"That's not true. It's part of who I am. It's who my mother was."

Conrad picked up the gin bottle from the counter and held it in front of him. "Yes. I can see that. You're part of who your mother was."

Vicky stared at him.

"I see," she said. Her voice was shaking. "Another drunken Indian."

He put the bottle down. "I didn't say that."

"Yes, you did."

"Vicky, I come home and I see booze everywhere, when you promised to quit. I see you scribbling on my schoolwork, I see you passed out on the couch. What am I supposed to say — "

"I guess you say what you've been really thinking all these years. Those drunk Indian genes have bred true. I'm not white enough after all."

"You're distorting what I said."

"No, I'm not. You weren't exactly being subtle. I'm part of who my mother was, right? You could have said I'm part of who my father was, but you didn't. He drank more than my mother did, for Christ's sake."

Conrad didn't answer. He sat down on a kitchen chair, propped his elbow on the table and leaned his forehead into his hand.

Vicky stood watching him for a moment, and then she turned and walked quickly down the hall to the bathroom and slammed the door shut behind her. It was dark, only a faint yellow illumination from the street creeping in through the window, but she didn't turn on the light. She put her hands on either side of the sink and looked down into it. She wanted to be sick. She tried to make her stomach twist into nausea, but it wouldn't. All she could feel was the throbbing in her head, a hard pulse beating at her temples.

She turned on the tap, fumbled for the glass on the counter and took a long drink. Then she stood staring into the sink, trying to make her mind blank. In the distance she heard a church bell tolling: she counted the strokes. Ten. She'd slept for hours.

Finally she ran a bath, got undressed and lay down in it, her head resting on the back of the tub, the water up to her chin. She listened for the sounds of Conrad in the other rooms. She thought she heard the fridge door open and close, a rustle of papers, his footsteps crossing the living room, but what she was waiting for most she didn't hear. She didn't hear him come to the bathroom door, pause, knock, and say, "Vicky? Are you okay? Can I come in?" She didn't hear him open the door, sit on the edge of the tub and say, "Tell me what's wrong, Vicky." The way he always did. The way he always had.

The water cooled; she ran some more hot and lay back in it. She heard the light click on in the bedroom, which shared a wall with the bathroom, and she looked up at the wall, imagining Conrad on the other side of it. Getting undressed. Putting on his pajamas. Taking out his clothes for tomorrow and laying them on the chair by the door. Getting into bed. Setting the alarm. Picking up his book, the Arthur C. Clarke novel she'd bought him at the Caserne. Reading for twenty minutes, give or take a minute. Turning out the light. Was he thinking of her, lying miserably in a tub of water only a few feet from him? Was he feeling any remorse at all for what he'd said? Maybe he was thinking he'd like to bloody drown her. First put out the light and then put out the light: like Othello. *Your husband ist in on it.*

She sat up abruptly, the water slurring over the sides of the tub. Stop it, she thought, stop it. She did feel nauseous, then, but she swallowed the feeling and made herself get out of the tub and, shivering, fumble for a towel, for her clothes.

When she left the bathroom she noticed a little hem of light under the bedroom door, but by the time she had taken the two steps to bring her even with the door the light had gone out. She doubted it was a coincidence.

She went into the kitchen, which smelled of grilled cheese; she realized she hadn't had supper, so she made herself a tomato sandwich and ate it disinterestedly at the kitchen table. The pile of arithmetic papers was gone; Conrad was obviously not taking any chances. But he had left the crayons strewn in the middle of the table. She doubted that was a coincidence, either. She picked one up and began doodling on the back of a list of new releases from a Canadian video rental store. She thought of the woman she had seen today in the Staatswald, her fingers just like this, holding her pencil.

Vicky wondered, suddenly, if she could draw the woman. She had taken those art courses, after all. She dropped the crayon and picked up a pencil.

When she was finished she was amazed at how accurate her drawing seemed. The round shape of the face, the large mouth with the pronounced Cupid's bow, the nose that was narrower than normal, the pucker on her right cheek that might have been a scar, the way the hair fell across the shoulders — they all seemed right. It cheered Vicky, looking at the picture, as though she had gotten back something from a day that had otherwise gone so wrong. The only thing she didn't like about the sketch was the woman's eyes — they were a little too large, too far apart. Vicky remembered what Annie had said about evolution and predators and women's eyes.

She pulled out another piece of paper and tried to draw the murdered woman, but she was less successful this time. She closed her eyes, tried to see the photograph, which she had peered at so closely, but it kept dissolving into grainy dots. She erased so often the paper began to gray and wrinkle.

She left it, finally, and tried to draw the murderer. Perhaps because she could only draw him in partial profile, she found it easier, and her first rendering seemed fairly accurate. But there was something about the nose: she erased the end of it carefully, tried again. There was a kind of bend, a skewing to the left, perhaps, making the nostril seem larger. There. She leaned back, scrutinized the drawing. That was him; that was the murderer. It chilled her to look at him, as though she might have invited him into her house, again, to reclaim his image.

She folded the two pages up and put them in her belt-bag, although she didn't know to whom she might show them. Constable Klug had probably written her off as an impossible drunk now. And who at the DND would care? Andrew was her best bet, but despite what he'd said she doubted that even he could completely believe her any more, and she could hardly blame him. Lieutenant Crosby? Phil? The MPs? They were all career army men; they had too much to lose by seeming to give credence to the hallucinations of a woman.

She went into the study, sat down at the desk. It was after midnight, but she had slept so long she felt wide awake. The thesis: it was supposed to be what anchored her, the sane predictability of work. Or was it the most dangerous thing of all, isolating her in a little intellectual hothouse, breeding little unnatural flowers? She flipped open the red file on Chapter 1, "Introduction and Premise Material," which was full of notes she'd rummaged through a hundred times before settling on a direction. On top was the page she'd spilled half a cup of coffee on last week. She let her eyes skim to the bottom of the paper:

... consider Johnston/Bergstrom comments about how the female voice can break through the patriarchal discourse in film, which is riddled with cracks from internal inconsistencies and tensions. This is the Rupture Theory.

The Rupture Theory: Vicky had liked the term. Maybe she should have given it more than a cursory mention in her introduction. Well, too late now; she'd committed herself to a virtually opposite position.

Her eyes lifted to the paper-clip tray, where the small bead rested. Then they moved to *The Cinematography Reader*, where she could see, between pages 104 and 105, the slight opening. The slight rupture, letting in, letting out, all kinds of dangerous possibilities. Like the rip in time she had thought about earlier today in the Staatswald where the woman had been murdered, and where a woman *had* appeared, but she was a trick, a conjurer's slight of hand, a *trompe l'oeil*. Vicky stared harder at the book, the small disruption among its pages. Maybe the rupture would get larger and larger, until she could stick her whole head in and see the truth. Or maybe it would get so large it would swallow her entirely —

She had to write something. Just one damned sentence. Yesterday all she'd done was scribble down an idea for later. She opened the Chapter 3 file and pulled the notepad grimly toward her. All right. Masquerade. She'd just quoted the loathsome but obligatory Freud. Women striving to be masculine. Ego. Repression. She checked her outline, bounced her pencil against her cheek, and then began to write.

While women who use the masquerade of excess femininity are meant to be seen as evil, as dangerous temptresses, women who appropriate male behaviour also face reprisals. In Hitchcock's The Birds, Psycho *and* Marnie, *for example, as we will see in Chapter 5, what happens to Melanie and Marion and Marnie is the swift and inevitable punishment of independent pleasure.*

MONDAY

SHE HAD HOPED that Conrad would leave her the car again, but when she got down to the garage she'd found it gone so she had to rely on her bicycle. It didn't feel as solid as it had before the accident, and the rear wheel was a little loose, but it was rideable, and she had to get some groceries today; they were out of almost everything. If the bicycle proved unreliable by the time she got to Conrad's school, she decided, she would pick up the car to collect the groceries.

But the bicycle worked fine, and she felt some of her old pleasure at being on it, at the physical push and release of her muscles. There was still a tenderness in her right thigh from where she had fallen, and at first she grimaced every time she pushed down on the pedal, but by the time she was passing the *Minigolf Eingang* at Friedrich-Mauer Park several blocks away she barely noticed the squeezes of pain. She tried not to tense every time she heard a car behind her, not to look nervously around, but she wasn't entirely able to stop imagining someone following her. Like the camera eye following the protagonist, she thought wryly, the camera eye, which was turning her life from a detective film, where the protagonist and spectator share knowledge, to a suspense thriller, where the spectator knows more than the now-helpless heroine.

When she got to Goethestraße, the increased traffic made her turn west onto the Radweg, the bicycle path that eventually led down to the river. It had rained overnight, and the air here smelled fresh and clean. Large mountain ash trees lined the path, dripping splashes of water onto her face, and the red berries glistened in the slanting morning sunlight. Behind the trees the Schutter River rustled and hummed, clattering as it went over rocks.

When she met other cyclists they invariably smiled and nodded and said, "*Guten Morgen*," and sometimes the peculiar, "*Grüß Gott*." She smiled and said the same thing back, wondering if they could tell from two words that she was a foreigner.

The path was taking her only indirectly to the Canadian grocery store and Bank of Montreal she was heading for, but she didn't really care that it was a longer route. It would, she realized, bring her to within a block of Annie's. Annie would probably be at work. Still — she might not be. What the hell, Vicky thought; I'll stop.

There was no answer to her knock, and she was just turning away when the door opened.

It was Andrew.

"Oh," she said, with a silly little laugh. "Hi. I'm sorry to, um, come by like this, but I was just passing and I thought I'd see if Annie happened to be home."

"She's at work," Andrew said, squinting at her. He was wearing a striped dressing gown over his pajamas, and it was obvious he had just woken up. He rubbed one eye with his fist, boyishly.

"I'm so sorry to disturb you. You were asleep, weren't you? I'm so sorry, really — "

"It's okay. I should be up by now. I was working late last night, that's all. Personnel reassignments. Godawful work."

"Well, just tell Annie I dropped by. No reason, just to seduce a cup of coffee from her." *Seduce.* What a word to use. Maybe she had hoped Annie actually wouldn't be home and that Andrew would be —

"Don't leave. My coffee's as good as Annie's. In fact, it *is* hers. She left a carafe full. Come in." He stepped aside, held the door open.

"Oh, I shouldn't. I was just going to pick up some groceries."

"Come on. I won't bite. One cup of coffee, free, twenty minutes." He grinned at her, winked.

Oh, god, she thought. "Okay, one cup of coffee, free, twenty minutes, and you won't bite."

"Unless, etc."

"Unless nothing."

"Nothing can be something."

"Oh, really?" They weren't even making sense, she thought, as she stepped over the sill. Come into my parlour, said the spider to the spider.

The kitchen, which was about twice the size of Vicky's, was immaculate, and it startled her, since she knew Annie's opinion of housekeeping, but then she remembered the Pilskis had recently hired a housekeeper to come in three times a week. The red floor tiles gleamed; the appliances on the counters were wiped clean and pushed back into the recesses built for them; a vase of blue and white irises sat on the shelf by the window.

"Sit down," Andrew said, gesturing at one of the chairs around the kitchen table.

The belt on his dressing gown had come loose and one end was dragging on the floor, but he didn't retie it. She was suddenly aware of what she herself was wearing: a sweatshirt with about two weeks' accumulated B.O., sweat pants with the knees sagging out of them. Andrew poured two cups of coffee.

"Just black," she said, before he could ask. She stared at his naked feet, feeling such guilty fascination she might as well have been looking at his genitals. She could see the delicate bones and tendons, the blue veins just under the skin, the long toes with their square-clipped nails.

She made herself look up, at the bowl of fresh fruit on the table, three slightly green bananas, two huge pears, a nubbly skinned avocado. The word "avocado," she remembered, came from the Aztec word for "testicle." Oh, for heaven's sake. She looked away, settled her eyes on the framed sampler on the wall opposite her. It had been made, Annie had told her, by Andrew's aunt, and it said, *Love your enemies in case your friends turn out to be a bunch of bastards.* Annie had originally hung it up over the calendar in Andrew's office, where a senior officer saw it the next day and frowned and said it was inappropriate and what would the Americans think if they saw it?

"Here you go." Andrew set the cup in front of her and sat down. "So," he said, leaning back. "How are things?"

"Oh, just getting weirder and weirder. Did Annie tell you about the woman I saw in the forest yesterday?" She hadn't intended to say that, but there it was, dropping off her tongue as though she had no motor control at all.

"Yeah. That is pretty weird, all right."

"It must sound incredible." And as though she were fishing for reassurance. Maybe she was. She took a gulp of coffee, which was still uncomfortably hot. Her upper lip felt as though she'd given it a second-degree burn.

"Well, yeah, I suppose it does. Have you told anyone else at the base about her? Crosby, Dr. Lester?"

Why would he mention Dr. Lester? Maybe he thought she needed a heavier medication.

"No," she said, a bit stiffly. "I realized it might only encourage people to think I imagined the other woman's murder."

"I can see your point."

"It happened, Andrew. All of it."

"I wasn't saying it didn't."

"But you're skeptical. You've got to be by now. Even Annie's skeptical. Everyone's skeptical." She took another swallow of coffee, a large one, punitive.

Andrew began to run his thumb up and down the side of his cup. "If only there were some proof — "

"Wait. I have something. Not real *proof*, of course, but it's something."

She unzipped her belt-bag and took out the two sketches. They looked more sloppy than she remembered, and she reminded herself uncomfortably that she'd still been somewhat drunk when she drew them. Even so, she thought, they weren't bad; they were what could be called "good likenesses."

"This is the woman I saw yesterday. And this is the soldier. The murderer." She passed him the sketches. He looked at the one of the woman first, then, longer, frowning, at the one of the soldier.

"I don't suppose you recognize him," Vicky said.

Andrew shook his head. "If there were more there," he said. "A frontal view we could try matching to our files."

"I know. But it's the best I could do."

"I could keep this, if you like, and get some photocopies made and distribute them to some of the NCOs. Unofficially. Just in case it rings some bells. It might be someone they had trouble with before."

"Would you? I'd appreciate that."

"As for the woman's picture, well, she could be anybody. But I'll take that, too, if you like."

"Oh, well, that's okay. Besides, as I look at it now I don't think I got the eyes right. Maybe I'll try again." She shoved the page into her belt-bag.

Andrew leaned back. Vicky tried not to look at the way the buttons on his pajama top gaped. "What did Conrad say about what happened yesterday? I imagine he's getting pretty alarmed."

"I didn't tell him. I didn't tell anyone except Annie."

"Why didn't you tell Conrad?"

"We .... Well, it was late when he came home. And, well, we sort of got into a fight."

"Oh — I'm sorry. I didn't mean to pry."

"It's okay." And then, to her dismay, she could feel the tears swelling in her eyes.

Andrew got up, put his hand on her shoulder. "I'm so sorry. I didn't know you were having trouble."

"We're not, really." *Except that he thinks I'm a drunk and I think he's part of some neo-Nazi conspiracy.* Vicky forced herself to smile. She imagined it looked grotesque. She stood up, making him drop his hand. "I should go."

They were only a few centimetres apart. She could feel his body as though it were pressed against her. It had the faintly musky smell of sleep. She tried to step back but the chair was in her way. Its rungs cut into her calves.

"Vicky," he said softly. "I want to make love to you."

"I want that, too."

She must have said that; there was no one else in the room who could have. *I want that, too*: it was some deep, hungry part of herself that had spoken: *I want, I want.*

Andrew put his arms around her and began kissing her. Through the thin pajamas she could feel his erection. She remembered, suddenly, vividly, her affair with the Psychology TA, the way, as he pulled down his pants, his erect penis would leap out, practically saying "boing." Andrew's hands moved under her sweatshirt and cupped her breasts. She wasn't wearing a bra, and she had to stop herself from whimpering with the hot pleasure of his touch.

"We can't."

It took all her will to say that, to turn her head aside, to lift her arms and place them not around his neck but against his chest, push him away.

"Why not?" He didn't let her go. His breathing was heavy and uneven.

"We're married to other people." Why should that sound so feeble, so naive? "You're Annie's husband. Annie's my friend."

She tried to slide away from him, but he wouldn't let her. His hands were still under her sweatshirt, moving on her skin. She clenched her teeth to stifle the embarrassing sounds she felt, she heard, in her throat. If he touched her nipples she would have an orgasm on the spot, she thought. She forced herself to concentrate. She was married. Annie was her friend. This was Annie's husband.

She reached awkwardly behind her and pushed the chair out of the way, and stepped back and sideways. Andrew let her go, then, dropping his hands. Vicky moved behind the chair, holding onto its back.

"You look like a lion tamer, ready to keep the beast at bay," Andrew said.

Vicky made herself laugh, let go of the chair back. "Well, I don't know when last you've eaten." She flushed; her remark had a meaning she hadn't intended. There was no part of Andrew she could look at and feel safe. She came out from behind the chair and edged toward the door. Andrew didn't try to stop her. Was there a small, desiring part of her that was disappointed? Relief and disappointment: they were one emotion, she remembered thinking at the party Friday. What you felt when you were being saved from yourself.

"I admire your decision, Vicky," Andrew said suddenly. "You probably don't believe that, but it's true." His fingers flexed on the back of the chair Vicky had abandoned. "Loyalty to a friend is ...." He frowned and lowered his eyes to the floor, as though the rest of his sentence might be written there. But he didn't continue. There had been a quietness, a sadness, in his voice that Vicky had never heard before.

"Is?"

"I do love Annie, you know. You probably don't believe that, either, but it's true."

She nodded, not knowing what to say.

"Well," he said. Then he looked up and laughed, his face reassuming its usual confidence.

She wished she could say something to bring back that moment of openness between them, but she knew it had passed and that she should be glad it had, that it was the openness of an abyss and if she'd stepped into it she would have been lost. So she just shifted her feet and said, "Well, I better go."

"Shall I tell Annie you stopped by?"

"Oh — I guess not."

Andrew nodded. Their eyes met. It was, Vicky thought unwillingly, a collusive look, a look confirming secrets.

She was halfway back to Schwarzwaldstraße before her body settled down, before she overcame the urge to run into the bushes and masturbate. If she'd been a man maybe she could have done it. Men jacking off in the bushes were disgusting but understandable, but women — well, that would simply be depraved. What an embellishment it would make to the army's file on her if someone saw her. But what could you expect, she imagined them saying; she's the wife who went into the grocery store wearing curlers.

It was that grocery store she was heading for now, just two blocks away, and she began to feel angry even thinking about how she would have to grit her teeth and push open the door with the big, rude notice signed by the base commander. One day, she thought, she and Annie would have to organize the wives to come here at the same time wearing curlers. If the store wouldn't let them in they could pull out their curlers and burn them in army helmets. They could issue advance press releases; the *Lahr Zeitung* could send a photographer; the papers at home could pick up the story: "Dependants Defy Curler Curb."

Sure. Some day.

She pulled up in front of the Bank of Montreal, beside a small Fiat from which a large man was struggling to tug himself with as little success as a foot trying to pull itself from a laced shoe. She gave him a limp smile which fortunately he ignored, and then she went into the bank. Waiting in line, she tried not to think about Andrew. Then it was her turn and she withdrew two hundred deutschmarks. The Americans used the U.S. dollar at all their European bases and stores, but the Canadians had apparently been more sensitive to their hosts and converted to the local currency. She found it hard to imagine what anything cost in Canadian dollars anymore.

Outside again, she was relieved to see the large man had apparently escaped from his Fiat, and she walked over to the grocery store next door, not looking at the sign posted on the glass. The store was a bit larger than a 7-Eleven back home and carried similar brands of foods. A frowning clerk was cleaning up a smashed milk bottle in one of the aisles; it was likely that the child screaming somewhere in the vicinity was responsible. Vicky picked up a plastic shopping basket and made her way down the canned vegetables aisle: peas, creamed corn — she had to remember the limitations of her bicycle carrier and that she would be pedaling uphill for several blocks. She picked up a bag of potatoes and a cauliflower, then turned down the meat aisle. She was almost at the limit of what she could carry, she thought, tossing in a pound of hamburger. A litre of milk and that would be it. Next time she'd have to bring the car.

She turned toward the check-out counter. And stopped dead.

There were four people lined up at the checkout, five if you counted the screaming child beating its fists at its exhausted-looking mother, who was last in line. In front of her was a short, round woman with a shopping cart piled full into the same shape she was. In front of her was a man, just setting down on the counter the two loaves of bread in his arms. It was unusual to see men shopping here — but then she'd recognized him as Phil and remembered he was on his own now.

What shocked Vicky into immobility was not seeing Phil but seeing the woman in front of him. She was picking up her cloth bag of groceries and saying something to Phil.

She was the young woman Vicky had seen yesterday in the forest. It seemed to her, for a few seconds, as though everything around her were dissolving into a pointillist painting, everything real and solid disintegrating into a blizzard of dots.

The clerk had totaled Phil's order and he was paying for it now. The young woman was by the door, fumbling to close her purse. The clerk handed Phil his bag, and he went to the door and held it open for the woman, who smiled and said something and then went out, Phil following.

It had been impossible for Vicky to hear what they had said because of the distance they were from her and because of the crying child. Had they come in together? Did they know each other or did they just begin to chat at the counter? And what was the woman doing here, anyway? The store was restricted to Canadian soldiers and their dependants. Could she be using someone else's card? Vicky set her basket on the floor and ran to the window.

They were standing outside the store still talking. Phil had his back to Vicky, but she could see the woman clearly. It was unmistakably the woman she'd seen yesterday, the same blond hair pulled back behind one ear, the same round face with the pucker on the cheek, the same narrow nose and dark eyes and large mouth that was smiling, then laughing, at something Phil had said. Then she lifted her hand in a little wave and headed for a white car with German plates parked up the street. Phil began walking in the opposite direction.

What should she do? She pressed her palms flat against the window and stared out. If they looked around now they would see her splayed against the glass like a huge insect.

The woman got into the car, pulled away from the curb. Vicky ran outside. Stop, stop, she wanted to shout, but it was too late for that. She ran over to her bicycle, thinking she would follow her, but the car was already almost out of sight. She would never be able to keep up, and even if she could, then what?

"You want this or what?" The store clerk was leaning out of the doorway holding Vicky's basket.

"Yeah, I guess," Vicky said. She went over and took the basket. She supposed she should apologize, but the youth's scowl made her decide not to bother.

She paid for the groceries, aware of people looking at her oddly. Two children of about four who might have been twins stared unblinkingly at her, clutched their mother's slacks, and, in perfect synchrony, popped their thumbs into their mouths. She gave them the kind of insincere smile she imagined their mother had warned them about.

As she loaded the groceries into her bicycle carrier and headed back down Schwarzwaldstraße, her mind was in a turmoil. A few days ago she would have trusted Phil with her life. And now? Was Phil "in on it," too? Perhaps it was no coincidence that she had run into him outside the Caserne yesterday. Perhaps he was there because he had sent the woman into the forest. The woman: Vicky had let her get away again. Who *was* she? Phil's new girlfriend? They didn't behave that way. Perhaps they really had just met in the check-out line. But how could Vicky know? She couldn't ask Phil.

But she could ask Claire. Of course. If Phil knew this woman the odds were Claire did, too. Claire knew everything about everybody. It was, Annie told her once, what Claire did: find out about people — if she were an army personnel file she'd be stamped "Top Secret." She could show Claire the picture she'd drawn. She should call Claire, anyway, to tell her she was sorry about the way the army was forcing her to leave.

Maybe they were forcing her to leave because she knew too much. Maybe she, like Vicky, had found out a dangerous secret. Maybe, as the saying went, she knew where the bodies were buried.

The thought made her shiver. She pushed hard on the pedals, standing up as she rode. Why had she bought the damn potatoes? They were heavy as rocks. She considered leaving them at the side of the road, but she couldn't make herself be so wasteful. She swung onto the bicycle path where Schwarzwaldstraße crossed the river, and she made good time there, although she almost ran over an old man riding in front of her so slowly his bike wobbled.

"*Verdammte Frauen!*" he shouted after her.

By the time she got home she was dripping with sweat.

She put away the groceries, fast, not caring that the can of creamed corn rolled away into the back of the cupboard. She was panting, the sweat still pumping from her, her heart crashing against her ribs.

Just one drink, to calm herself, before she called Claire. She poured herself a tumbler of wine and took it to the phone. By the time she sat down the glass was almost empty. Just one, she told herself, please, just one.

She called the Europa Hotel and asked for Claire Grady. The man who answered said something she didn't understand, and finally, after a wait so long Vicky had just decided to hang up, she heard Claire's voice.

"Claire! It's Vicky. How are you?"

Claire laughed, humourlessly. "If you know enough to call me here, you know how I am."

"I couldn't believe it. I mean, I thought you and Phil were arranging everything so, so logically."

"Logically. I suppose Phil still thinks this is logical. The army, after all, is the epitome of logic."

"Could we meet? For lunch today, maybe, if you're free?"

"Free! Of course I'm free. Everyone's afraid I'm contagious."

"But you've so many friends, Claire — "

"You eliminate your husband and you eliminate your social existence here," Claire said bitterly. "I'm history, my dear. And armies never had much use for history."

"Oh, Claire — it can't be that bad." Vicky finished her wine, twisted the phone cord guiltily around her fingers. If she hadn't had an ulterior motive, would *she* have phoned Claire? She hoped so. Of course, she had less to lose than the real long-haul military wives, for whom what happened to Claire, to Claire of all people, must be a particularly compelling cautionary tale.

"Well, it *is* that bad," snapped Claire, sounding so unlike her usual composed self that Vicky moved the receiver from her ear and stared at it. "Anyway," she continued. "Lunch, sure. I'd love to. Can you pick me up?"

"I don't have the car. Can we meet at the hotel?"

"Oh, please, no. It's such a grotty place."

"How about at the Storchenturm, then? It's just a few blocks from you. I can be there in half an hour."

"I'll be counting the minutes, my dear."

When Vicky arrived, Claire was pacing the sidewalk along the low brick wall beside the tower, slapping her hand onto the wall with each step. Two sparrows hopped along close behind her fingers, hoping she had left some crumbs. Behind her the ivy cascaded down, a green waterfall spouting from cracks in the mortar of the ancient tower.

If Vicky hadn't been expecting to see Claire she probably wouldn't have recognized her. She was wearing an old jogging outfit with a grass stain on one knee, and her hair, unevenly parted and pinned behind her ears with two bobby pins, needed to be washed. Her face, devoid of its usual make-up, had an unpleasantly stretched look, as though it were being held in embroidery hoops. This was a woman, Vicky thought, who had always dressed immaculately, always had her hair in a careful, flattering style, always wore make-up that made her look elegant. She had been the kind of older woman the younger men hoped their wives would grow into, an asset to a man's career; and she had been the kind of older woman the younger women liked, too, because she was charming and motherly and held out the promise that wife-hood in the army would not be as bad as it seemed.

"Well, where should we go?" Vicky said cheerfully, hopping off her bicycle. She hoped her face wasn't contradicting her tone of voice.

"How about the Edelweiss? It's just a block away. Good food, not too pricey."

"Sure." Vicky walked her bike along beside her and they headed down the half-cobbled, half-tiled pedestrian Markt-straße.

"I'm so glad you called, my dear," Claire said. "I was just going crazy in that little room. Mostly I'm just so *angry*. I mean, Phil and I had this agreement, I'd stay until the kids were through school, but when he suggested it would make sense to get the divorce over with now, to let the kids get used to it, I said, fine, I'd just stay on until spring, then Tom would be off to university and I'd go back to Toronto with Jenny. And then one day I show up at work and there's this notice on my desk that I'm fired, that I have to leave the country. And Phil just whines that it's not his fault. I was so furious I packed my bag and stormed out, but that was stupid, I should have made *him* leave, I played right into their hands, and Phil just says that, well, I wanted the divorce, too, and that I knew what it meant, but I *didn't*, I mean, I didn't know *this* would happen, because we'd agreed I'd stay until the kids finished school, and I certainly didn't expect that after twenty years he'd let the DND do *this*, although he says I should have known what to expect, but we had an *agreement*, damn it, and if I'd thought that just like that, by losing my husband I'd also lose my job and my kids and my home, I'd have waited, or, or, got things in writing, not that that would have helped, I suppose, since we're dealing with army *policy*, after all — "

Her words had come out in a tumbling rush, and Vicky could only listen in dismay. She wondered if she should show Claire the picture after all. Maybe she had already had more than she could cope with.

But when they got to the restaurant, Claire took a deep

breath, held it deliberately the way people do when they have the hiccups, then let it out in a protracted sigh and said, "I'm sorry. You must think I've gone a little crazy."

"Of course not," Vicky said authoritatively, although it occurred to her that she was probably the least qualified person in Lahr to evaluate sanity.

The restaurant had a small patio in the back, and they took one of the three tables there. In the middle of theirs sat a vase of delicate alpine flowers, and the menus had what looked like real edelweiss laminated in the right hand corner. There were only five dishes to choose from, though, each followed by a long description that Vicky supposed was the obituary of ingredients.

Claire ordered for them in fluent German, which she had made a point of learning when Phil was posted here, just as she had made a point of perfecting her French when they were posted, briefly, to Mons in Belgium. When the two Germanies had united and seriously entertained the notion of holding dual membership in NATO and the Warsaw Pact, Claire had laughed and said to Vicky, well, her next language might be Russian. Vicky looked quickly down at her serviette, as though Claire might see the cruel memory on her face.

She heard Claire say the word "*Wein*" to the waiter. *Wein*, which also meant "to cry." Well, a drink was what Claire needed now, Vicky thought. And she, she'd have a glass, too, just to be polite, if Claire had ordered enough.

"So," Claire said, when the waiter had gone, "here we are, my dear." She laced her fingers together on the table and smiled. "And how are you?"

Vicky laughed, trying to think of the best response. Before she could say anything, Claire exclaimed, "Oh, good heavens, you had that bizarre experience of thinking you saw a woman murdered! Annie told me. What happened with all that?"

Thinking you saw. Vicky wondered if that was how Annie had phrased it. "I did see a woman murdered. I don't think anyone believes me, but it's true. I just can't prove it."

"And the army, being the army, demands proof."

The wine had come, and Claire poured them each a glass. Vicky took a sip, resisting the urge to gulp it like water. If she was still considering showing Claire the picture, she would have to be clear-headed. Well, why not right now? Claire looked as though she could handle it.

"Actually," Vicky said, setting the glass down carefully, "maybe you can help me with something." She unzipped her belt-bag and took out her drawing. "Yesterday I drove up into the Staatswald again, and I saw another woman there, and later I saw her talking to Phil. And, well, I drew a picture of her and I was just wondering if you might recognize her."

She had left a lot out, the most important parts, really, and she could tell Claire was puzzled. But curious, too — she craned her neck and reached for the picture even before Vicky had unfolded it, and then she studied it, frowning.

"I'm not sure if I got the eyes quite right," Vicky said, watching Claire nervously, "but otherwise I think it's fairly close."

Finally Claire put the picture down, but she still kept looking at it. "I might have seen her before," she said. "But darned if I can remember where."

"Could she be, well, Phil's new girlfriend?"

Claire poured them more wine, took her time. Then she smiled a little, not pleasantly, and said, "If Phil has taken up with someone new, I don't think it would be a woman."

Vicky's mouth gaped. "He's *gay*?" The word came out in a whisper. In the military this was still the love that dare not speak its name.

"You'd be surprised how many men here are. The wives

and the kids are a perfect cover. So perfect even I didn't find out until a few years ago. I just thought he had a low sex drive."

"Does anyone know? In the army, I mean?"

"Some people must, I suppose. They might try to get rid of him if he came out of the closet, but he's discreet. The brass like him, the men like him, he does a good job. And if his wife was happy, well .... And, actually, I wasn't really *un*happy. Phil was a lot kinder to me than most straight husbands. And I had my job, the kids, friends. And a low sex drive." She laughed bitterly. "Still, when he finally told me the truth I was a complete wreck. For a while I was just living on drugs, thanks to Annie. You know Annie. She could open her own pharmacy." Claire smiled, ran her forefinger around the top of her glass. "Anyway, I got over it. Phil and I agreed to stay together until the kids were older. And of course I had to keep his secret."

"How does he know you won't report him now?"

"He doesn't, I guess. He's so close to retirement maybe he thinks it won't matter much. It's the kids who'd be hurt the most."

"Could someone blackmail him over this, do you think?" Someone like the woman who was murdered, Vicky was thinking. She had tried to make the question sound casual, hypothetical, but when she reached for her wine glass her fingers were shaking.

"*Blackmail?*" Claire stared at her. "Well, I suppose it's possible. Although I think he'd have told me about it. I was, after all, his best defense. And we were, well, friends." She leaned back in her chair. "That's why I'm so upset that he won't fight this policy that's screwing me up. He's a coward, I suppose. If he weren't he would have come out a long time ago."

"But they'd have discharged him, wouldn't they? It's not that long ago since they've had to stop throwing homosexuals out of the military. And even now I expect gays aren't exactly encouraged to come out."

"Of course not. Army attitudes haven't changed. They'd overrule the Charter if they thought they could win in the courts."

"So Phil isn't intending to admit anything."

"If he did, they might not be able to fire him but they'd make his life hell." Claire sighed. "Jesus, I wish he'd have had the guts to be honest about himself years ago. So what if they'd discharged him? It would have been a liberation for all of us."

The waiter brought their meals then, and Claire said, "I think we can do with another bottle of wine, can't we?"

Vicky nodded. She could feel what she'd drunk lovingly nudging her brain. She wondered how Claire's wine glass could still look spotless, while her own was greasy with fingerprints and marks from her lips. Even in adversity, Vicky thought admiringly, this woman managed to be elegant.

"*Noch eine Flasche, bitte*," Claire said.

•

She wanted to tell someone, but she had promised Claire she wouldn't. Even Annie didn't know. She paced around the apartment, muttering to herself. Phil — gay! Could that possibly have anything to do with the murder? And how did the second woman fit in? How did Phil know her? Several times as she stalked past the telephone she had to resist the urge to call Phil and demand he tell her what he knew, what was going on.

But no, of course she couldn't. She had to stop thinking

of him as an affable friend. He was someone with secrets, the kind of secrets that may have gotten someone killed. If she was even afraid to tell Conrad about that wretched note, then how could she trust Phil, a man she had known only a little more than a year?

Conrad. She glanced at her watch. He would be home soon. Even as her mind registered the fact she thought she heard his key in the lock, his step on the stairs. But when she went to look there was no one there. It was just his *Vardogr*. A *Vardogr* was supposed to be a kind of ghost double that arrived at destinations shortly before the person did. It could-n't be seen, only heard, and was thought to be caused by the person's eagerness to arrive. Although she doubted if Conrad was especially eager to arrive. The last few days he had not exactly found this a welcoming domestic refuge. Well, neither had she. She tried not to think about the things Conrad had said to her yesterday. And not to think about Andrew, what had happened between them just a few hours ago.

Well, if his *Vardogr* was here Conrad would soon be, too. She began peeling potatoes for supper, trying to concentrate on the movements of her fingers, the peel curling thinly away from the knife, the white flesh of the potato.

She had just put the potatoes on to boil when she heard him at the door. When it opened, Frau Daimler's voice carried up the stairs, a tangle of German from which Vicky was unable to translate a single word. She could make out some of Conrad's replies, though, probably because they were mostly monosyllabic: "*Ja*," "*Nein*," "*Vielen Dank*," and final-ly, the one that alarmed her, "*Ich muß Vicky fragen.*"

"Hi," she said, casually, when Conrad came into the kitchen. "What is it that Frau Daimler wants you to ask me?"

Conrad put down a stack of scribblers on the kitchen table. "Your German is better than you let on."

"Not really. You're the only one I can ever understand."

"Well, she's invited me, us, if you want, to supper tonight. Someone gave them some fish and she says there's too much for them."

"I've just put on the potatoes to boil."

"That's fine. I'll tell her I can't come."

"Go if you want. We can have the potatoes tomorrow."

"Well, I don't really *want*. I just have a hard time saying no."

"It's all right. I don't care. Less work for me. I can have a sandwich."

"You're sure you don't want to come?"

Vicky shook her head. "You know it would just be awkward."

"Well, all right. I'll tell her I'll come." He turned to the stairs, then hesitated. "I've a gift for you," he said.

"A gift!" Conrad wasn't someone who gave unexpected gifts. She wondered if he meant it as an apology for his nasty comment yesterday about her mother. "*Gift* in German means *poison*," she added, instantly wishing she hadn't.

Conrad raised an eyebrow at her, but when he spoke his voice didn't sound annoyed. "Your German *is* better than you let on."

"I only remember the odd stuff. So where's the gift — the *present*?"

"You have to promise not to be offended."

"Must be quite a present."

He reached under the pile of scribblers and pulled out a thin book and handed it to her. It was a colouring book.

Vicky laughed. She could see the relief on Conrad's face. "Well, that's very thoughtful," she said. "Although I might have outgrown the need."

"Well, just in case it strikes you again."

"Thank you." She took the book, flipped through it, feeling suddenly awkward.

"I'll go down and tell Frau Daimler I'll come, then."

"Conrad."

"Yes?"

What could she say to him? *Your husband ist in on it.* "Nothing. Have a good supper."

She could hear them downstairs later in the evening as she sat in her study re-reading the article by Irigaray. She put in her earplugs and tried to concentrate, but the dull rasp of conversation rubbed its way through, and she found herself reading paragraphs over and over without understanding, getting frustrated and depressed. But she was afraid to let the thesis go for even one day, as though its significance would evaporate, her whole vocabulary of academic discourse fly apart into abstraction.

She let the book drop to her desk. Her eyes rested, again, on the bead in the paper-clip tray. She was surrounded by clues, everywhere there were clues: the bead, the note, the car accident, the second woman, Phil. Surely she should be able to put it all together: Colonel Mustard in the bedroom with the gun. Of course it should be a colonel. Of course it would be a gun. Of course it could be a bedroom.

She shuddered. She had come so close to calling Conrad back tonight, blurting it all out. It was intolerable, living with someone about whom you allowed such suspicions. How long could she let it go on?

A burst of loud voices rose from downstairs. She recognized Conrad's, familiar yet not, in his mother tongue. Or would they call it, like the fatherland, the father tongue? Then the rhythm of the voices changed, and she thought they might be singing. Was it *Deutschland Über Alles*? Or just *Ach, Du Lieber Augustine*?

She shoved the earplugs in further, so hard it hurt, until all she could hear was the strange, subterranean hum and beat of her own body. She pulled the notepad toward her, began doodling in the left margin, a picture of a tree with large pendulous leaves, turning one into an eye with frilly lashes. Finally she started to write, slowly, laboriously at first, then more quickly and with real enthusiasm when she began to talk about specific films.

> *Of course, since women in film are intended to be only the fetishistic objects of the male gaze, they are not themselves permitted to look, to be spectators. They are to be looked at, to be spectacles. Perhaps the best example of this can be found in the old cliché of a woman wearing glasses, the most obvious — and literal — example of a woman who can look, can see. The glasses (whose function seems entirely symbolic, having nothing to do with impaired vision) make her not just sexually unattractive and unreceptive; they make her intellectual, a woman who has appropriated the male gaze, who can see instead of being seen. In* Now, Voyager, *for instance, Bette Davis is "cured" by a doctor who removes her glasses, transforming her from a "spinster aunt" into a beauty, into an object of male desire. In* Humoresque, *Joan Crawford's character continually removes her glasses, turning repeatedly from spectator to spectacle.*

She lifted her pencil, twirled it between her fingers. Her mind was full of examples, possibilities, directions she could go. Why wasn't writing always like this, a fluent rush of ideas? She scribbled a superscript "3" after "spectacle," found her footnotes page, and continued to write, quickly, dotting her *i*'s and crossing her *t*'s ahead of the letters.

3 An interesting parody of this device occurs in the more recent film Strictly Ballroom, *in the scene in which the protagonist removes the glasses from his partner, transforming her instantly from a dowdy, poor-complexioned woman into a beautiful one. More significantly, he transforms her from a strong, creative woman to one more docile and passive, concerned now mainly with her appearance and with pleasing. Conversely, in films where glasses are similarly removed from a male character (the Clark Kent-Superman example is the obvious one), he turns from indecisive and weak to aggresssive, confident, active.*

She paused. Footnotes were like minor characters wanting to take over the story. She made herself return to her main text. But, although she knew where she wanted to go with her argument, she found herself suddenly writing more slowly, losing focus. As she wrote the last sentence, she felt an unease close to real fear, that crawling-up-the-back-of-the-neck fear, as though she might no longer be writing something removed from her own life.

The large number of films in which women are blind may represent an idealized female image, the perfect woman-as-spectacle. More sinisterly, women who insist on retaining the gaze, on looking, are, like Hitchcock's women or women in horror films, punished, often with death.

TUESDAY

WHAT MADE HER decide she had to confront Conrad was what happened that morning.

He had left the car for her and got a ride to work with Paul Garten, and she had done a few errands and stocked up on groceries. She was struggling with the three heavy cloth bags at the back door, cursing as one of the straps caught on the outside door handle, when she felt the weight of the bag in her right hand suddenly ease. She whirled around, off balance, and saw Erich Daimler standing beside her, lifting the bag.

"Oh!" she cried.

Startled, he let go of the bag and stepped back. "I am sorry," he said. "I did not mean to give you fright. I wanted only to help."

"It's okay. I was just surprised." She peered at him, pressed back against the wall. His dark eyes seemed to have sunk deeper into his face since she had last seen him, and there was a stale odor of cigarettes about him. She had rarely seen him smoking, but today he smelled of something that had been sifted from the ashes in a fireplace. "I didn't know you spoke English," she said, fumbling for her keys. In fact, she thought, he had made a point of pretending he didn't.

"I have learned some," he said, smiling in a way she did not feel was particularly friendly.

The door beside him opened a few centimetres. Frau Daimler's face appeared in the crack. She glanced at Vicky and smiled nervously, then said something to Erich. He made an irritated gesture with his hand and said, "*Noch nicht.*" Vicky knew what that meant. *Not yet.*

She turned her back to them and shoved her key into the lock. Not yet what? The back of her head felt hot, as though their eyes were burning into it.

"I wish to ask you something," Erich said, his voice compelling her to turn and face him. He licked his lips.

"Yes?"

"I have heard that you, that you — " he cleared his throat " — are Indian. Is this true?"

Vicky stared at him.

"From whom did you hear this?" she asked, enunciating each word clearly.

Erich shrugged, the rigid smile on his face looking as though it would have to be ripped off forcibly, like a band-aid. "I only wondered if this was true," he said.

"What difference does it make?"

"We only want to know if this is true. You do not look like an Indian." Erich licked his lips again. "You are staying here, in our house, you see. We must know."

"Does it make any difference?"

"We did not know this about you when you rented our house. We must know if it is true."

"I see."

"*Was sagt Sie?*" Frau Daimler asked, eagerly, through the crack in the door.

"*Sie sagt,*" Vicky said, "that it's none of your fucking business."

She turned, wrenched the key in the lock.

"*Was hat Sie gesagt?*"

Erich said something in answer to his mother, but Vicky didn't try to understand it. She jerked her grocery bags through the door and slammed it behind her. She ran up the steps, trying to shut out the blurred voices downstairs.

She put the groceries away, carefully, concentrating on what she was doing. Then she sat down on the sofa and pulled her knees up to her chest. She could smell her sweat, overwhelming, sour: an old defense mechanism to drive away one's enemies.

She made herself remember the conversation, play it again in her mind, word for word. It had only taken a few moments, but in her memory it was huge; it would need the storage space of whole days, weeks.

She looked around the room, at the familiar walls with the pale blue flowered wallpaper, with the large painting of an alpine landscape by a local artist which Frau Daimler had insisted they keep. Vicky had felt comfortable here, at home, and suddenly it all seemed hostile. It was theirs, the Daimlers', not hers. *You are staying here, in our house, you see.* She was contaminating their home, that was what they meant. *We did not know this about you when you rented our house. We must know if it is true.*

Had Erich understood her answer? Even if he had missed her exact words, her tone and actions needed no translation. And what now? Would they demand she leave, take her impure *unter-Mensch* blood out of their house? And what about Conrad?

What *about* Conrad? Had he told them about her last night? Had he still been thinking about their argument and mentioned her unsatisfactory ancestry? She dropped her legs and leaned back against the sofa, closed her eyes. *Your husband ist in on it.*

She had to talk to him. She *would* talk to him. Tonight. She couldn't stand one more day of this.

I want a drink, a drink, a drink: the word throbbed in her forehead. She forced herself not to give in. In an hour she had an appointment with Dr. Lester, and that would be just what he'd want, her smelling of gin and babbling about the master race. She considered canceling, but she knew he would be annoyed and wouldn't give her another appointment for weeks. She didn't even need to see him; it was just to get a renewal of her Anaprox and Valium prescriptions, which he refused to authorize at the pharmacy without an office visit first. She had to go. Besides, if she canceled she would sit here and drink herself unconscious.

She had a shower, lathered on enough deodorant to plug the pores on an elephant, put on fresh clothes and pinned two barrettes in her hair, remembering that Dr. Lester, proud of his extra courses in psychiatry, had told Annie that good grooming was a sign of good mental health. They had had great fun dressing Annie for her next appointment: a skin-tight skirt and sweater, with no bra; bright blue eye shadow that swept up in two wings from under her brows into her hairline; thick, dark red lipstick that made her mouth look swollen; her hair backcombed and decorated with a green ribbon and several pin-on braids she had bought as a joke. But at the last minute Annie had chickened out, run into the bathroom and washed her face and combed out her hair and changed her clothes. The most Vicky could persuade her to do was to keep the green ribbon in her hair. Dr. Lester had remarked on it, saying it made her look younger.

Vicky tiptoed downstairs and then fled outside, not daring to look behind her, not wanting to imagine what the Daimlers might be doing, saying, now.

As she got in the car and put on her glasses she remembered

what she had written in her thesis last night: with her glasses she had appropriated the male gaze; now she would be able to look, to see; wearing spectacles prevented *being* a spectacle. Too bad, she thought, starting the car, that she hadn't been wearing her glasses when she saw the woman murdered; then life really could imitate art. And too bad she didn't have bifocals, double-vision glasses; think of the symbolic potential there.

She drove slowly to the Caserne, concentrating on the road, her driving. All she wanted was her damned prescriptions renewed. She parked behind K-2, noting Andrew's blue Mercedes only a few cars over. His office, in fact, on the third floor, was almost straight above Dr. Lester's on the ground floor. That thought had, of course, occurred to her every time she went to see the doctor.

When she entered the waiting room, the receptionist, a small, young woman with pink hair, was on the phone, which she kept tossing from one ear to the other. Her fingers twisted themselves into the phone cord; she writhed on her seat; her feet seemed to be trying to tap themselves free of her ankles. What medication did Dr. Lester have *her* on, Vicky wondered. She'd get a tic if she kept watching her. At last the woman hung up the phone, smiled energetically at Vicky, and with long, curved fingernails tweezed her file from the pile on her desk.

"Have a seat," she said. "The doctor will just be a moment."

The only other patient in the waiting room was a pregnant woman who looked too young even to be menstruating. She was thin, and pale as snow. Even before she blew her nose and wiped at her eyes Vicky knew she had been crying. Vicky stared down at her lap. What should she do? Would it be kinder to pretend she didn't see or to offer some words of comfort? She felt such a sudden and unexpected sympathy for the woman that if the receptionist hadn't told Vicky to go in then she would probably have done the latter. Behind her she could hear the receptionist say something to the woman, and the woman say loudly, shrilly, "No!"

She sat in the little cubicle fidgeting, still hearing the woman's voice. *No*: it wasn't a woman's word. It was a word for troublemakers, for women who were going to get punished, for women who didn't know their place. Longer ago than she wanted to remember she'd read an interview with John Lennon about the first Yoko Ono exhibit he'd attended, how he'd climbed the ladder to the ceiling where Ono had printed one tiny word, "yes." If the word had been "no," Lennon said, he would never have wanted to meet the artist. Wow, Vicky had thought then, how lucky for Ono, to have gotten it right.

"Vicky." Dr. Lester's voice made her jump, guiltily, as though he had caught her snooping through his desk.

"Hi."

He looked carefully through her file as he stood in the doorway, frowning, turning the page, murmuring, "Mmm," ambiguously, several times. He was a short man with a soft, delicate face, for which he seemed to be compensating with an excess of body hair and a dour expression. He was wearing a white lab coat with a pale yellow stain on the right upper pocket. Psych 101, she remembered (irrelevantly, she hoped): people will do nearly anything, even kill someone, if told to do so by men in white coats, by men in the uniforms of science, of medicine. Yes, Dr. Mengele. Of course, Dr. Mengele.

"So," Dr. Lester said, snapping closed her file and sitting down opposite her. He crossed his legs, pulled his lab coat carefully over the top knee. "What's the problem today?"

"I'd just like my prescriptions for the Anaprox and the Valium renewed, please."

Dr. Lester set her file on his desk and splayed his hand on it. "You think you still need these prescriptions?"

"Well, yes. The Anaprox really helps with the pain of my periods, and the Valium, well, it's something you recommended — " oh, shit, she thought: wrong thing to say " — and it's been very useful," she went on, ingratiatingly. "I use it sparingly, but lately I've been under a bit more stress, and — "

"Ah, yes," the doctor interrupted. He allowed himself a smile, the kind that only touched the lips, and those with apparent reluctance. "The incident in the forest. About — " he flipped open the folder, glanced inside, and continued with barely a pause " — five days ago. I imagine that would have intensified your stress level."

Vicky stared at her file, on which Dr. Lester was again resting his hand. How dare he put that in his medical records! As though he had been called out that day to see *her*. She could just imagine how he had recorded it: "Psychotic delusional episode." She wondered to whom else he had given his report.

She made herself look away from her file, fix her eyes on the doctor's right ear, from which an astonishing amount of black hair sprang. "Yes," she said, trying to keep her voice neutral. "Seeing a woman murdered does intensify your stress level."

"Do you still think — that is, are you still sure that's what you saw?"

"I couldn't be more sure."

"You realize there's no corroboration for this. I checked with Lieutenant Crosby again this morning when I saw you were scheduled to come in today. You should consider the possibility that you didn't see what you thought you saw. Persisting with your claim might be, well — "

"Detrimental to my health." She couldn't stop herself from saying it. If he only knew.

He shifted, recrossed his legs. His eyes, Vicky realized, were exactly the same colour as her file folder, a pale matte gray. "I think you know what I mean, Vicky. If your story can't be proved, it's not going to be believed."

"Well, Andrew still thinks there's something to it. I drew a picture of the man and he's circulating it." Why had she told him that? It was none of his business. But she knew why — to see exactly this expression on the doctor's face: one of surprise, discomfiture.

"Andrew? You mean Captain Pilski?"

"Yes."

"I see. You drew a picture for him." Dr. Lester's fingers drummed lightly on his desk. He was more disconcerted than she had expected. It was nice to have friends in high places. "Well, good, good. I hope something comes of it. Meanwhile, I'll write out these prescriptions for you." He tore two pages off his pad and scribbled something down, handed them to her.

"Thank you."

The doctor stood up, held the door for her. "Now, you'll make an appointment to see me again in a month, all right? Of course we want to keep an eye on how you're doing."

Of course. An innocuous phrase, one she, too, was academically adept at using. It was just a way of boosting one's own probably feeble argument; it was a bluff, a shoring up of leaky logic, a dry insinuation that only an idiot would disagree.

"Of course," she said, rubbing at the corner of her eye with her forefinger in a way she hoped looked casual. "And who exactly is 'we'?"

"What? Oh — " Dr. Lester laughed. "The doctorial 'we,' that's all. Who did you think I meant?"

"Oh, nobody, I guess." Great, she thought: now he would sit down and write in her file, "Classic symptoms of paranoia."

She made an appointment with the twitchy receptionist for a month later and left the office. As she walked down the hallway she thought of Andrew in his office above; she thought of how, if they were slightly different people, she would run upstairs and they could make love fiercely on his office floor. She quickened her step, looked down at the floor, where the baseboard was warping, bending away from the wall. In a few years, who would care if the baseboards were warped or if she and Andrew had made love upstairs? This building would be empty. All the plotting and plodding and planning coming only to that, an empty building. Well, that was good, wasn't it? The army's real goal should be to make itself redundant.

She got her prescriptions filled at the little drugstore, then walked out to the parking lot, where she was relieved to see Andrew's Mercedes was gone.

When she turned to open her car door she noticed, at the end of the parking lot, the weeping, pregnant woman from the doctor's office. She was standing beside the driver's side of a car, clutching the door where the window was rolled down, and speaking to the man behind the wheel. He reached up and scratched at his neck in an odd way, by flicking his fingers upward. The gesture seemed familiar to Vicky. She peered at the man. It was Lieutenant Crosby, the man who'd led the search for the body in the Staatswald. He was involved in a messy divorce, Andrew had said. The pregnant woman was crying again, and Vicky looked away, feeling, as she had in the doctor's office, an unexpected sympathy and sadness for her. By the time Vicky got into her car and backed out of her parking space, Crosby had gone, and the young woman was walking away, her large stomach seeming to pull her, resisting, along behind it.

Driving home she felt increasingly depressed, thinking

about what was waiting for her: the Daimlers, with their accusing, predatory stares from their doorway. But, even worse, there was the promise she had made to herself, that she would confront Conrad today, not just about the Daimlers but about the note.

The car was going slower and slower, and twice other drivers honked at her and glared as they swerved to go by. At last she pulled over and sat for a while, leaving the car idling. She remembered her new prescriptions and opened the Valium bottle and took one. She stayed there for about ten more minutes, her eyes closed, listening to the swish of traffic, to the roar of a plane low overhead heading west to the airfield, and then she sat up and put the car in gear and headed home.

She was sure one of the Daimlers would be waiting for her as she came around the side of the house and opened the back door. But the yard was empty, the hallway, too, and the door to their suite remained closed as she unlocked her own.

She went upstairs and into the study and pulled the note from between the pages of *The Cinematography Reader*. Without opening the paper, she slid it into her belt-bag. Now all she had to do was wait until four o'clock, when she had agreed to pick Conrad up at school. Now all she had to do was wait, and not have a drink. Well, one drink, maybe, just to take the edge off. Two at the most.

.

It was closer to four-thirty than four by the time Conrad came out of the school. Not that Vicky minded. If he was late he would have to apologize, and she was grateful for any advantage. She had sat in the car rehearsing what she would say, the tone of voice she would use, whether she would try to sound upset or indignant or even amused. Whatever else, she mustn't let this turn into the kind of argument she had had too often with Conrad, one in which he would make her sound, make her be, unreasonable, petty, childish. This was not a quarrel about who had left the towels wadded up in the bathroom or who had bought something foolish or who (guess which who) had had too much to drink.

Two boys came towards her car, shouting at each other, verbs and nouns and adjectives all some variation of "fuck," slapping at each other with their book bags. The T-shirt on the child closest to her read, "It isn't how you play the game. It's whether you WIN or LOSE." She watched the boys in the rearview mirror, going home to their fathers who had paid for those shirts, fathers who were soldiers, after all, granite-jawed fathers who would say, "Second place is for losers, boy."

Conrad was coming out the front door now, talking to Paul, who reached up and ran first one hand, then the other, over his perfectly tidy hair. He waved to Vicky. She smiled and waved back, hoping he wouldn't come to the car to chat. He and Conrad conversed for a few minutes more, then headed for their own vehicles. Vicky's fingers tightened on her belt-bag. She could almost feel the note inside, wedged between her wallet and her bottle of Valium.

"Sorry I'm so late," Conrad said, getting into the passenger seat. He was wearing grey slacks and the navy cardigan she'd damaged by trying to bleach out the ink stain on the right cuff. "One of my mothers was having a nervous breakdown in Paul's office. Of course, if Patrick were my son I'd have a nervous breakdown, too."

"Patrick. Wasn't he the one who set the fire in your wastebasket?"

"That's the one." Conrad sighed and leaned his head back. "Well, take me home."

"Actually, I was hoping we could go somewhere else first. Just for a coffee, maybe? There's something I want to talk to you about."

Conrad sat up, looked at her. "I suppose so. Talk about what?"

"I'll tell you when we get there."

"Very mysterious. Is it something to do with the Staatswald business?"

"I hope not," Vicky said, trying to keep her voice steady, light even.

They went to a small, low-ceilinged restaurant a few blocks away. Because of its proximity to the Canadian Cultural Centre, it was a convenient place for the wives to go after their aerobics classes, but now Vicky and Conrad were the only customers. On each table were small Canadian flags on sticks inserted into bud vases. Conrad picked one out, twisted it between his fingers. It twirled like a red and white sparkler.

"Do you remember," he said, "that time we were in Halifax and went into the information office and those American tourists standing beside us saw some of these for sale and said, 'Isn't their flag cute? I wonder if it comes in any other colours?'"

Vicky smiled. "Yeah, I remember that." If Conrad had deliberately tried to charm her away from her purpose he couldn't have done a better job.

The waiter, an elderly, red-cheeked man who was likely the owner, spoke to them in fluent English, which Vicky would have preferred he didn't know, but after he brought them their coffees (and menus "just in case") he disappeared into the back, where they could hear the murmur of a television.

"So," Conrad said. "Tell me."

She had known him almost twenty-five years. She had trusted his judgement over her own. And she loved him, perhaps a little absentmindedly, and not the way marriage manuals might define it, but wasn't it still love? And now she sat across from him in a restaurant because she had decided that what she had to tell him was so dangerous, so frightening, it had to be done in a public place.

She opened her belt-bag and took out the note.

"The day after the murder I found this shoved under the door." She handed the note to him.

He unfolded it, read it. Vicky watched his face, trying to read his reaction. He was frowning: that was all she could see, his eyebrows pulling together, wrinkling the skin between them.

"What is this? What's it mean?"

"I was hoping you could tell me."

"I don't understand. What am I 'in on'?"

"That's what I want to know."

"Vicky — you've had this for, what, four days, and you only show it to me now. Why didn't you show it to me right away?"

"Don't try to make *me* feel I did something wrong! What was I supposed to think — "

"You were supposed to think this was some ugly game someone was playing and to tell me about it."

"I was afraid to."

Conrad stared at her. Vicky forced herself to meet his gaze. The television in the back of the restaurant continued speaking, saying things Vicky could not understand.

"Afraid," Conrad said at last, quietly. "You were afraid of me?"

"No, not really." But how else, then, if *not really*? "I saw a woman murdered, Conrad! Nobody believed me. Then this creepy note appears — I didn't know what to do, what to think — and every day something else frightening happens. I haven't even told you what happened yesterday. How am I supposed to judge what's making sense anymore, who to trust — "

"And you didn't trust me."

"I don't know, I don't *know!*" It was all going badly, exactly the way she had told herself it mustn't. She wanted to scream, to cry. She looked down into her coffee, black and opaque, and pressed her hands around the sides of the cup, felt the warmth move slowly into her fingers.

"Vicky — for god's sake. Do you honestly think I could be involved in a *murder*?" He threw the note onto the table. Inside she could see, bent by the fold, the word "husband," the last letters peeling away from the glue.

"No, no, not really, but .... " She raised her eyes to him again, made herself concentrate, loosen her hands from the cup. "After we came back from Dresden you were ... different. So withdrawn, so, I don't know, you suddenly had all this anger, and I began thinking about what happened in Weimar with the black waiter, the way you told me it was none of my business. And the woman who was killed was black, I think, and then there was that nasty crack you made about my mother, and you spend so much time down there with the Daimlers, in fact something happened with them this morning that made me think I was right about them — "

"What happened with the Daimlers?" Conrad leaned forward. He had sat rigidly, listening, his eyes fixed on Vicky's face. There had been words — "Dresden," "Weimar," "black waiter," "mother" — that had seemed to be like tiny pins she'd stuck into his cheeks, into the sides of his mouth, making the small nerves wince, pull away. But it wasn't until she'd mentioned the Daimlers that he interrupted her.

"Erich accosted me as I was coming in with the groceries. He asked if I was Indian. When I asked him what difference it would make, he said he had a right to know because I was staying in their house, and that they didn't know this about me when they'd rented to us."

"He said *what*?"

"That he had a right to know if I was Indian because I was staying in their house. You obviously said something to him about my impure background."

"Of course I didn't," Conrad said.

"Well, how else would he know about it?"

"I don't know. You told people at the party. Maybe Paul and Hilda told him."

"Well, it hardly matters. Erich made it clear I was unwelcome in their house."

"Are you sure you didn't misunderstand?"

"I didn't misunderstand."

Conrad looked down at his hands lying on either side of his coffee cup. His shoulders slouched forward, as though they needed to protect his chest. The door of the restaurant opened then and two women came in, speaking English, talking about Vancouver, home. The waiter greeted them effusively, and Vicky and Conrad sat silently while he brought them menus, took their orders. It seemed to take hours. The tension in Vicky's back was pushing a hard fist of pain into her neck. The waiter came over and asked them if they'd like more coffee.

"No, thanks," Conrad said. Neither of them had even taken a sip from their cups.

A drink, Vicky thought, I want to order a drink; but the man, fortunately, had already moved away. She took a big swallow of her tepid coffee and waited for Conrad to speak.

Finally he straightened his shoulders a little and shifted in his seat. Then he nodded at the paper between them on the table and said, his voice low and tight, "So what do you think that means? That the Daimlers and I are part of some Aryan plot to take over the world, to kill all the non-white people?"

Vicky laughed, too loudly. "Of course not. But how do you explain the note? Who sent it, and why?"

"It came the day after you saw the murder?"

"Yes."

"Someone trying to confuse you, maybe, misdirect you."

"But it had to be someone who knows not just where I live but the right door under which to slip the note. Maybe the Daimlers had something to do with it."

"Why? They're my friends — "

"Maybe until they found out you married someone with tainted blood."

"I thought you said they just found that out today."

"They *confronted* me with it today. I don't know when they found out."

"But last night they had me to supper. They were so ... kind." Conrad's eyes dropped to the table, to the small Canadian flag in the vase.

"Well, I don't understand how their minds work. Maybe they don't blame you. Or maybe we'll come home and they'll have changed the locks and thrown our things into the street."

The waiter came back to their table. "Perhaps you will want to order something to eat now?" he asked.

"No," Conrad said. "I don't think so. We should be leaving."

Leaving. Going home. To what, to where? The two women at the other table suddenly laughed loudly at something, startling Vicky.

"Is that all right?" Conrad was asking her. "Do you want to go now?"

"Yes, sure." She took another gulp of coffee and picked up the note and folded it back into her belt-bag. Conrad watched her, then stood up and paid the waiter.

"Thank you," said the man, more heartily than necessary. "I will miss you Canadians when you leave." He sighed. "I will probably have to close my business."

On the way home they were quiet, looking straight ahead at the streets, the traffic. It was likely only because they didn't speak until they were almost home that made what Conrad said then seem significant, as though he might have been thinking about it for a while.

"Did you show the note to anyone else?" he asked.

"No."

When they got back to the house they did not, at least, find their belongings thrown into the street. They sat in the garage, not opening the car doors.

"Do you want me to talk to them tonight?" Conrad reached up and adjusted the rearview mirror, as though he wanted to watch someone in the back seat. Vicky resisted the urge to look behind her.

"What would you say?"

"What do you want me to say?"

"It's a question of what *you* want to say," Vicky said.

Conrad sighed. "All right. It's just ... going to be so ... unpleasant." He started to say something else but stopped.

They went into the house, nervously, watching where they stepped, as though something might explode under their feet. Vicky was just putting her key into the lock, thinking, for one awful moment, that it wasn't going to turn, that the lock *had* been changed, when she heard a slight noise behind her and then Conrad's voice saying, evenly, "*Guten Abend.*"

She whirled around, and there was Erich, standing in his doorway. She expected to see his mother peering over his shoulder, but she was nowhere in sight. The light behind him made his face dark, only the eyes clearly visible, as though the light might be shining right through them.

"*Kann ich zu dir sprechen?*" Erich said.

"*Und Vicky? Auch zu ihr?*" Conrad asked.

"*Besser nicht.*"

Conrad turned to her, where she stood with her hand still on the key in the lock. "Erich wants to talk to me," he said. "Alone, apparently."

"Of course," Vicky said tightly, aware her reply was ambiguous.

"I'll come up as soon as I can."

"All right," she said. She went inside and shut the door, but she didn't go up the stairs. She stood listening to the low voices in the hallway, but even if they had been in English she wouldn't have been able to make out the words. She climbed the stairs, counting them, a mantra to distract her.

She put yesterday's potatoes back on the stove, took out the hamburger and began dividing it into portions. As she watched her fingers shaping and reshaping the patties, as though she had to make them identical, she thought about her conversation with Conrad in the restaurant. His reactions were what she had hoped for, weren't they? Astonishment, disbelief, annoyance that she hadn't told him sooner: weren't they the reactions of a man who was not "in on it"? So, did she believe him, trust him now, completely, unequivocally? She squeezed her hands slowly, into soft fists, watching the hamburger ooze out between her fingers. So — *did* she? If she had to choose between yes and no, would she choose yes? She closed her eyes.

I want to choose yes, she thought. Please, god, let me be able to say yes.

She thought of Conrad downstairs with Erich, making god knew what bargains on her behalf. She should have refused to leave. Erich might be lying about their conversation; she had played right into his hands, allowing herself to be dismissed, to be Conrad's Dependant, to be talked about instead of with.

It was half an hour before Conrad came back. Vicky had just started setting the table and she stood, the cutlery clenched in her hand, watching him come up the stairs. He came over to the kitchen table and sank into his usual chair.

"Well," he said.

"*Well?*"

"We won't have to move."

"Is that all he said?"

"It was Hilda who told them. I don't imagine she had any idea they would react as they did."

"What else did he say?"

"He was disappointed in me. That I would marry outside the race."

"I see." Vicky sat down opposite him. She couldn't seem to make her fingers let go of the cutlery.

Conrad was staring straight ahead, but his eyes seemed to be focused not on Vicky but on something in the air in front of her. When he spoke his voice was so low she had to bend forward to hear.

"I suppose I just didn't want to see that in them. Especially when Paul and Hilda came over and we would talk about it on a more ... intellectual level. It didn't sound like racism when Erich called it the jealous gene theory or when we talked about immigration or third-world birth rate levels or how every country and nationality becomes obsessed with *Lebensraum*. It was all just words, ideas. We had discussions. We argued." He stopped, still staring into the air. Vicky sat still, afraid to move, to remind him she was there.

"You said I was angry after Dresden," he said at last. "You're right. Something happened to me there. I can't really explain it. It's like I had my childhood stolen, my whole family killed, and because Germany lost the war I was never allowed to be angry about it. The suffering of Germans like me was — shameful, somehow. Maybe with the Daimlers the forbidden could be spoken. If some of the things they said made me uncomfortable, well, I could overlook those. With them I could be angry. I could be German again. Oh, I don't know. I don't expect you to understand."

Vicky loosened her hand slowly from around the cutlery. "Maybe I do," she said.

Conrad nodded. She wasn't sure if he'd even heard her. He looked exhausted, his eyes red and staring, as though he had forgotten how to blink.

"Maybe we should eat," Vicky said. "The potatoes can't take another delay."

"Yes," Conrad said. "All right."

The potatoes and carrots were overcooked, lumps of white and orange mush on their plates, but neither of them remarked on it. As she looked at him across the table she thought: how could what he's told me be anything but the truth? She wanted to put down her fork and take his hand and say something comforting and kind, but she was never good at that sort of thing, and she was afraid that she would sound phony or patronizing, and that in any case Conrad's pain was beyond the comfort of any words from her.

Mostly just to push away the heavy silence, she told him what had happened yesterday, about seeing the second woman in the forest, about her lunch with Claire, remembering just at the last minute her promise not to tell anyone Phil was gay. Conrad listened and nodded, but she wondered how much he was really hearing, what he was thinking.

Conrad helped her with the dishes, and then, sitting beside him on the sofa, she helped him mark his Social Studies map exercises.

"I'm sorry I said what I did about your mother," Conrad said suddenly. "I didn't mean it. I was just upset about your drinking."

"I know."

"I liked your mother. Maybe I thought she was like me. Adrift, somehow. I was sorry for her. I was sorry for you."

"So you married me because you were sorry for me?" She smiled, thinking he would have to deny it.

"Yes, I suppose so."

"You married me out of *pity*?" She leaned away from his side so she could look at him.

"Well, yes. Was that so terrible? I wanted to save you from becoming your mother."

"To save me."

"Surely after all these years this doesn't surprise you?"

"Well, no," she lied. "Although I rather thought you married me because you loved me."

He didn't answer for a moment. "I suppose pity is a kind of love," he said at last.

Vicky sat looking at his profile, that perfectly sculpted face. She was afraid to ask, but she knew she had to: "And now? Do you still pity me now?"

Conrad brushed his hand slowly across the paper on his lap, wiping away invisible eraser crumbs. "I pity myself," he said.

That's no answer, she wanted to say. But she didn't. She pretended to concentrate on marking her Social Studies paper. When she finished it she realized she had marked as correct a map that put Saskatchewan in Ontario and Manitoba in Alberta. She made herself change the check marks to X's: wrong, wrong.

They worked in silence for another half hour, and when they were finished Conrad yawned and said he was going to bed. Vicky sat on the sofa listening to the bathroom sounds: the toilet flushing, the water running in the sink, the scrubbing sound of his toothbrush, the silence that meant he was flossing his teeth, the clicking out of the light. The nightly routine that was part of her routine, because she lived with him, because she was his wife.

I was sorry for you.

He was right; it shouldn't have surprised her to hear that, after all these years. But it did.

Pity is a kind of love. She remembered how, all those years ago, she had said so glibly to her university friends, "Conrad is capable of love but not complexity." She couldn't have been more mistaken. Perhaps it was just the opposite.

At last she got up and went into the study. She took the note out of her belt-bag and put it back between pages 104 and 105 of *The Cinematography Reader.* Maybe she should have thrown it away. She believed now (didn't she?) that her husband was not "in on it." The note was written by someone trying to confuse and misdirect her, as Conrad said, wasn't it? And her suspicions about the Daimlers: well, he'd admitted she was right; he'd taken his share of the blame; he'd explained everything. The man who had liked and pitied her mother when no one else did could not have changed so much.

Sorry for her. Sorry for you. I wanted to save you from becoming your mother.

If Conrad hadn't saved her, would she have become her mother? Would that have been as awful as Vicky, as Conrad, as her mother's family, as perhaps even her mother, seemed to think? Maybe it was the same sad paradox as being saved from oneself. My mother was someone I loved and then learned not to love, Vicky thought. I didn't even let myself pity her, the way Conrad did, not even pity, which may or may not be a kind of love.

She put her head down on her desk and began to cry, quietly, so Conrad wouldn't hear.

When she stopped she didn't feel better, only tired. She blew her nose and pressed her arm across her eyes to blot the tears and walked a few times around the room. Why, in the midst of everything else that was happening, should she have these sudden and overwhelming feelings for her mother? When she looked down at her thesis folders she thought: filmic identification, the face in the mirror, the first other: mother. She had fought and denied that first basic identification. It was supposed to be a victory, but it wasn't. It was, had always been, a grief, a loss.

She couldn't make herself continue writing. Instead, she opened the Chapter 7 file labeled "Mother/Daughter," with its research she intended using in a discussion of *Stella Dallas* and *Mildred Pierce*, and skimmed her notes on *Das Mutterrecht*, a term Conrad had given her. It meant "Mother Right," the practice of matrilinear descent, common in pre-history and still observed in some cultures, and was based on the kinship belief that only those who came from a common womb were true family. Then her eyes fell to the quote from Hirsch about Demeter and Persephone, and she read it with a slight and joyless smile.

> *This mother-daughter narrative is resolved through continued* opposition, interruption *and* contradiction. *As we follow Persephone's return to her mother for one part of the year and her repeated descent to marriage and the underworld for the rest, we have to revise our very notion of resolution.*

WEDNESDAY

ANNIE HAD INSISTED Vicky come over after supper to break in the fancy new VCR that had just been delivered. Andrew had bought it at one of the U.S. bases for, Annie said, "practically nothing." As holders of NATO identification cards, the Canadians were allowed to shop tax free on both Canadian and U.S. bases, as well as from German merchants, who would happily arrange to deliver expensive items through the bases so that the purchaser could avoid the 14 percent German sales tax (as well as, of course, Canadian sales taxes). It was a particularly appealing kind of cross-border shopping, since there would also be no import duty when the goods were shipped back, courtesy of the DND, to Canada. Vicky knew she was probably foolish not to be taking advantage of the shopping opportunities, but neither she nor Conrad seemed interested in acquiring things simply because they were bargains. Which might be fortunate, she thought wryly, in case the Daimlers changed their minds about letting them stay.

Annie's new VCR took them over an hour to hook up.

"This better be worth it," she said, shoving the movie they'd rented into the slot. "If that place gave me one with French subtitles again I'll be so pissed off."

Vicky smiled. It was annoying, she had to admit, to watch Hollywood movies while their eyes kept being drawn to the subtitles. Annie's favourite translation came, she claimed, in an old war movie, where the hero leaps into a trench, pointing behind him and shouting, "Tanks!" The French subtitle says, "Merci!" Vicky suspected the story was apocryphal, but with Annie you could never tell.

This movie, *Basic Instinct*, did not have subtitles, but it was unlikely they could have made the movie less enjoyable. It was, Annie said as the credits rolled, "nasty, brutish and long."

"Who can women identify with in these things?" she demanded. "Like, am I the woman uncrossing her legs in front of the cops so they can see I'm not wearing panties? Right, that's what any woman would do when she's being interrogated for murder."

"Or are you the cops? The ones who, like the camera, get to look? Is it a willing suspension of gender that makes us able to watch these things without puking?"

"I mean it," Annie said, frowning, looking for "Rewind" on the remote control. "We've got to start making our own movies. When you get your thesis finished you'll know how, right?"

"Talk about unclear on the concept of 'thesis.' Writing about anything useful is strictly prohibited."

Annie found the right button and the machine silently began to rewind. "Well, how hard can it be, eh? This VCR is so smart I could probably program it both to write the script and to film it. We could be the stars. Conrad and Andrew could be the love interests. Or the sex objects."

Vicky laughed, but nervously, at the thought of Andrew as either a love interest or a sex object. He was, to her relief, working late tonight at the base. She reached over to the coffee table for another chocolate-covered cherry, took a bite.

"Do you think pity is a kind of love?"

"Huh?"

"Oh, just something I was wondering about." But she knew Annie wouldn't let her dismiss it so easily.

"Why were you wondering?"

"Just — something Conrad said."

"Uh-huh." Annie was watching her. "Well, I suppose it depends on how you define pity. Or love."

"Would you say pity could be part of the kind of love a marriage is supposed to have?" She couldn't have made it more obvious, she thought, annoyed with herself, that she was talking about herself and Conrad.

Annie took a chocolate, bit into it thoughtfully. "Sure," she said. "It's not exactly marital love at its most exalted, it's more over there in the *agape* category, but it's a kind of caring, something positive. Shit, Linda, you know Linda, well, she insists it's love that makes Gerald beat her up every week and love that makes her put up with it. Give me pity over that kind of love any day."

"I suppose so," Vicky said. The VCR clicked off and a red light began to flash. "Why is it doing that?" She was glad of the distraction.

"Damned if I know." Annie pushed some more buttons on the remote. The flashing light went out. The machine made a low humming noise and then ejected the tape and sent it flying across the room. Annie and Vicky screamed.

"My god," Annie said. "What oft was thought but ne'er so well expressed."

"Built-in quality control," Vicky said. "I'm impressed."

Then they began to laugh, and they couldn't stop, falling over onto the couches on which they were sitting, laughing until their eyes watered and their stomachs hurt, and that was how Andrew found them when he came into the living room.

"What's so funny?" he said, setting down his briefcase, which looked as if it were made out of an expensive and polished wood, like a piece of furniture, its locks and hinges carefully hidden.

"Oh, nothing," Annie gasped. "The VCR is a feminist, that's all."

Andrew picked the tape up off the floor. "I assume that means it needs to be fixed."

His comment sent them into new bursts of laughter. Finally Vicky, wiping at her eyes, made herself sit up, and said she ought to be heading home.

"Don't leave on my account," Andrew said.

"It's late. Conrad will think his car and I have been arrested again."

"Call us if you need a character reference," Annie said.

Andrew went into the kitchen and poured himself a drink. His face looked pale and tight, and he stared at the refrigerator door as though his mind were still elsewhere struggling with a problem.

Vicky walked through the kitchen to the front door, trying not to remember the last time she and Andrew had been together in this room. Her hands began to sweat. She clasped them behind her back, then immediately dropped them to her sides as she realized how that posture would have made it seem she was thrusting her breasts at him.

"Did you distribute the picture I gave you?" she asked.

"Oh. The picture. Yes. No luck, I'm afraid."

"Did you give Phil a copy?" Then to make her question seem less pointed she added, "And Lieutenant Crosby?"

"Yes, yes, of course." He took a big swallow from his drink. "Dr. Lester phoned me today, too. To ask for a copy. I assume you told him about it." He sounded irritated, angry even.

"Yes. I hope that was okay. I just happened to mention it to him."

"I don't trust the man, that's all."

Vicky stared at him. "Why not?"

Annie had come into the kitchen now, too, and she said, "I don't trust him either. He's a pill-pusher and I bet he feels up all the young women."

"That makes me safe, I guess," Vicky said.

"From the pills or the feeling-up?" Annie asked, and Vicky laughed, but uncomfortably, a nervous reaction.

Andrew took another swallow of his drink, finishing it, and handed the glass to Annie, whose hand had already reached for it, automatically, anticipating his movement. She set his glass on the counter.

"Well," Vicky said. "I'm off."

They said their good-byes, and she went out to the car, fumbling in the dark for the keys. She started the car, slipped on her driving glasses and pulled into the street. It was almost one o'clock. She hoped Conrad hadn't woken up and wondered what trouble she was in now.

It was a warm, overcast evening, with a light wind blowing from the west, and as she turned onto Schwarzwaldstraße she rolled down the window and opened the sun roof. There was virtually no traffic on the road, and she drove slowly, easing up to the stop lights. A car came up fast behind her, passed and cut back in without signaling, accelerating through a light turning red; when Vicky stopped at it the car was already out of sight. A kilometre farther on she noticed it parked at the side of the road, and if the driver had still been in it she would have given him or her a glare.

She was just nearing the little bridge over the Schutter River when she heard a sound, a soft clap, and suddenly the car pulled sharply to the right. She knew immediately what it must be. A blow out. She hung onto the wheel and steered the car towards the shoulder. The right front wheel hit the curb, but she was able to brake the car gently to a stop before it mounted the narrow sidewalk. Thank god she had been going so slowly, she thought.

She sat there a moment trying to calm her racing heart. Then she turned off the motor but switched the lights to stay on, opened the door and stepped outside. She could see right away, even in the poor light, that she'd been right. The left front tire was completely flat. Damn, damn, damn. She'd thought the new kind of tires didn't get blow outs. She knelt down to see. It didn't really look like a blow out, although when she ran her fingers around the tire she could feel a jagged edge of rubber that seemed to have exploded outward. Well, what did it matter what had happened — the tire was flat.

She stood up and looked around. It was a rather deserted part of the road. There was a large house across the street, but it was fenced in and dark. It was hard to distinguish much beyond the two splashes of light on the road made by her headlights because the two streetlights beside her, as well as several behind her, were apparently burned out, a fact unusual enough to give her a nudge of anxiety.

It was probably a good kilometre to the nearest phone. And then whom would she call? Her German wasn't adequate to order a tow truck, and waking Conrad and making him deal with it was unfair even by her standards. She could at least attempt to change the tire herself, although it had been years since she'd tried, and then the car's hubcaps had been locked on and she couldn't find the key.

She knelt down again to see if the Passat's hubcaps were locked on.

The bullet slammed into the car door a few centimetres above her head.

Vicky stared at the small, round black hole. It took her a second to realize what it was. She screamed and dropped to the ground. Another bullet tore into the fender beside her. She screamed again, the sound muffled by the pavement and sounding even to her own ears more like a moan.

Should she get up and run, should she crawl to the passenger door of the car and try to get in and drive away, should she stay down and try to hide under the car — her mind dashed frantically among the possibilities.

Perhaps because it afforded the most immediate protection, she found herself wriggling under the car. She thought she heard another bullet hit the back of the vehicle. She hadn't heard the crack of a gunshot, but that might only mean he was using a silencer.

She couldn't stay here. The gunman couldn't be far away. It wouldn't take him long to reach her. She inched her way along the ground on her stomach to the other side of the car, banging her head twice on the undercarriage. She could smell gas. One of the bullets must have hit the tank.

When she reached the far side of the car she realized the curb was blocking her. She began to whimper, a terrified, low keening sound she did not recognize as her own voice. She was facing the back of the car; if she crawled out that way she might crawl directly into the path of her assassin. If the last bullet hit the trunk he must be somewhere behind the car now.

Desperately she pushed herself backwards, toward the front of the car. When she tried to use her arms and elbows all she did was raise her torso too high to clear the undercarriage, so she had to writhe along using her stomach and her hips. As she got closer to the front, the car had even less clearance because of the flat tire. It must have been shot out, of course, as the streetlights must have been —

She tried to keep to the passenger side, where the car was

higher. The cuff of her pant leg caught on something and she wrenched it free. A stone in the road ground into her thigh. She turned her head as far as she could, but it was impossible to see anything behind her except the dark pavement and, somewhere in the distance, the beam of the headlights on the ground.

Then beside her she could see the right front wheel: she must be almost clear. She turned her body slightly sideways, reached out, grabbed the bumper and pulled herself out.

She half expected to feel a bullet tear into her, but as she pulled her feet up under her to crouch by the right front headlight she could see nothing, no movement, anywhere around her. Why hadn't she turned off the headlights? They must be making her visible for blocks.

She crawled underneath the direct beam of light to the sidewalk, her ears straining to catch any sound. Nothing. She pressed her back against the right fender.

Maybe he wasn't sure where she was. Maybe he was trying to stay hidden, too, and wasn't as close as the bullets made it seem. A rifle could shoot for at least a kilometre.

Maybe it was over. Maybe the shots had been just another warning —

Don't be such a fool. If you hadn't bent down when you did, the first shot would have hit you in the head.

It was frighteningly quiet. In the distance there was the faint sound of traffic, but not one car had passed since she'd stopped. Somewhere to the west a plane was going over, and the wind was riffling through the leaves of the trees on the other side of the sidewalk.

Trees. It would be safer there than here.

She looked quickly around again, and then, crouched over, her fingertips grazing the ground to keep her balance, she ran across the sidewalk.

From the corner of her eye she saw a dark figure running across the street, onto the sidewalk to her right, about half a block away. She forced the scream back and dived forward, into the bushes. As she fell she heard the whine of a bullet over her head. It hit a tree, making a muffled sound, like a grunt.

She'd fallen on some branches and skinned her knees and the palms of her hands, but she was already stumbling to her feet, pushing forward into the undergrowth. She held her arms out in front of her, fending off branches. Her eyes had adjusted to the darkness, but still there was little she could see. The moon was behind heavy cloud. She pushed farther into the trees, pausing only for a second to listen for noise behind her. She could hear him, smashing among the bushes and branches.

He was too close for her to try and hide. She was wearing a dark sweater but her jogging pants were a light gray and could flag her even in this darkness. He might even have a night-vision scope on his gun. Her only hope was to run, to gain enough on him to get beyond his sight or hearing. The farm on which she'd grown up had been surrounded by a forest like this. But the real and imagined animals from which she had run there had not had guns.

The growth was getting thicker, and the downward slope was increasing, affecting her balance. The loafers she was wearing weren't as good as laced shoes; her heels kept twisting under her.

She ran into a tree that knocked her reeling and sent her glasses flying off into the darkness. She sank to her knees, fighting to control the dizziness, to swallow back the lurch of nausea. When she put her hand down to steady herself it went into something wet and cold and soft, and she jerked it back, on instinct. Her heart hammered at her, keeping her conscious. She got clumsily to her feet. The air smelled heavily of dampness and decay. She stepped on a log so rotted her foot went right through it.

There seemed to be more brambles now; they ripped at her clothes and arms, but she stumbled on, flailing at the dark woods around her. Behind her she thought she heard the man curse. She didn't pause. What was behind her was infinitely more terrifying than what was in front of her.

Suddenly she knew where she must be heading. Down to the river. She had taken the bicycle path along there only two days ago. Was the path on this side of the river? It crossed over at some point. She tried to remember. The path was on this side, she was fairly certain; it crossed over with the street bridge about a kilometre farther on.

So ahead of her was an open bike path — where she would be an easy target — and the river. Should she try for the river, try to cross it? It was probably only about half a dozen metres wide here, but she had no idea how deep or how swift. She was a poor swimmer; if she lost her footing she could drown, and she would be an easy target as she floundered her way downstream. Even if she did make it across, the other bank, if she remembered correctly, was covered in thick brambles and nettles.

No, the river would have to be a desperate last resort. She had to try to avoid the path and the river for as long as possible. The forest was full of unknown hazards, but at least it was as hard for him as for her, and possibly, just possibly, his motivation to kill her, now, here, was not as great as her motivation to live. She didn't think he had gained on her. But neither had she gotten farther ahead of him.

She veered to her left, counting on the feel of the slope under her feet to direct her in a somewhat parallel course to the river. If the killer was following her purely by sound he would be able to narrow the distance between them by cutting left now, too, but she would have to risk it.

Her hair had come loose from its clip, and a strand caught on a branch, wrenching her head to the side. It felt as though the whole right side of her scalp were being ripped off. She grabbed hold of the strand of hair, tore it free. A large bird flapped into the air from the bush in front of her and made her cry out and stumble backwards, but she recovered quickly and pushed ahead, squeezing between two trees so close together she felt the bark grating on her sweater.

Suddenly, without warning, the woods ended. Beyond, she could see a large open space, a field, perhaps.

She stopped abruptly, which saved her from tripping over the low stone fence marking the field's boundary. Behind her she could hear her pursuer, thrashing through the trees.

She couldn't stop to think. She had to move. About sixty metres into the field was a large building, too large for a house — a warehouse, perhaps. Or a sports arena. That would explain the field. She had to hope she could reach the building before the man burst from the woods. If she didn't, she'd get a bullet in the back.

She stepped over the stone fence and began to run, as fast as she had ever run in her life. She could feel the emptiness around her, full of threat. It was lighter here, too; she felt as exposed as if it were daylight.

Her feet on the grass hardly made a sound, and she could clearly hear the noises now behind her in the woods. If they stopped she would have only a few seconds before he fired. Dropping to the ground here would only delay what would happen for a few more moments.

Pain began to burn in her side. Her struggling lungs felt as though they would burst through her ribs. She'd underestimated the distance, and it was slightly uphill. Please, her mind was saying, please. Her feet felt leaden, every step an effort. She seemed unable to take in enough oxygen.

The sounds behind her stopped.

The corner of the building was so close. She dodged sharply left, then right, a tactic she must have seen in movies.

Three more strides. Two. She leaned forward, reaching for the corner of the building with her left hand to spin herself around to the safe side.

The first bullet slammed into the building beside her head, scattering chips of plaster into the air.

The second bullet hit her in the upper left arm.

She leaned, gasping, against the side of the building, and it took her a few seconds to realize the sensation in her arm, which her adrenalin did not yet allow her to understand as pain, wasn't from something she had done to herself in the woods. She could feel blood running down her arm. She began to whimper, hysteria rising in her. He'd got her. In a minute he'd be here to finish the job. She had the urge to sink to her knees and just let it happen. She hadn't planned beyond reaching the building, and now she was wounded; she couldn't run any farther.

She clenched her teeth, forcing her mind to be clear. She was hit in the arm, not the leg. She could still run. She had to keep running.

She headed for the far side of the building. She could hear a car go by somewhere, perhaps to the north. If so, it was likely on Schwarzwaldstraße, which curved slightly to the south after the point at which she'd left it. But if she headed back there she'd be in the same position as before, only without even her car to hide behind. The vehicle that had just gone by might be the last for an hour.

Her best bet would be to head for the woods she could see ahead of her. The field that lay between it and the building seemed less than half the width of the one she'd crossed. Perhaps in the woods this time she could find a place to hide. Right now her arm only felt numb, but she could feel the blood dripping from her fingers. It would weaken her. She couldn't outrun him indefinitely. If he was a soldier he would be in better physical condition than she was.

She was almost at the corner of the building, preparing herself for the sprint into the forest, when she stumbled on something piled along the side of the building. She fell, twisting her body to land on her right, uninjured shoulder. She lay there, stunned, trying to see what she had fallen over. It looked like construction materials: a pile of bricks and lumber, several large bags of what might be concrete mix, and, leaning against the wall beside these, some large sheets of metal.

She could hide behind the sheets of metal.

He wouldn't expect that. He would think, as she had, that the dark woods so close by offered the best protection. He wouldn't know he'd hit her; he would think she'd want to keep running. But what if he did think to look here — if he stumbled over the lumber and bricks as she had and decided on a quick check behind the metal sheets just in case —

She had to decide. Now.

She got up, stepped onto the pile of lumber, and lowered herself carefully into the narrow triangular opening created by the leaning metal sheets, which were less thick than she'd thought; they were probably just tin. Her hips caught on the wall and on the sheets. She was too big; she wouldn't fit. But she forced back the panic, pressed herself down. She'd lost too much time to change her plan now or to try to enter from the other side of her makeshift lean-to; she had to *make* herself fit. The sleeve of her sweater snagged on a nail or ragged edge on the wall and she jerked herself free, hearing something tear, not bothering to look.

The tin made a grating noise as she squeezed against it, but she was moving lower. Her toes touched the ground. Suddenly her hips came free and she sank into a crouch, her back against the wall of the building.

This was it. This was the hiding hole that would either save her life or see the end of it.

Had he heard her steps on the lumber, the sound of the squeaking metal? How close was he?

With her right hand she felt on the ground around her for something she might be able to use as a weapon — a piece of wood, a brick, a nail, anything — but all she could feel was bare earth, with occasional small patches of grass or weeds. The boards on which she'd climbed to enter her hiding place were far too large for her to use, and she didn't dare try to straighten and reach for the top of the pile to fumble for anything that might be there. Besides, what could she possibly find that would be a match for a gun? Her only hope was to remain still.

Her heartbeat sounded so loud she involuntarily put her right hand over it, as though she might muffle it. It was her ragged breathing that might give her away instead, she realized, and she cupped her hand over her mouth and bent her head down and to the side, directing her breath away from the opening above her head. He would be breathing hard, too — she would just have to hope he wouldn't be able to hold his breath long enough to listen for hers. She was aware of something clinging to her face, a cobweb, and she ran her hand quickly over her face and wiped it on her sleeve and then cupped the hand again over her mouth.

Her left arm had begun to throb, and when she tried to pull it closer to her chest the spurt of pain made her dizzy. She could feel the blood running into, out of, her palm. She clenched her teeth and tried not to imagine what the wound looked like, where the bullet had gone, what it had done. She'd heard about bullets made to explode once inside a body, to do maximum damage.

She concentrated only on breathing — long breaths sucked into her mouth from under her cupped hand and expelled hotly out against her fingers — and on listening. Silence. Her own breathing, her heartbeat. Where was he? Shouldn't he have been here by now?

A footstep. Another. Running. He was here.

He had come around the corner of the building, but, unlike her, he had not kept close to the wall. Of course — why would he? He wasn't running from anyone; it made sense for him to swing wide of the building to get a better view around the next corner. Perhaps he wouldn't even see the pile of construction materials — he would be looking ahead, toward the woods, imagining her there or running up toward the road —

The beam of a flashlight began playing along the wall beside her. It dropped to the pile of bricks and lumber, moved closer to her, closer, then was gone.

She could imagine it on the metal sheets, could feel it burning through them to find her. She turned her head, slowly, to the opening on the other side of the sheets. The cartilage cracking in her neck made her go rigidly still: could he hear, could it sound as loud to him as to her? Abruptly the light appeared where she was looking, falling from the sheets onto a small pile of gravel, then onto the wall of the building.

Keep going, oh please, please, just keep going.

But it didn't. It moved back, disappearing as it hit the metal sheets. Her eyes followed its imagined course across the metal, willing it to stop, retreat. But just as she was thinking it might have done so, it dropped again, onto the lumber close to her head. And stopped.

Bloodstains. Perhaps he had seen her bloodstains.

He was coming closer. She could hear his heavy steps. She could hear his breathing, harsh and uneven.

She closed her eyes. She was going to die. She could see images of her life: her mother, her father, Conrad, the man whose truck had run into her father, the house she lived in at university, her two roommates there, Annie, the woman in the yellow sweater, the title of her thesis —

A hand grabbed the metal sheets and wrenched them aside. She put her right arm up across her head, a useless shield against discovery. The flashlight beam hit her directly in the eyes. She squinted dumbly into it, an animal blinded and entranced, an easy shot for the hunter. She could see nothing but the light, the man behind it simply a piece of the larger darkness. His breathing was loud, fast.

"You bitch," he said. "You fucking bitch."

He set the flashlight down slowly on the ground. As the light wavered she could see him reaching with his other hand for the short, steel-handled rifle slung over his shoulder. He took hold of it and swung it forward in one easy motion so that it pointed at her.

She screamed. Again and again and again. She heard a shot and she knew he had probably hit her but she kept screaming, horrible, raw sounds; even when she saw him drop the rifle and fall slowly to his knees, then forward onto his face, she kept screaming; even when she heard Andrew's voice saying over and over, "Vicky, Vicky, it's okay. He's dead. I killed him. I saw him start to follow you. Vicky, listen to me, it's okay," she still kept screaming.

·

In the hospital they gave her some nice drugs. She felt very happy, not at all like screaming.

She smiled at all the nurses and thanked the polite German doctor who had fixed her arm so that she felt as though she could play tennis against Steffi Graf. When the man from the military wanted to take her statement she assured the doctor she felt well enough to answer a few questions, so she did, although later she had no memory of the man's visit.

Conrad came, looking pale and frightened and rumpled (because it was, after all, four in the morning), and she apologized for leaving his car full of bullet holes on Schwarzwaldstraße.

"Thank god you're all right," he kept saying. His face was the colour of talc.

"I'm fine, I'm fine," she said. "I thought I was dead, I had my life flash before my eyes and everything, just the way it's supposed to, but, no, really, I'm fine."

Then Annie came, lying to get in by saying she was Vicky's cousin, and Vicky said how happy she was that Annie's husband had saved her life.

Annie couldn't stop crying. "I shouldn't have let you leave," she said. "If I'd known what was going to happen — Oh, god, Vicky, how horrible, I'm so sorry — "

"It's not *your* fault, Annie. Stop crying. Andrew killed him. It's all over."

A nurse came in with something in a hypodermic and Vicky laughed and said, "Oh, goody, I hope that's for me."

"You really must both leave now," the nurse said. "Mrs. Bauer must rest."

Conrad kissed her awkwardly on the forehead. "Thank god you're all right," he said again. His eyes were shiny, tears suddenly lapping against them.

Annie leaned over and kissed her, too. "Oh, Vicky," she said.

"Good-bye," Vicky said. "Thanks for coming. I'm fine, really. Don't worry."

When they were gone the nurse gave her the injection. "I really am feeling quite fine, you know," Vicky told her. "You've done an excellent job."

The nurse smiled. "Try to sleep now." She pressed her palms together and leaned them against her cheek, making Vicky giggle. "*Schlafen*," the nurse said.

But it was a long time before Vicky could sleep. Her mind would not let itself feel exhausted. It hummed with words, with the strange images, hypnagogic, preceding sleep. At one point she managed to reach over to the bedside table for the pencil and pad of paper that lay there, and she wrote, "thesis," then underlined it three times. After a moment she wrote:

Blow Out *is a movie. (cf.* Blow-up.*) Remember that pro-tagonist's original quest is to record a woman's perfect scream of terror.*

AFTERWARDS

SHE HAD A LOT OF VISITORS, all of whom, in retrospect, had of course believed her.

Even Constable Klug came to see her, congratulating her on her courage, not mentioning their last embarrassing phone call. Even someone from the army with two gold braids on his hat and a thick gold bar on his cuffs, which she knew meant he was important, one of the General Officers, came to see her. He shook her hand, solemnly, and then took a step back, as though he had just placed a wreath on a cenotaph. His conversation seemed to consist almost entirely of conjunctive adverbs: nevertheless, therefore, indeed, however, moreover. When Vicky asked him if she was going to get a medal he smiled gravely and said, no; nevertheless she deserved one.

Even Phil and Claire came to see her, together, whether by intent or by accident Vicky wasn't sure, but they both stayed and were civil to each other, and Vicky tried to forget her dark suspicions about the man who stood beside her bed toying with the daisies he'd brought and looking almost comically incapable of anything sinister. Even Dr. Lester came to see her, although primarily to stake out his medical territory; Vicky was, after all, a sort of celebrity now, especially after the army and the German police had gone back into the Staatswald and discovered, less than half a kilometre from where Vicky had seen the woman murdered, her shallow grave.

"You'd have found it that day if you'd really looked," she told Lieutenant Crosby, who was the one to bring her the news. But she was less accusatory and self-righteous than she might have been because she was still on the nice drugs, which made her feel forgiving.

Lieutenant Crosby asked her if she felt up to looking at pictures of her attacker — "taken when he was alive, of course" — to try and identify him positively as the woman's murderer.

Vicky could feel herself tensing, even with the nice drugs, but she agreed to do it. She stared at the four pictures, head and shoulder shots, two full face and two in profile, for a long time, trying not to see that ordinary young human face above the flashlight, above the hands reaching for the rifle, not to hear that mouth speak the words promising her death.

"Yes, that's him," she said, handing the pictures back. "I didn't see him that clearly, but I recognize the nose, the way it seemed to have a little bend in it."

The lieutenant looked at the pictures again, too, carefully, one after another. A young nurse with an overbite small enough to be charming and a uniform several sizes too large came into the room, whose door was adamantly propped open all day. "*Bilder*," she said, smiling at the pictures, overly accenting the first syllable of the word to give it a happy sound, because weren't pictures people brought to hospitals of happy things, of babies and smiling friends and vacations?

"*Ja, Bilder*," said Lieutenant Crosby, gathering them quickly together. "*Nichts interessantes.*"

"*Schade*," the nurse said. She removed a sheet of paper

from the clipboard hanging at the foot of the bed, smiled enough to display her charming overbite, and left the room.

The lieutenant tapped the top picture lightly with the back of his right hand. "His name's John Eldridge. A private. His corporal says he was a loner, secretive. He got into trouble in Comox for beating up a girl. And he liked prostitutes, apparently."

"Enough to kill them," Vicky said. She thought of the woman in the yellow sweater. She'd been identified as "a known prostitute" from Offenburg, "of East Indian extraction." No one seemed to think it necessary to find out anything more about her. No one Vicky asked could even recall her name. But she knew now, whether she wanted to or not, the name of the woman's murderer. John Eldridge. She would never be able to forget it.

Crosby was turning to leave, when for some reason Vicky remembered the pregnant young woman she had seen with him. Perhaps if she hadn't been on the nice drugs she wouldn't have had the nerve to ask him about her, but she was on the nice drugs, and she did.

The lieutenant's posture seemed to become even more erect, his firm mouth to tighten even more, but when he spoke his voice did not sound annoyed. "She's left her husband and gone back to Canada," he said. "With her mother. I may be a grandfather by now for all I know."

"She's your daughter," Vicky said. She had, of course, imagined something more sleazy.

"The military is hell on families," Crosby said. He flicked his fingers up along his neck. "You're lucky your husband is a teacher," he said. "He can leave."

"So can you."

He smiled at her wryly and didn't answer.

She had agreed to let the DND Public Information Officer handle her story officially and not to give any media interviews, so by her third day in hospital the flurry of attention had abated and only Conrad and Annie came to see her any more. She could probably have gone home sooner except that an infection and a low-grade fever had set in. Although the bullet had chipped the bone, it had gone right through her arm. She knew she should consider herself very lucky.

But her doctor had cut her off the hard-core painkillers, so she was feeling the pain more now and was growing restless and irritable. Her room made her feel claustrophobic, its walls the relentless pink of compulsory relaxation. Her mouth seemed constantly dry, with a potatoey taste in it. She badly wanted a drink, although she didn't dare say so to anyone except Phil's drooping daisies, their white petals like strands of shriveling hair around their yellow faces, in the vase beside her bed. When Conrad said, trying to amuse her, that the DND was buying him a new Passat, she only grunted and said they damn well better buy her a new bicycle, too.

At night now she began to have nightmares, someone terrifying chasing her and her feet moving only in slow motion, the kind of dreams, her father used to say, that chip your teeth. She would wake up moaning, drenched in sweat, her heart running as fast as when she'd fled across the field. A few times she dreamt about Andrew, hard, erotic, exciting dreams that stayed with her too long after she woke.

Andrew. The one person who hadn't come to see her. Yet it was Andrew she wanted to see more than anyone else. He had saved her life. She didn't think she'd even thanked him that night. She remembered him saying her name over and over as she crouched screaming beside the pile of lumber, but the next thing she could remember was being wheeled into the hospital, and Andrew was already gone. It wasn't, of course, a case of him being the anonymous rescuer; the army was calling him a hero; there was an article about him in the *Lahr Zeitung* and, Annie told her that Saturday afternoon, *The Globe and Mail* was sending a correspondent the next day to interview him.

"Captain Shaw's wife said she's betting he'll make major because of this," Annie said.

"I wish he'd come to see me," Vicky said, deciding to be blunt about it, her more subtle hints to Annie having had no effect. "I just need to thank him, that's all."

Annie got up and looked out the small hospital window. She was wearing a floppy blue sweatshirt and, unusually for her, a skirt, midi-length, of faded denim.

"He's been so busy," she said. "A million reports to fill out. And he doesn't like all this hero stuff. I'm surprised, but he doesn't." She picked up the video magazine Vicky had been reading, rolled it into a cylinder and beat it lightly into the palm of her left hand. "*You're* the real hero, you know. All those things that happened and you didn't give up. You shouldn't have agreed to let the army handle your story. Spin control, that's all they'll do. You should have sold it to the *Enquirer.*"

"I kept the movie rights," Vicky said. "Diana Rigg's going to play me. Emma Peel, gifted amateur. Who do you want to play you?"

"Me? I'm not in this movie." Annie dropped the magazine onto the night table.

"Of course you are. The sympathetic friend and confidante."

"Well, okay. Roseanne."

"Not exactly my choice," Vicky said.

"This isn't a democracy, Dar-lene."

Laughing made Vicky's arm hurt. "But we'd have to change the ending," she said. "This one was too regressive. Mrs. Peel wouldn't stand for it. I was like Bujold's character at the end of *Coma*. We both sat there helplessly and had to be rescued by a man."

"The men have to have something to do." Annie turned to look out the window. "I should go. I think I parked in an *Achtung, you vill be shot* zone." She glanced quickly at Vicky. "Sorry," she said.

"It's okay."

Annie came over to the bed. "I'm just so glad you're all *right*. When I think of how close it was — " She swallowed. "I mean, if Andrew hadn't decided to go after him — "

"But he did. That's all that matters."

"I suppose so. I'm just so glad it's *over*. All those creepy things that happened to you. There's an explanation for everything now. And it's just *over*."

After Annie had gone, Vicky lay looking at the ceiling, where a tiny spider had managed to evade the housekeeping staff and was crawling slowly toward one corner.

Annie was right, there was an explanation for everything now. John Eldridge had killed the woman in the Staatswald. She was a prostitute; he had a history of violence against prostitutes. He had found out, probably easily enough through gossip at the base, Vicky's name and where she lived. He'd left the note implicating Conrad under her door to mislead her, to frighten her off. He'd watched her pick up the photographs, followed her home, broken into her apartment and stolen them — they'd found them in his quarters. When she wouldn't quit, when she went to the German police, he'd bumped her with his car. He would have enjoyed the sadistic games he was playing with her. He'd hired the second woman, probably another prostitute, to go up into the Staatswald to shake Vicky's confidence even more, to convince her she hadn't seen what she had. When none of that worked, when she drew the picture of him and it began circulating, he knew he had to silence her permanently. The picture alone wouldn't have been enough to identify him positively, but her testimony might have been.

Yes, there was an explanation for everything now. Still.

She couldn't shake the feeling there might be more to it. If Eldridge was just a private how would he have been able to take the time to follow her as often as he did? How would he have known which door at the Daimler house was hers? A lucky guess? Could he have followed her right into the back yard once and watched her go into the hallway and unlock the inside door? And the second woman — Vicky was sure she'd talked about the incident with her in her statement to the DND official right after she'd come to the hospital, but she suspected nobody was bothering to follow that up because the woman wasn't necessary to the case; maybe they had decided her presence in the forest was coincidental or that Vicky *had* been imagining things by then. She couldn't remember if she'd mentioned seeing the woman with Phil. She must have.

The case was closed. If there were a few loose ends, what did it matter? They were the kind of details that could be tucked easily enough into the overall fabric. The killer of the woman had been found, and punished. Wasn't that really all she wanted?

The spider had reached the corner of the ceiling now, and it stayed there, unmoving, so long that Vicky finally stopped looking at it. She closed her eyes. Her arm hurt, the wound beating like another heart in a dull rhythm of pain. But her fever was down, and, if she promised to be good, to keep her arm in a sling and immobilized, not to sleep on her left side, to let Conrad do all the housework for the next few days, she would be allowed to go home tomorrow.

Home: the Daimlers' home. She wondered how they had reacted to the news of what had happened to her. She thought she recalled Lieutenant Crosby saying someone from the German police had gone over and taken a statement from them. "The *Polizei* at the door," she could imagine them whispering. "That is what comes of having non-Aryan blood in the house."

The thought almost made her smile. Well, they wouldn't dare to evict her now. She would be too famous. Diana Rigg would play her in the film.

When Conrad came to see her half an hour later and she told him what she had been thinking about the Daimlers, he smiled, although rather thinly. "Do you still want to keep living in their house?" he asked.

"We don't have many options. Have you talked to them? Would they let us stay?"

"Oh, yes, they'll let us stay. They find it all very exciting. They're proud to be involved. They came clamouring to me for details as though we'd never had that last conversation."

"They're pragmatists," Vicky said. "They see the world as plot-driven. Their filmic identifications shift to coincide with the prevailing POV."

Conrad frowned. "I promised the doctors I'd bring you back immediately if I found you even thinking about work."

Annie must have said something to Andrew because the next day, not long before she was supposed to check out, suddenly there he was, standing at the foot of her bed. He was wearing his uniform, his hat tucked formally under his left arm, and he looked, Vicky thought, more handsome than Tom Cruise in *Top Gun*.

"They should name a missile after you," she said, the first stupid thing that came to her mind.

"Pardon?" He reached across his chest with his right hand and touched the brim of his hat, as though Vicky had told him it needed adjusting.

"Nothing, nothing. Just a movie Annie and I had talked about. Sit down."

He took the chair beside her bed, sitting down, she noticed, without leaning forward at all, which a fitness instructor had once told her was a sign that you were in excellent shape.

"You're looking well," he said. He took the hat from under his arm and set it in his lap.

"Yeah, right." Her hand reached up without her telling it to and tugged at a strand of hair lying limp and unwashed on her shoulder. It probably looked, she thought, as though she were trying to pull the hair over the orange juice stain on her nightgown. Probably she was.

"Well, considering."

She laughed. "Of course. Considering."

He laughed, too, leaned back a little, relaxing.

"I haven't thanked you yet. For saving my life."

He looked down at his hat, turning it in his hands. "You're welcome," he said.

"When I think of how close it was, it seems like some ... like a miracle."

Miracle. Good lord, couldn't she have found a better word? But Andrew just kept looking down at his hands, the thumbs slowly crimping the brim of his hat like a pie crust, and said, "It was luck, that's all. I was just turning to go back inside the house when I saw him in the car behind yours across the street."

"And you recognized him from the profile I drew."

"Well, there was enough likeness for me to remember the picture. And when I saw him follow you, I followed him. When he passed you I thought I must have been wrong, and I was just going to turn around when I saw his car parked at the side of the road."

"The car that passed me and then parked. Of course. That was him. I'd forgotten all about the car. It was red, the same colour as the one that hit me on my bicycle. I should have made the connection."

"You can't be suspicious of every red car you see."

"So how did you find us?"

"If I'd kept going, of course, I'd have run into you right away."

"And he might have shot both of us."

Andrew lifted his hand, let it drop. "Anyway, I decided to just go around the block to see if I could find where he'd gone — there were so few houses around there, as you know — and by the time I got back out onto Schwartzwaldstraße in front of you he'd already gone after you into the woods. When I saw your car abandoned, with the lights on, I knew even before I saw the bullet holes that something had happened, and luckily I could still hear him in the woods."

"I'd be dead if you hadn't."

He nodded, whether in agreement or just to acknowledge hearing her she wasn't sure. When he didn't say anything more, she went on, trying to make her voice light, "Annie tells me you don't like the hero treatment."

"I killed a man. It shouldn't bother me, but it does."

"Oh," Vicky said meekly. She hadn't thought about that,

about how it must feel, even for a soldier, even to save a life, to kill someone. People must be telling Andrew over and over how brave he had been, that he'd risked his own life, but no one was telling him how hard it must be to know he'd killed a man.

He looked up at her then, at last, and she could see the emotions struggling in his face. For a moment she thought, alarmed, that he might cry. But he only cleared his throat and said levelly, "I shot him twice, that's what I keep thinking about. Because I didn't need to. The first shot got him in the chest. He dropped the rifle. But then I took careful aim and shot him in the head. I didn't just want to stop him, I wanted to kill him."

"But you did what you were trained to do. You did the right thing. You had to be sure he couldn't pick up the gun again."

Still, it had chilled her a little, hearing him say it, *I didn't just want to stop him, I wanted to kill him.* But it was for you that he did it, said another voice inside her, one that came from some bad movie, one that swooned: this man cared enough about you to want to kill for you and isn't that wonderful. No, it's not wonderful, she told the bad movie voice angrily. Nothing about this is wonderful. Grow up.

"I know. I tell myself that. I'm not sorry he's dead. So I don't know why I'm sorry I killed him."

"I'm not sorry he's dead, either. And I'm sorry you killed him only if you are."

He smiled then, the kind of smile that could have been a grin except for the irony stiffening the edges. "There *is* the hero stuff. Maybe I'll get to like it."

She laughed. "The hero stuff. Sounds like a good title for the movie Annie and I were planning about this."

At the mention of Annie's name, Andrew glanced towards the door, as though he expected Annie to be standing there.

Vicky looked over, too. But it wasn't Annie who appeared there as though summoned. It was Conrad.

Andrew stood up. "Conrad," he said, nodding once.

"Andrew."

What kind of greeting was that? Vicky looked from one to the other, trying to read what they might be thinking behind their careful features. *Conrad. Andrew.* No women she knew, no matter how fond or distrustful they were of each other, would greet each other like that. It was some male code, some gender shorthand she would never be able to understand.

"Well," she said to Conrad, "I hope you've come to take me home."

·

Walking up the stairs to their apartment required almost as much energy as Vicky had. She felt surprisingly weak and feverish. She collapsed onto the sofa and decided she had no choice but to let Conrad look after her. He had borrowed from Paul Garten over two dozen movies Paul had taped from a pay-TV channel in Toronto over the summer, and Conrad said he had offers from about ten other people, including Paul's wife, Hilda, to come visit or do errands.

Vicky was about to say something about the Gartens and their friendship with the Daimlers, but decided against it. Paul was Conrad's boss, after all, and he and Hilda had always been kind to her. Hilda couldn't be blamed for having bigoted relatives. She mustn't let herself start imagining Hitlerian conspiracies again. The murdered woman had been dark-skinned, yes, but that had nothing to do with the Daimlers, or the Gartens, or Conrad.

Still ....

No. It was over. John Eldridge was dead, and it was over.

She told Conrad she would just as soon be left alone while he was at work. A nurse from the hospital would be coming over the next afternoon to change her dressing, and beyond that, she assured him, she would just lie around and rest. She had to admit that the pile of movie cassettes on the coffee table looked appealing, and she promised herself she wouldn't think about her thesis once while she watched them.

That night she had trouble sleeping, the nightmares flaring almost as soon as she closed her eyes. Even lying there awake, with Conrad snoring lightly beside her, she felt the fear creeping toward her from the darkness. Was that a step on the stair? Was someone in the kitchen? Were there voices whispering just outside the bedroom door? She tried to talk herself out of it but it only got worse. Finally she got up and turned on all the lights in the other rooms and checked the lock downstairs. He'd gotten through this lock before, though, hadn't he, gotten through so easily he didn't leave a trace — She brought down a knife from the cutlery drawer and slid it along the door between the two wood strips of the frame.

Upstairs again, she changed out of her sweat-drenched pajamas into dry ones, although it took her almost twenty minutes using only one hand and trying to button the top across the sling. She left a note for Conrad warning him about the knife in the door, and then took a sleeping pill and went back to bed and this time slept until morning.

Conrad had already gone to work by the time she got up. He'd left the knife lying beside her note and had written, "Take it easy. Put the knife back in the door if you need to." She smiled. It was hard to believe she'd been so frightened last night. Of what? A dead man. She put the knife away, poured herself a coffee from the carafe, and ate some raisin toast at the kitchen table, glancing through the mail that had come while she was in the hospital. Nothing interesting. Well, she didn't want interesting. She wanted peaceful; she wanted boring.

Her arm felt quite pain-free today, and the nurse who came in the afternoon to change the bandage told her she seemed to be healing well. Vicky still couldn't bring herself to look at the wound. She would have to eventually, of course, and she knew it would upset her. For the rest of her life John Eldridge would have his mark on her.

After the nurse left she lay down on the sofa and looked through the pile of carefully labeled cassettes Paul had left for her. *Lethal Weapon 2.* No thank you. *Black and White In Color.* Seen it. *Betrayed.* Seen it? She tapped the box, tried to remember. Oh, yes. A Costa-Gavras film. Debra Winger playing a woman who marries a kind and loving widower in a kind and loving community that turns out to be all white supremacists. Vicky was amused, for a moment, to think Paul might have given her this film deliberately, a subtle reproof, but it was hardly likely Conrad would have told him anything about her suspicions.

She settled for something called *Miss Right*, which turned out to be a dull, vignettish sex comedy that nearly put her to sleep. That was okay, she thought: she wanted peaceful; she wanted boring.

When Conrad came home he brought along a casserole Hilda had made for their supper.

"That was awfully nice of her," Vicky said, making herself mean it.

"She's making something for tomorrow, too," Conrad said. "I told her it wasn't necessary but she insisted." He took the casserole from the oven, spooned some onto their plates and sat down.

"If I play my cards right I may never have to cook again," Vicky said. "Mmmm, this is good."

"I'm glad you're feeling better. The knife in the door did worry me."

"Nightmares." Vicky shrugged. "I'll have them for a while, I suppose."

Conrad nodded. "I suppose so." He was cutting his broccoli into little pieces and pushing them around his plate.

"Why aren't you eating?"

"There's ... something I want to talk to you about. I should have told you earlier but you had enough on your mind."

"What?" Vicky put down her fork and stared across the table at him. He wouldn't meet her eyes. Peaceful and boring, she thought: I only wanted peaceful and boring.

"Are you sure you want to hear this now?"

"You can't not tell me, not after you brought it up."

"Paul isn't going to go back to Canada. He's applied for German citizenship. Hilda's German, of course, so it's virtually automatic for him."

"And?"

"He's been offered a job in Frankfurt, with the Education Ministry, starting next fall. A very good job."

"And?"

"He's able to hire some curriculum consultants from abroad. He wants me to come work for him. It's a three-year contract, maybe longer if I want. I told him I'd take it."

"I see." The casserole on her plate suddenly looked inedible.

"I should have discussed it with you first, I know, but he needed an answer and, well, I said yes."

"You're not going back to Canada."

He shook his head, prodded a lump of hardened cheese around the rim of his plate.

"You know I'm planning to register for the Ph.D. program in the fall in Edmonton."

"Of course I know. But I ... need to stay here longer, that's all. It's — " He set his fork down, pushed it as far as it would go under the edge of his plate. "I just feel there's a part of me here that I've only started to understand. I need more time."

"Alone."

It took him a long time to answer. "I think that might be best."

She took a shaky breath, let it out. When she spoke her words sounded rushed, bumping into each other. "Conrad, I know I've been a pain the last year, the drinking and everything, but I can stop, really I can. I'll start being more responsible, I know I haven't been pulling my weight — "

"Vicky, please — this has nothing to do with you."

"Of course it does. So you stay here. What about me?"

He smiled at her, a smile she had come to know too well over the years, one that looked sad and tired and burdened by knowledge. "You've always done what you wanted. You don't need me. I just make it easy for you not to be independent."

"I see. I'm still a child and you're still daddy. Except now daddy wants to leave home."

Conrad looked away. "There's some truth to that."

Vicky forced the tears back; he would think they were the defences of a child, pitiable. *Pity is a kind of love.*

"Do you want a divorce?" she asked, trying to keep her voice steady.

"I wasn't thinking of that. Unless you want one."

"I don't know," Vicky said. She swallowed. "No, I guess not. I'm just so ... used to you. To you always being there."

"It's not as though we haven't lived apart before, Vicky. We've lived apart more than together."

"I know. But — "

But it was always I who decided when and for how long, Vicky realized. She had always assumed Conrad would be there when she wanted him and would leave her alone when she didn't. Now he was only asking the same of her.

"I'll send you the money for your Ph.D. program," he said. "I'll be making a very generous salary."

"They've promised me a TA position. You've paid for my schooling long enough."

"Whatever you think."

They sat at the table for a long time, looking at anything but each other. At last Vicky got up and took her plate to the sink, and then Conrad followed with his. They stood close to each other, not touching.

"I hope it works out for you," Vicky said. "Frankfurt and everything. Really. I hope you find what you want there."

"Thank you." Did he sound surprised? Maybe he wasn't used to hearing her wish him well when her own interests weren't also at stake.

She wanted a drink. No, she couldn't, not after she'd just told Conrad she could quit.

She would phone Annie. Annie would tell her how she'd fly out to Edmonton to visit from wherever Andrew got posted and how they didn't need men or booze to survive. Maybe Annie would even mean it, although Vicky wouldn't bet on it.

"Do you want to watch one of the movies?" Conrad asked.

"Why not?" Vicky said. Yes, why not? She would sit down and watch a movie with her husband. Next fall was a long time away. She'd rarely planned more than a year ahead in her life, anyway. *Carpe diem.*

·

But later that night, sitting in her study, her confidence seeped away, and she felt a terrible aloneness. Conrad wouldn't be coming back to Canada with her. She'd be going home by herself. Of course he was right, they'd often lived apart before, but never countries and oceans apart, and never because he was the one who wanted it. They might come back together again, even live together again, but something had changed. What had changed was Conrad, whom she had always imagined as fixed and predictable as the compass foot in the Donne poem, with herself the wandering arm. His firmness was supposed to draw her circle just, or something, and make her end where she'd begun.

Well, she thought, perhaps if he goes away for a while to find his missing childhood and I go away to find my missing adulthood we might come back to each other in better shape. It made her feel a little better to think of it like that, something they would both find instead of lose.

She picked up the glass of wine on her desk and raised it to her lips, then looked down at it, blurry because it was so close. The sweet smell filled her nostrils. She exhaled deeply and lowered the glass, not breathing, until the need in her chest made her gasp for air. Need, she thought, that's the question: what I need as opposed to what I want. Only children saw them as the same thing.

She got up, went over to the window, pushed it open, and poured the wine into the dried-out soil of Frau Daimler's window box. It almost made her laugh, it was such a show-don't-tell movie cliché, the alcoholic pouring his drink down the sink and we know, oh we just know, he'll never touch a drop again. Well, the flower box at least was an original touch. She sat down at her desk again and set the empty glass beside the paper-clip tray.

The pearl was still in the tray. She should do something with it now, she thought, something final, an act of closure, a way of saying good-bye to the woman reaching her hand out to her in the Staatswald.

But she left it there, and she would think, later, that she had done so because she had known the woman's story wasn't quite over, that justice had not yet, quite, been done her.

But that would be only later, in the assurance of retrospect. Now she told herself she was simply getting sentimental or theatrical or morbid; it was just a pearl, after all, in a paper-clip tray.

She pulled the notepad toward her, read what she had said about *Now, Voyager* and *Humoresque* and Hitchcock, about punishments for seeing. It seemed like months instead of days since she had written those words. She opened the file on Chapter 3, thought for a while and then began a new paragraph.

> *It can be argued, furthermore, that the female filmgoer, simply by looking at the screen, an inherently voyeuristic activity, is similarly appropriating the male gaze. Maybe her punishment is the movies she has to watch.*

Vicky re-read the last sentence. Then she drew a line through it. Her thesis supervisor didn't have a sense of humour. Just saying "movies" instead of "films" would horrify him. When a student in their class had said the only difference *she* could see between movies and films was that the former showed women's genitals and the latter showed men's, he had been severely unamused.

But after a moment Vicky thought, what the hell, and she replaced the sentence with one a little more pompous but essentially the same:

> *It could also be argued (and not entirely frivolously) that her attendant punishment is the films she sees.*

TUESDAY

S HE WOULD OFTEN wonder what would have happened if she just hadn't answered the phone the next day.

She would, she supposed, have gone on much as before. She'd have worked on her thesis every day. She'd have avoided the Daimlers and told herself she'd have to put up with them for only eight more months. She'd have seen more of Paul and Hilda and conceded them to be as liberal as Conrad had always told her they were. She'd have gone to movies and lunches with Annie and laughed at her cynical jokes about the army. She'd have tried not to give in to her attraction to Andrew. She'd have taken more pictures of Lahr and sent them to her grandmother, along with letters she had less and less hope (and, if she was lucky, less and less need) of having answered. She'd have gone to Dr. Lester like a good girl for her check-ups and pills. She'd have struggled to keep off the booze and been, except for one or two lapses, reasonably successful. She'd have looked at Conrad yearningly sometimes and wondered if, after all, theirs was a love that would survive their will to outgrow it.

Some of these things, of course, did happen. But some of them did not. And they would trouble her dreams for the rest of her life, mixing in strange ways with the faces of John

Eldridge and the murdered woman and the second woman, and she would wake up not crying out in fright but with a sadness heavy as stone.

It was Claire who phoned.

"My dear! How are you?"

"Mending nicely, thanks," Vicky said. "How are you?"

"Mending nicely, too, I suppose. I'm not quite the emotional wreck I was when we had lunch. But, listen, I'm flying back to Canada this Thursday — "

"Thursday!"

"Yes, I know it's sudden, but I thought I might as well get it over with. The kids seem to be okay with it, and I'd have to be gone in a week or so anyway. Well, I was wondering if you felt up to going out for lunch today. A farewell lunch. I've the car. I could pick you up."

They went to the same restaurant they had gone to before, the Edelweiss, and the waiter gave them the same table on the patio at the back. Claire ordered for them, a creamy potato soup.

"Wine?" she asked. "Shall I order a carafe?"

"Not for me," Vicky said. "I'm trying to be good."

Claire smiled. "*Und zwei Kaffee, bitte*," she told the waiter. "*Ohne Milche.*"

"I can't believe you'll be gone in two days," Vicky said.

Claire sighed and leaned back. She looked quite different from the last time they were here, Vicky thought. She'd had her hair touched up and done in a modified French braid; she was wearing earrings and a necklace and an attractive blue suit dress with gold trim on the lapels. She looked, essentially, like her old self.

"I know, my dear. I can hardly believe it, either. But I'm rather looking forward to it, now that it's all settled. Phil has suddenly coughed up a big lump of money and reservations on a commercial flight, and my old friend Karen — she was before your time — thinks she's found me a job in Toronto. She's another dumped army wife. She's organizing a campaign for ex-wives to get their share of their ex-husbands' army pensions, which are *huge*, by the way. Right now ex-wives, no matter how many years they hung in there, how many times they had to uproot themselves and their kids and move, get absolutely nothing."

"So you won't, either."

"No, my dear. Not a sou. After all these years." She leaned forward and smiled. Vicky could hear the slithery sound of nyloned legs being crossed. "But, listen. I'm trying not to be bitter. And who knows, maybe Karen's campaign will pay off. But she'll have a lot of opposition. We can't let her do it alone. You know: '*My* name is Spartacus.'"

"Pardon me?"

"Oh, you know — the old movie. To protect Spartacus all the slaves step forward and claim to be him."

"Yes, of course," Vicky said, feeling foolish. Old movies were supposed to be her thing.

"Anyway. Enough about me. You're the one with the exciting life! I can't believe how well you've handled it. In the hospital you looked so calm, so relaxed."

"Drugs," Vicky said. "They wore off."

"Still — when I think of what happened — " She gestured at Vicky's arm, the bandage and sling. "How close you came to being killed, by that madman. Did you read the interview with his mother? I saw it in the *Winnipeg Free Press*, but I assume it was a wire service story."

"No." Vicky didn't want to hear about it, but Claire had already started to tell her.

"She was a battered wife. You could see where the son learned his attitudes to women. The father was army, too."

The waiter brought their soup then and Vicky, relieved, concentrated on eating. Claire, watching her, shifted the subject delicately, began talking about hospitals and doctors and then the job she was hoping to get in Toronto, something to do with Quebec and translations for the government.

Vicky nodded, tried to look interested, because she *was* interested; she cared about Claire, admired her resilience. She thought about telling Claire that she, too, would be returning to Canada alone, but decided against it. She had resolved not even to tell Annie until she was more sure of her feelings. So she smiled at Claire, asked her when her daughter would be joining her in Canada.

So it wasn't until they were almost home, only a few blocks from Haydnstraße, that Claire, putting on the signal light to turn off Werderstraße, said, "Oh, I meant to tell you, although I don't imagine you still care, not after everything else that's happened, but I remembered where I'd seen that woman you saw with Phil. You know, the one you drew the picture of?"

Vicky sat forward so abruptly the seatbelt locked, squeezing her injured arm. "Who is she?"

Claire smiled slightly. "She's Andrew's mistress."

"What?"

"I saw them quite by chance. I was delivering some work requisitions in Offenburg and I was having lunch in a little hotel café and who should I see coming down the stairs with their overnight bags but Andrew and this woman. Well, talk about embarrassing. It was impossible to pretend we didn't see each other. Andrew made some feeble introduction, I don't think he even said her name, and then they fled. Anyway, when I told Phil about seeing them he admitted he knew about her. Maybe he'd even introduced them, I can't remember. So that's why he knew her in the store. I wouldn't have thought she'd be from Lahr, though. I'd have imagined

Andrew to be too discreet for that. But I'm sure it's the same woman you drew. I remember that large mouth, that mark on her cheek, maybe it was a scar, or a dimple. You caught it in your drawing."

Vicky felt terribly cold. When she reached her right hand up to clutch the seatbelt the chill of her fingers soaked through the thin cotton fabric of the sling, through her blouse, reaching deep into her. Goose bumps raced up her arms. Horripilation, it was called, she remembered numbly: a word she had learned because it had made her laugh.

"Are you all right?" Claire asked, alarmed, looking at her.

"Yes, yes, I'm fine. A little tired, that's all."

She could barely remember getting out of the car, or saying good-bye to Claire, or walking around the side of the house, or fitting the key into her lock, or going up the stairs. She sat down at the kitchen table and picked up a water glass and squeezed her fingers around it tightly.

She was Andrew's mistress.

Andrew had saved her life.

She was Andrew's mistress.

Couldn't it have just been a coincidence that it was Andrew's mistress who was up in the Staatswald that day? Oh, please, couldn't it?

When she'd shown Andrew the woman's picture he must have recognized her, but he'd given no sign of it. Still, that was understandable, wasn't it? He couldn't very well say, oh, yes, of course, that's the woman I'm having an affair with. But she was connected to a murder; he wasn't just being discreet about an affair —

He'd told her that on the night Eldridge tried to kill her he'd lingered on his outside steps long enough to see the man in the car, to see him follow her. But she couldn't remember Andrew coming out with her at all, let alone staying there long enough to watch her drive away, and besides the street had been dark, very dark —

When someone had stolen the pictures, hadn't she told herself that only Phil, who was with her the whole time, and Andrew knew where the pictures were? He was delayed by the other captain but he could have made a quick phone call telling someone where to find them. And hadn't it occurred to her another time that Andrew might have told someone something about her, what was it? — oh, yes, that she was going to the German police? But it had been a joke, hadn't it, her suspecting him? She hadn't for a moment thought there could really be anything to it (the heroine running for sanctuary to the one man she trusts, and he opens the door and smiles and she sees the incriminating dossier on the kitchen table; he smiles and she sees the contract killer sitting on the couch; he smiles and she sees his Dracula teeth) —

It was absurd. When Andrew had come to the hospital to see her he'd been genuinely upset about what had happened; she couldn't believe he could have faked it so well, been such a convincing actor. Besides, if he did have foreknowledge that Eldridge would try to kill her that night, what reason could he possibly have had for letting the man go after her, get within seconds of killing her, and then killing *him*? He wasn't that desperate for a promotion, surely. The thought almost made her laugh: yes, she was just imagining conspiracies again, with Andrew this time — Andrew, who'd saved her life; Andrew, with whom she was probably a little in love. She was upset to hear about the mistress, that was all.

She remembered, suddenly, the feel of his hands on her, the electric way her whole body had wanted him, still wanted him — She pushed away the memory. She had to be clear-headed. She had to find reasons beyond her sexual desire either to blame or to exonerate him.

All right: Andrew couldn't be involved because: one — he had no motive. Two — he had saved her life; he wouldn't have been involved in trying to take it. Three — he'd been helping her, been her friend; he'd kept checking up on things for her at the base. It was his distributing John Eldridge's picture that had flushed the man out. But then why was he angry when Dr. Lester asked for a copy of it?

Unless he hadn't distributed the picture at all.

She unclasped her hand from the water glass. Her fingers were numb, stiff. When she looked up the number for Lieutenant Crosby she had to lick her forefinger to turn the pages.

"Mrs. Bauer! How nice to hear from you. How are you feeling?"

"Much better, thank you. Look, I know this is an odd question, but — " She swallowed. The numbness seemed to be spreading up her arm, into her chest, her throat. "I was just wondering if Andrew gave you a copy of the picture I drew of John Eldridge before, you know, before Eldridge was killed."

"No-o. He didn't. I'm afraid I've never seen the picture." He sounded apologetic. "Does it matter?"

"No, it's nothing. It's not important. Thank you."

She had to try several times before she replaced the receiver properly in the cradle. Then she only sat staring at it, not taking her hand away.

She'd asked Andrew directly if he'd given Crosby the picture. He'd said yes.

She sat there for a long time, trying to make her mind empty, as though she needed to make room, prepare herself, for the conclusion waiting at the end of the silence.

Andrew was involved in this. He had to be. Andrew, not Conrad, was the one who was "in on it."

Annie: could she know anything about this? No, of

course not, but she would have told Andrew things about her, things he had used.

Vicky looked at her hand, still on the phone, as though she had known that she would have to make another call.

She had to tell Annie what she knew. Perhaps Annie would have an explanation. If she didn't, then she had a right to know what Vicky knew. Annie would be appalled; Annie would refuse to believe her; Annie might never forgive her. But this had gone beyond the stage of worrying about either of their feelings.

It was two-thirty. Annie would still be home; she was working the night shift this week. Vicky dialed the number. Her heart was pounding, making her injured arm throb. She listened to the ringing: one, two, maybe she wasn't home, three —

"Hello?"

"Hi! It's Vicky." Her voice seemed several octaves above normal.

"Oh, hi. How ya doing?"

"Okay, fine. Look, can you come over? Right now? It's urgent."

"Yeah, I guess. Are you all right?"

"I need to talk to you. Please. It's important. Really important."

"Okay. I'll be there in twenty minutes. Keep your knickers on."

Vicky paced the living room floor, turned the radio on, off, on again, Elvis singing, "Are You Lonesome Tonight?" and, inanely, she found herself humming along. Her hands were so cold: her body must be sucking the blood from her extremities and sending it to the vital organs, the way she heard happened in hypothermia. Was her brain a vital organ? It would need all the blood it could get. She took her left arm carefully out of the sling and ran hot water over both hands until they felt less like clubs of ice hanging from her wrists.

A drink, that's what she needed, just to warm herself up — No. No drink. Get a grip.

When she heard Annie's knock on the door, she jumped as though it were the last thing she expected. She made herself go slowly down the stairs, open the door. There was Annie; it was only Annie, wearing jeans and running shoes and an old beige shirt and her denim jacket in the seaweedy colour they had decided to call gang green; only Annie.

"So what's so important?" Annie said, following her up the stairs. "The army want you to hand over the movie rights?"

Vicky tried to laugh. "No, no, nothing like that."

Annie sat down on the sofa, put her feet up on the coffee table and clasped her hands behind her head. "So, what then?"

Vicky sat on the chair facing her across the coffee table. She felt cold again.

"I want to talk to you about Andrew," she said.

"Yeah? What's he done now?"

"Well, I had lunch with Claire today — she's going home on Thursday, you know."

"Yeah, I know. I suppose for her sake it's just as well."

"Anyway, she told me — oh, Annie, this is so hard — I don't know how to tell you — "

"What? Tell me what?" Annie unclasped her hands and dropped her feet from the coffee table.

"Well, I'd drawn this picture of the second woman I saw at the Staatswald, you know, I told you about her."

"Yes, yes — "

"And I showed it to Claire because I'd seen Phil talking to the woman, so I thought Claire might recognize her. Well,

she did. She remembered where she'd seen her before. It ....
She said the woman was Andrew's mistress."

Annie sat perfectly still, staring at Vicky, her face blank.
She might as well have been staring at the wall.

"I'm sorry," Vicky said, when Annie didn't speak. "But I
thought you should know. I thought — "

"I know about his affair," Annie said abruptly. "From a
so-called well-meaning friend. Adrienne. I don't suppose you
remember her. *She* was sorry to have to tell me, too. I assume
you both mean the same affair. Her name's Christa. She's
from Offenburg. She had a two-week contract to do some
work for Phil, once, at the Baden-Söllingen base."

"Oh, well, I'm glad, I mean, glad you already knew, that
it's not a surprise."

Annie gave a short, bitter laugh. "It's no surprise. I wish it
were."

"Anyway," Vicky said, "I saw her that day at the Staatswald. Claire was sure the picture I drew was of her." Vicky
licked her lips. Her tongue felt thick, dry, carrying with it
saliva like glue. "Why was she up there that day dressed as she
was? Why did she lie to me about who she was and where she
lived? Someone must have told her to go up there, maybe
every day, maybe only the day I was hanging around the base
first. She has to be involved with the murderer. And — I
think Andrew may be involved, too."

"What do you mean, Andrew involved?"

"I mean, the woman connects him to everything, doesn't
she? I just think, maybe there are things he hasn't been honest
about. Like this woman. He saw the picture I drew of her
and he pretended not to know her. And then, the other picture I drew, of the man, the murderer — Andrew told me he
gave a copy to Lieutenant Crosby, but Crosby never saw it.
Annie — help me. Tell me how to explain this."

Annie's eyes seemed to have opened wider, the pupils become larger, darker. Her whole face, Vicky thought suddenly, looked gaunt, haggard, the face of someone who has lost weight too quickly or through illness. "Andy saved your life," Annie said. "How could he be involved with any of this?"

"I don't know," Vicky said miserably. "But why would he lie about those things?"

"To protect his precious Christa, I suppose. He kept saying he'd end it with her but I knew he hadn't." Annie got up abruptly and went into the kitchen. Vicky could hear her opening cupboard doors, pouring herself a drink. When she came back with it, in the water glass Vicky had left on the kitchen table, she didn't sit down, only stood beside the sofa, picking at a thread on the back.

"I'm sorry," Vicky said. "It's just .... This woman was helping Eldridge. Is it simply a coincidence that she's also having an affair with Andrew?"

"All right, I'll confront Andy with it — "

"No! I'm afraid," she said, not knowing until she said the words how true they were. "I'm afraid of having him find out that I know."

"I see." Annie wouldn't meet her eyes. She stepped around behind the coffee table and sat back down on the sofa. "So what do you intend to do?" Her voice was unsteady.

"I don't know. I should tell someone else. One of the army investigators. Someone at the German police, Constable Klug, I suppose."

Annie took a big swallow of her drink. It was something clear, vodka or gin. She set the glass on the coffee table and fixed her eyes on it.

"I wish you wouldn't," she said.

"I've got to, Annie! I can't just pretend this woman never existed, especially now that I know who she is."

"Why can't you? The case is closed. Eldridge was the murderer and he's dead. Nobody cares about Christa. She's completely irrelevant."

"But Annie, she's *not*. She ties Andrew into this — "

Annie stood up, her knees jarring the coffee table. The sudden movement made Vicky flinch. "Why do you have to *do* this?" Annie cried. "Andy saved your life. How can you repay him by ruining *his* life, and mine?"

"Oh, Annie," Vicky whispered. "I don't want to hurt you."

"Then don't!" Annie strode to the window, stood looking out. She clasped her hands behind her neck. Vicky could see the knuckles whiten, the tips of the fingers turning red from the pressure. When Annie turned, she was attempting a smile. It looked so desperate Vicky had the urge to put her hand over Annie's mouth, to stop the frightened grimace. But she only sat there, rigidly.

"Why can't you just let it go, Vicky? For god's sake. What does it matter now? Eldridge is dead. What have Andy and I ever done to you to deserve this? I thought we were friends, Vicky. And Andy — I know you wanted him, don't deny it. He told me how you came on to him — "

"I didn't!"

"Andy didn't have to go after Eldridge that night. He could have let him go ahead and kill you. Vicky, please — let it drop. *Please.*"

"You know all about it, don't you? You know as much as Andrew does." Vicky heard herself saying the words, and she wanted to pull them back, because they weren't true, how could they be true?

They looked at each other for a long time. A door closed downstairs and a blur of German voices receded outside. A crow lit on the big oak tree outside the window and called hoarsely across the yard, sounding unnaturally clear.

Annie began to cry. She pressed her hands to her face and sank slowly to the floor. Vicky watched her for several moments, and then she stood, picked up Annie's drink and went over to her. She sat down on the floor in front of Annie and set the drink beside her.

"Tell me," she said.

Annie shook her head, continued to cry. Vicky waited. She pressed her hands together and shoved them between her thighs and waited. Her heart was beating, not fast, as she might have expected, but slowly, patiently, the way a well-trained dog might beat its tail on the floor, waiting.

At last, after a long time, Annie said, "It was all my fault. He'd never even have met that bastard if it hadn't been for me."

"How did you meet him?"

Annie wiped her face on the sleeve of her jacket, and then she reached inside the jacket, into an inner pocket, and pulled out a small plastic bag of white powder. She tossed it onto the floor between them.

"It makes that — " she gestured at the drink " — seem like a joke," she said. She gave a little harsh exhalation, a laugh or a sob or both, something that seemed forcibly pressed from her body.

"I see." Vicky stared at the white bag.

"I thought about getting you hooked," Annie said. "It wouldn't have been hard. I'm an expert on addictive personalities. But I didn't."

"Why didn't you?" Vicky asked. She couldn't take her eyes from the bag.

"You were my friend," Annie said. "I broke one of those three Good Army Wife rules. Don't get attached to where you're living. Don't expect to have a career of your own. Don't become too close to your friends."

Vicky swallowed. It hurt, as though something large and jagged were in her throat. She pulled her eyes from the bag and forced herself to look at Annie. "Eldridge was your supplier?"

"Eldridge had a good little business going. He knew the perfect market, too. The wives. No DND drug testing to worry about with them. He seemed like such a nice guy, wanting to make us ladies happy. And, oh, he did, he did." She ran her forefinger, gently, along the side of the plastic bag. "You don't know what it's like for most of us here, Vicky. You think you do but you don't. You're a visitor. A tourist. You don't know what it's like to be totally dependent on your husband and the whims of the army. This stuff — " she ran her finger back along the bag " — makes it easier. Such a lot easier."

"And then Andrew found out?"

"He was furious. It would ruin his career, etc. But I couldn't stop. So Andy said he'd help me. I don't know how he did it, but suddenly Eldridge was working for him. No one but me knew that, of course. Andy got to like the money, the excitement, the power, I suppose."

"Eldridge ... was working for Andrew." What Vicky had seen on Andrew's face in the hospital may have been genuine, then, she thought coldly. She'd seen the remorse of a man who'd killed a useful employee.

"When the rumours started about how the base was closing, everyone panicked. Andy and Eldridge had a pretty substantial clientele. The woman who was killed, she was an addict, hooking to feed her habit. Once the base was closed, there would go both her dope and her customers, so she tried to blackmail Eldridge, she threatened to go to the German police."

"And Phil. How was he involved?"

"Phil? All Phil wanted to do was hang in until he could retire. He did what Andy told him to and he kept his mouth shut. He seemed to think Andy was perfect or something, god knows why."

Vicky could think of a reason why, but she didn't say anything.

"Andy was afraid Claire knew too much," Annie went on. "She'd had her little romance with this stuff, too, you know — so he told Phil to get her out of the country. Phil did what he was told, that's all."

"Claire was your friend — how could you let them treat her like that? And me, all those things that happened to me, to scare me off or make me think I was going crazy. That was all Eldridge and Andrew — and you — working together. *You*, Annie. You say you're my friend, but, my god, you'd sit there listening to me tell you things and you knew why they were happening, you fed them information on where I'd be, if I was crazy enough or scared enough yet — "

She began hitting at Annie, slapping at her with her right hand, not caring where the blows landed, on Annie's arms, legs, face, shoulders. Annie put her arms up over her face but she didn't try to stop the blows. She began making little whimpering noises, pulling her knees up to her chest. Vicky's hand closed into a fist, and she hit harder, pounding, her anger beating itself out of her.

At last she stopped, revolted at what she had done but not enough to wish she hadn't. Annie was huddled against the wall, hugging her knees, into which she had pressed her face. She was saying over and over in a low voice, "Don't. Please don't."

"All right," Vicky said. She picked up the glass which had held Annie's drink and which had gotten knocked over and she set it on the bookcase beside her.

Annie lifted her head from her knees. Her eyes were red and swollen, her hair stuck to her damp skin, and her nose was bleeding slightly. She reached clumsily into her jacket pocket and found a crumpled kleenex and pressed it to her nostril. Vicky wondered, not really caring, if she or the drug had caused the nosebleed.

They sat in silence, not looking at each other. The air in the room smelled stale, dead, as though the oxygen had been leached from it.

Finally Annie said, "I didn't know anything at first. I swear I didn't. But Andy kept asking me about you, and at first I thought it was just because he was interested in starting, you know, an affair with you, but his questions were so odd, always about what you were saying about the murder, what you were going to do .... "

"And so you figured it out. And you did fuck-all about it."

"Maybe I didn't let myself know that I knew. I just, I just did what Andy told me. Like Phil, I suppose. Oh, I don't expect you to understand."

"Oh, I understand. You were just following orders. Like any good soldier. Like any good collaborator."

"I was a coward, I know that. But I couldn't betray Andy. And I was afraid. I was afraid of Eldridge."

"But Andrew was controlling Eldridge."

"Not completely."

"Maybe all you were afraid of was getting your dope cut off. For that you'd have let Eldridge kill me."

"No! I swear I didn't know what he was planning!"

"But Andrew knew, didn't he? It was probably his plan."

"No! He promised me, he *promised* — "

"Andrew was getting scared, wasn't he? Maybe Dr. Lester was getting suspicious. Maybe he knew a little too much about where his patients were getting snappier drugs than the ones he was pushing." She could tell from Annie's face that she was right. "And I was getting closer to exposing Andrew, too. Sending that woman up to the forest was stupid, he must have realized that afterwards, he was just getting desperate."

"He saved your *life*!"

"He changed his mind about letting Eldridge have me. Why did he change his mind? Maybe he'd intended all along to kill Eldridge, but why didn't he wait until Eldridge killed me?"

Annie began crying again but making no sound, her face twisting and the tears pulsing down her cheeks. "All I know is that he was standing in the kitchen that night after you'd gone, with his forehead pressed against the refrigerator, and suddenly he just said, 'No,' and he bolted out the door. He took pity on you, I suppose."

Vicky smiled, without amusement. Pity. Which may or not be a kind of love. She looked at Annie, crumpled against the wall as though someone had tossed her there. Annie, her friend.

"We were going to make a better movie, Annie," she said. "What happened?"

"I had the wrong script," Annie said. "I had the *Bright Lights, Big City* script. I had the *Stand By Your Man* script."

Vicky noticed something glinting on the sleeve of Annie's denim jacket, and without thinking she reached over to pick it off. Annie cringed back.

"Your contact lens," Vicky said.

"Oh." Annie didn't bother to look. Vicky took the small chip between her thumb and forefinger and set it on the bookcase. Annie blinked several times, heavily, and said, "My other one's gone, too."

"I don't see it anywhere," Vicky said.

"It doesn't matter."

"Did you bring your glasses?"

"It doesn't matter."

Vicky remembered her own glasses, torn from her face and lying now somewhere in the woods between Schwarz-waldstraße and the Schutter River. She remembered Annie saying, what seemed so long ago, "Honestly, I don't know why we weren't just born blind to begin with." Maybe she should have seen Annie's words as a clue; maybe she should at least see them as that now, retrospectively; knowledge happened that way in the movies, didn't it, the "Aha" and the rising music and the protagonist not finding a new clue so much as having to be ready to understand an old one. The movies, yes, the goddamned movies.

Annie suddenly pushed herself clumsily to her feet, banging her shoulder on the window sill. "I feel sick," she said. She grabbed her purse from the sofa and stumbled to the bathroom.

Vicky didn't get up. She felt drained, exhausted. She let herself slide down onto her side on the floor and lay there, her legs pulled up, her hands folded into a hard pillow under her head. She focused her gaze on an old cobweb lacing up the right angle of the floorboards in the far corner. Her eyes began to feel itchy, the way they did when she had been reading or writing too long, and she closed them, but the feeling didn't go away.

Eventually she felt the spilled drink soaking through her blouse and she sat up. The smell of it — gin — made her want, with an intensity that made her tremble, a drink. Her own nasty drug. What hateful things had it made her do; what excuses had she made for it? She remembered the party at the Gartens', how she had responded to the sight of the cocaine, how she might have asked to use it if she hadn't been interrupted. That's how easily it could have started. Addictive personalities, Annie had said: that's what they both were. Maybe it was what drew them to each other. Identification.

She glanced over to where the plastic bag had been lying, but it was gone.

She stood up, quickly, and walked over to the bathroom. She could imagine Annie behind the door, her head bent over the counter, inhaling that white, temporary forgiveness.

The door was not quite closed. Vicky pushed it open, slowly.

Annie was sitting on the edge of the bathtub. On the counter beside the sink lay a revolver. It was black and shiny, the way a soldier's gun is supposed to be. Vicky couldn't take her eyes from it. It lay there sucking up the life and light and energy in the room like a black hole.

"I brought it in case you'd figured it all out," Annie said. "I brought it for me, not for you."

It took Vicky a moment to understand. *For me, for you*: they were the words used to talk about giving a gift. "Gift" in German meaning "poison".

"It isn't for either of us," Vicky said.

She picked up the gun, carefully. It was surprisingly light. Annie sat watching her, not moving.

Now that she was holding the gun all Vicky wanted was to get rid of it. She reached down beside the toilet and put it into the garbage can, into the empty tampon box she'd thrown there two days ago.

"In this movie, the women throw the guns into the garbage," she said. "Into their empty tampon boxes."

She sat down beside Annie and put her good arm around Annie's shoulders. "In this movie the women get up and go to the police. In this movie they take a shitty script and give it a better ending."

"I'll be losing everything," Annie said.

"Maybe you lost Andrew a long time ago."

"I know. I know I did. And myself along with it, isn't that

how the story goes?" Annie reached over to the toilet paper roll, tore off about a dozen squares with her right hand, and blew her nose. The roll kept turning, unspooling several feet of tissue onto the floor.

"We're going to change the story."

"The stuff. The coke. I can't live without it. I'd go insane. I would. You don't know."

"I do know. It'll be hard, as hard as anything you've ever done, but it's possible. There are places to help you. I'll help you."

"I don't know if I can do it," Annie said. "Any of it."

"You can."

They were quiet for a long time. Vicky's arm began to feel stiff but she didn't take it away from Annie's shoulders. She thought she heard a key in the lock downstairs, but no one came up the steps. It was Conrad's *Vardogr*, that was all, not Conrad, not yet, perhaps never.

She looked down the hallway, toward her study. The door was open and she could see the edge of her desk, the paper-clip tray holding the small pearl, the eight files full of the lives of women she had not forgiven for their weaknesses; the women whose voices were given to them by men; the Melanies and Barbaras and Marnies and Marions and Charlottes; the women with whom she would not identify.

"We can," she said, making her voice sound firm and confident. "Of course we can."

Was *of course* the bluff she'd once told herself it was? Probably. But that didn't mean it referred to a lie, an impossibility. It meant they would have to work at this, together, to make it happen. She took a deep breath, let it out, felt the warmth and the weight of Annie along her right side.

.

OTHER BOOKS FROM SECOND STORY PRESS